A Good
Name

Essential Prose Series 186

**Canada Council
for the Arts**

**Conseil des Arts
du Canada**

**ONTARIO ARTS COUNCIL
CONSEIL DES ARTS DE L'ONTARIO**

an Ontario government agency
un organisme du gouvernement de l'Ontario

Canadä

Guernica Editions Inc. acknowledges the support of the Canada
Council for the Arts and the Ontario Arts Council.
The Ontario Arts Council is an agency of the Government of Ontario.

We acknowledge the financial support of the Government of Canada.

A Good
Name

YEJIDE KILANKO

**GUERNICA
EDITIONS**
TORONTO · CHICAGO · BUFFALO · LANCASTER (U.K.)
2021

Michael Mirolla, general editor
Lindsay Brown, editor
Rafael Chimicatti, cover design
David Moratto, interior design
Guernica Editions Inc.
287 Templemead Drive, Hamilton, ON L8W 2W4
2250 Military Road, Tonawanda, N.Y. 14150-6000 U.S.A.
www.guernicaeditions.com

Distributors:
Independent Publishers Group (IPG)
600 North Pulaski Road, Chicago IL 60624
University of Toronto Press Distribution,
5201 Dufferin Street, Toronto (ON), Canada M3H 5T8
Gazelle Book Services, White Cross Mills
High Town, Lancaster LA1 4XS U.K.

First edition.
Printed in Canada.

Legal Deposit—Third Quarter
Library of Congress Catalog Card Number: 2021930933
Library and Archives Canada Cataloguing in Publication
Title: A good name / Yejide Kilanko.
Names: Kilanko, Yejide, 1975- author.
Description: First edition.
Identifiers: Canadiana (print) 20210109998 | Canadiana (ebook) 20210110007
| ISBN 9781771836012 (softcover) | ISBN 9781771836029 (EPUB)
| ISBN 9781771836036 (Kindle)
Classification: LCC PS8621.I5374 G66 2021 | DDC C813/.6—dc23

To Rachel and the sisters we lost

Content

PART ONE *1*
*One does not enter the water and
then run from the cold*

Chapter One—Chapter Seventeen

PART TWO *131*
*No one gets a mouthful of food by picking
between another person's teeth*

Chapter Eighteen—Chapter Thirty

PART THREE *207*
*When the drummers change their
beats, the dancers must also
change their steps*

Chapter Thirty-One—Chapter Fifty-Four

Epilogue *363*
Glossary *365*
Acknowledgements *369*
About the Author *371*

PART ONE

*One does not enter the water and
then run from the cold*

Chapter One

EZIAFAKAEGO OKEREKE PULLED the small towel from his trouser pocket and wiped the sweat off his face. He draped the damp cloth across the back of his neck. Living through twelve years of long and harsh Minnesota winters made the sweltering Houston heat hard to bear. He picked up the barbecue tongs and placed the last set of marinated pork ribs on the sizzling grill. There was a plus side to the humid weather. It brought back precious memories of Oji, his home village. After so many years of grey and black, he was dreaming in colour again.

"My guy, *jisie ike*."

Eziafa turned to smile at his best friend. Felix had acquired a full head of grey hair by 30. Eziafa was still startled every time he saw the hair. Felix refused to dye it.

"How goes the grilling battle?" Felix asked.

Eziafa scowled. His grill duty was Felix's fault. When he'd asked him to join the Houston Igbo Cultural Association, Eziafa's first response was no. The last thing he needed was insults from small boys jingling shiny coins in baggy jeans pockets.

To get Felix off his back, Eziafa attended an association meeting. By evening's end, Eziafa found himself paying membership dues. He could not say no when an elder assigned him grill duty for the party.

"Didn't you say you would help?" Eziafa asked.

Felix flashed crooked white teeth as he handed over a chilled bottle of palm wine. "No vex. Nkolika asked me to run an errand."

Eziafa pursed his lips. "Shameless woman *wrappa*. I knew you would have an excuse."

"People are raving over the barbecue," Felix said.

The compliment made Eziafa smile. "They are?"

"Yes. Maybe you should forget about driving a taxi and open a shish kebab hut?"

Eziafa downed a third of the palm wine and wiped his mouth with the back of his hand. "That's not why I moved here."

"I know. You can run the kebab hut on the side. We all need multiple streams of income."

His childhood friend had always been one to encourage. "I'll add it to my list of possible ventures."

Felix gave him a thumbs-up. "Obikwelu and I are going to buy more ice."

"I'll be here," Eziafa said.

Felix's wife, Nkolika, came for the final pan of ribs. "Well done o," she said, smiling.

Nkolika's fresh face made it seem as though she was getting younger as her husband was aging. She could have passed as an older sister to her teen daughters. Eziafa smiled his thanks.

After cleaning the grill, he went back into the high school auditorium which was vibrating with loud music and conversation. It was a wonder they managed to hear themselves think.

Grateful for the air conditioning, Eziafa made his way down the long buffet table. He heaped home-made food on two Styrofoam plates, and sat on the nearest empty chair. The women had outdone themselves.

The pounded yam's texture was just how Eziafa liked it. The starchy morsels didn't stick to his fingers. Generous amounts of spicy okra soup warmed his stomach. Eziafa licked his fingers. He would coax some take-home food from Nkolika.

A peal of laughter made Eziafa look up from his plate. The sound came from a young woman seated at the other end of the table. As she threw her head back in another burst of laughter, Eziafa's eyes were free to caress the caramel skin showcased by a bright yellow halter-top. Gnawing on a chicken drumstick he imagined his fingers grazing her soft skin. Even though she seemed oblivious to his curious stare, Eziafa forced his gaze away. She could be someone's wife.

He jumped at the tap on his shoulder. It was Felix. Annoyed, Eziafa kissed his teeth. "This man. You almost gave me a heart attack."

Felix grinned. "No vex. I wanted to let you know we're seated at a table by the door."

Eziafa had good reason to stay where he was. "I'll join you guys later."

Felix left. Eziafa stole a glance at the woman's ring finger. It was bare. Her phone conversation dragged on. Eziafa's growing impatience had him tapping fingers on the side of his chair.

As soon as she put her cell phone down, he pushed

back his chair, straightened his shirt over a round stomach and walked over to her. Hoping a big smile masked his nervousness he said: "Hello. I'm Eziafa Okereke."

She shook his offered hand. "Jovita Asika. I don't believe we've met?"

He held on to her soft hand. "No. It would be impossible to forget your face."

Jovita gave him a sceptical look as she released his hand. "I'm sure that's what you tell all the ladies you meet."

Eziafa grinned. Jovita was built the way he liked his women, voluptuous and several inches taller than him.

"Only the beautiful ones," he said.

"Hmm." Jovita pointed at the chair beside her. "I guess listening to a little more flattery wouldn't hurt."

Eziafa sat. "I'd love to have a private conversation with you."

"Oh. Okay. I do need to make a quick run to the ladies' room. Can we meet up at the bar?"

Eziafa jumped to his feet. "I'll be waiting."

Five minutes and forty seconds later, Jovita joined him. To save money, the association executives decided against an open bar. Jovita ordered an extra dirty vodka martini. She also insisted on paying for his bottle of beer. Eziafa felt better when she agreed that he would pay for their second round of drinks. A woman shouldn't be buying his drinks.

They sat in a small room off the auditorium. Ajar, the door did little to muffle the boisterous party sounds. Jovita lowered her cocktail glass to the small table. "So, what do you want to talk about?" she asked.

"You."

Jovita swirled her drink. The stuffed olives settled to

the bottom of the glass. "Well, before I give up my secrets, you must tell me about yourself."

He cleared his throat. "There is not much to say."

She gave him an encouraging smile. "Humour me."

Eziafa's nervous energy dissipated as he talked about moving to America and his life in Minnesota. Jovita revealed she was born and raised in Buffalo, New York. Like him, she moved to Houston in search of better opportunities. She worked as a real estate agent and an interior decorator.

"So, what do you do for a living?" she asked.

Eziafa shifted in his seat as he watched for the anticipated change in Jovita's expression. "I'm a taxicab driver."

"That's a fun job."

Eziafa frowned. "Are you mocking me?"

Jovita's hand settled on his bare arm. "No way. You can't interact with that many people without having some good stories to tell."

Eziafa cleared his throat. Jovita's warm touch was messing with his mind. If she moved closer, he would make up all the stories she wanted to hear. "I haven't started the job," he said. "But, it's why I moved to Houston."

Jovita smiled. "Ah. Welcome to H-town. There are lots of things to see and do here."

He was still adjusting to the sounds and sights of the sprawling city. "Maybe you can give me a tour?"

Jovita gave a non-committal shrug. "It would depend on my availability."

Eziafa leaned forward when Jovita took a second glance at her wristwatch. He wasn't ready for the evening to end. "You have to go?" he asked.

"Yeah. I hadn't planned to stay this long."

"You have other plans?"

"No. I'm just low-key mad. Earlier, I wasn't impressed when one of the older women mocked my attempts to speak Igbo. She said I was an A.B.N."

"What does that mean?"

"Dem dey call me, American-Born *Naija*."

Surprised by her perfect pidgin English, Eziafa hooted with laughter.

Jovita frowned. "It's not funny."

His laughter died. "Sorry. I didn't expect to hear those words from you."

"My parents speak pidgin to each other."

"You sound authentic. I'm sure your Igbo is also excellent."

"My Igbo sucks. I should have paid attention during the lessons my parents arranged. Still, I don't understand why, instead of teaching me the proper pronunciation, these women laugh at me. Then when they speak Igbo to me and I respond in English, they're quick to say I'm conceited." She sighed. "I don't even know why I keep coming to the meetings."

"It is good to associate with your people. Whether at home or abroad, there is strength in numbers."

"Not when my own people think I'm a second-class Igbo person."

Eziafa doubted the women meant Jovita any harm. "Don't mind them."

"It's easy for you to say."

"I can offer some free Igbo language lessons."

"Really?"

"Yes."

"Hmm. This American capitalist is curious about something. What's in it for you?"

Eziafa cleared his throat. "As a true Igbo man, I'm committed to the language's globalization."

Jovita's hearty laugh rang out in the small room. "That's plain bull."

"It's the truth."

The wall clock chimed six times. "Time for me to leave." She fished the last stuffed olive from her glass and popped it in her mouth.

Eziafa rose to his feet as she pushed back her chair. "Will your car turn into a pumpkin if you don't?" he asked.

Jovita rolled her eyes. "I no longer believe in fairy tales and I'm not leaving my pricey Louboutin shoe behind."

"That's too bad. I would have taken the bus to find you."

"You're funny," she said.

"It's been nice, no, great, talking to you."

"Same here."

Eziafa cleared his throat. "So, what's your phone number? I hope your boyfriend won't mind you taking calls from other men."

"This Nigerian way of soliciting information pisses me off," Jovita said. "Would it kill you to ask a direct question?"

He grinned. "It's not how we do things."

"That's what my parents say. God forbid you guys learn to do things differently."

Eziafa shrugged. "Why fix something that's not broke?"

"There is nothing wrong with growing," Jovita said. "To answer your unasked question, I don't have a boyfriend. And even if I did, trust me, he wouldn't tell me whose calls to take or not to take." Jovita pulled a business card from her purse and handed it to him.

He pocketed the card. "I can apply for the boyfriend position?"

"I never said I was looking for a man."

Eziafa lifted his chin. "With all humility, I can say my impressive resumé has changed many doubtful minds. You will want to keep it on file for future opportunities."

"Your confidence is admirable," she said.

"You inspire me."

Jovita cocked her head. "I do?"

Eziafa nodded. If he played his cards right, his self-imposed celibacy could come to a satisfying end. "You'll hear all about your massive influence during our first date."

Jovita was silent as they headed for the door. He held it open. "After you."

She raised her eyebrow. "A quasi-gentleman."

Eziafa licked his lips. "The truth is I need a grown woman like you. Someone brave and competent enough to unwrap this ... em ... complex package."

Jovita's eyes twinkled with mischief. "You should make that line the primary goal on your resumé."

Eziafa winked. "I love insider tips."

Chapter Two

THE **FOLLOWING WEEKEND**, an elated Eziafa drove a Crown Victoria sedan away from the auction site. Thanks to Felix's advice, he made the winning bid.

Felix read out directions to Dinesh's apartment building. The Sri Lankan, an automotive engineer in his home city of Colombo, was the go-to-guy for free vehicle inspections. In America, he worked as a sanitation engineer. Eziafa had laughed when he found out it was the politically correct term for a garbage collector.

While Dinesh tinkered under the car hood, Eziafa and Felix sat on lawn chairs and drank from icy cans of soda.

Eziafa gave Felix a grateful look. Friends like him were rare. "*Nna*, thanks for all the help," he said.

Felix inclined his head. "My brother, no be today. You would do the same for me. Now that we've sorted out the car, it's important you attend a safety class."

Eziafa wasn't happy to hear about another expense. "My pocket is light o," he said. "Is this safety class mandatory?"

"Relax. It's not a government program. One of us,

Mr. Osas, offers the free program to new cab drivers from the Nigerian community. I'm sure you will find it beneficial."

Eziafa settled back in his chair. "When can we go?"

"I'll find out the date for the next class," Felix said. "*Daalu.*"

Felix raised his soda can. "To progress."

Eziafa exhaled. "At long freaking last."

Felix gaped at him before bursting into laughter.

He and Felix encountered ten men and one woman at the community center's safety class. Noting the white plastic chairs in a horseshoe formation, Eziafa wondered idly if the woman was on her own or accompanying someone.

An elderly man in a plaid shirt and jeans stood beside a flip chart. Eziafa noticed that his mesh baseball cap sat at an odd angle. It looked as if the man was missing some part of his head.

Felix nudged Eziafa's arm. "That's Mr. Osas," he whispered.

Their teacher for the evening pointed at two empty chairs. "Men, welcome," he said in greeting. "We were about to start."

Eziafa and Felix took their seats.

Mr. Osas' gaze swept the room. "Good evening. Welcome to Taxicab Driver Safety 101. If you did not know, taxicab driving is not an easy job. To survive, you must understand the dangers and learn how to keep yourself safe. Working alone at odd hours of the night while in possession of cash makes you an easy target. Let us begin."

Minutes into the class, two young men seated next to

Eziafa began whispering. Eziafa glared at them. When their voices grew loud, Mr. Osas stopped mid-sentence. "Hey! You two over there. Keep talking. I can assure you that your poor mothers won't be laughing when your bullet-ridden bodies arrive in Nigeria."

The room fell into stunned silence.

"If any of you thinks learning this information is a waste of your precious time, you may leave now," he said.

Stone-faced, the noise-makers stayed in their seats.

Mr. Osas' eyes swept across the room. "Now that I have your undivided attention, we will go over the safety rules again. One day, they may save your life."

On their way home, Eziafa's mind was still on their teacher's odd appearance. "How did Mr. Osas get his head injury?"

Felix glanced at him. "He was shot in the head during a taxi robbery."

The words sent a chill through Eziafa. "He fought back?"

"No. The thief was angry that Mr. Osas only had twenty dollars on him. Imagine. The man would have died for chicken change."

Eziafa's heart thumped as he declared: "An early death will not be our portion. We will live and prosper in the face of our enemies."

"That's the hope," Felix said. "None of us moved to America with a plan for premature death."

Eziafa made the minor repairs Dinesh recommended and gave his vehicle a new coat of bright yellow paint.

At the end of his first week, after paying for gas and

other business expenses, Eziafa still had $600 in his pocket. Imagine. Six hundred American dollars. If he kept up the 12- to 16-hour shifts, the potential income was about $3,000 a month. In comparison to his paycheck at the meat processing factory, he'd finally struck gold.

Eziafa walked through a set of sliding doors leading into the drab brick apartment building. Before Eziafa left Minnesota for Texas, he and Felix had co-signed a rental lease for his one-bedroom apartment. Eziafa's credit score wasn't good enough.

The Southwest Houston area suited him. Populated by immigrants from all over the world, the neighbourhood allowed him to feel part of it when he walked the streets. He was no longer a visitor.

He retrieved a pile of mail from the lobby box on the way to the basement apartment. Eziafa wished there was someone there to welcome him with a smile. A woman who would ask about his day and listen to his stories while he ate her fragrant food.

After taking a shower, Eziafa sat at the kitchen table and ate a bowl of instant noodles before sorting through his mail. One by one, he flung the envelopes on the table. "Electricity bill. Phone bill. Renters' Insurance bill. *Chei.* The bills just keep coming."

At the sight of a crumpled airmail envelope marked with faded Nigerian eagle stamps, he sat up. Despite his regular telephone calls home, Nne insisted on sending him letters. He knew they gave his mother the opportunity to express her thoughts in full.

The letters from home evoked equal amounts of happiness and dread. The temporary happiness because they were a physical sign of his mother's enduring love. But her lofty expectations repackaged as harmless news reports fueled the dread.

The small, neat script belonged to his younger sister, Evelyn. She was their mother's letter-writer. He read the last two paragraphs.

> *My son, do you remember your childhood friend Nnamani? He, his beautiful wife and twin sons visited last week. You should have seen the fat envelope of money he gave your sister. As if that was not enough, the next day Nnamani sent his driver to fetch me for their housewarming party. When he asked after you, I told him you would be coming home soon. My son, we are all waiting.*
>
> *Eziafakaego, I held my peace when you said you could not come home for your father's burial. We buried him like a man with no son. Now, I wish to ask you for one thing. Come home and marry. Let me carry your children on my back before I join my ancestors.*
>
> *Your mother,*
> *Cordelia*

Eziafa fought the urge to crush the letter. Her expectations were why he'd left Minnesota. He could not plan a respectable wedding with the pennies earned from his minimum wage job at a meat processing plant.

A burning sensation radiated from Eziafa's amputated index finger. Sometimes, his foolish brain acted as if the finger was still there.

He flung the letter on the coffee table. He stared at a

two-photo frame on the table. The first was a ten-year-old picture of Eziafa's parents dressed in their church clothes. The second was a family portrait—Papa, Nne, Evelyn and him. Nne said she had given up on having another child until Evelyn showed up.

Even at five feet six, Eziafa stood a head above the others. His hand shook as he repositioned the frame slightly.

He'd wanted to go home to see his father off. Bedridden for five years, Papa gave him enough time to say a proper goodbye. But Eziafa sent the money he would have used for a plane ticket and family gifts to his mother. There were overdue medical bills to pay.

After Papa's death, there were numerous burial items to buy and just as many unreasonable demands on him from extended family members. Going home with near-empty pockets would only have added to his mother's sorrow.

Eziafa grimaced as he scanned the space furnished with mismatched yard sale rejects. The faded brown couch had a thick, hardcover book replacing a leg. A dark green chair pushed up against the wall hid a large hole in the back. The wooden coffee table had teeth marks from a previous owner's dog. Not a home that evoked pride.

He was 25 years old when he arrived in America. During those early years, Eziafa saw the string of menial jobs as stepping-stones, as an immigrant rite of passage. A succession of slammed doors told him otherwise. And no matter how hard he tried to move on to bigger and better things, he could not get the corporate jobs he wanted.

At first, he had seethed with fury and frustration. How dare this vast land not live up to the promises it peddled?

Twelve years passed. And he accepted the comfort that came with facing his sad reality: On any available ladder to success, his place was at the bottom.

Eziafa rubbed his tired eyes. The long distance from home became a blessing. He could lick his wounds without worrying about the presence of a jeering audience.

The scribbled words on the paper before him demanded answers he didn't have. Even in bed, with his head jammed into a pillow, he couldn't escape the echo of his mother's pleas.

Chapter Three

EZIAFA SPRAWLED ON his bed to dial Jovita's number. She answered on the third ring.

"Hello?" Jovita's voice was slightly slurred, as if she'd just woken up.

"Good morning. It's Eziafa."

"Uh?"

"Eziafa Okereke. We met at the Igbo Cultural Association party."

Jovita yawned. "Oh, yeah. I didn't expect to hear from you so early in the day."

"Sorry. I'd wanted to catch you before you left the house to conduct your business."

"I don't have any home showings today." Jovita gave another loud yawn. "I need my cup of coffee."

"I was wondering if you would like to watch a movie with me."

Eziafa heard the hesitation in her voice. "I had planned to clean my apartment and do some laundry."

"I'm good at folding clothes," he said.

"Do you fold yours?"

He was a wash-and-leave-in-the-laundry-basket-until-you-need-to-wear-it kind of guy. "Well …"

"I'll take that as a no. How about we meet at Flicks Cinemas? It's right on Texas Ave."

Eziafa knew the place. "What time works for you?"

"Well, a four o'clock movie would be great."

"I'll see you then," he said.

"Okay. Thanks for the invite."

Eziafa clicked off his cell phone and rolled off the bed. It was time to give his car a good wash. He ran a hand across his uneven afro. He was due for a haircut. One could always work around a bald spot. His receding hairline was a different matter. It looked as if something had gnawed an uneven path around his head.

Before leaving home to complete his chores, Eziafa ironed his outfit for the evening—a short-sleeved purple shirt and a pair of black trousers—and buffed his leather sandals with a cloth.

He couldn't remember the last time he was so excited to spend time with anyone.

Eziafa gulped as he watched Jovita's slow runway walk. The fabric of her knee-length dress flowed over generous curves. In combination with her sparkling brown eyes, the woman was a tantalizing sight.

Jovita's face lit up when she saw him. "Hey, you," she said.

Eziafa doffed an imaginary cowboy hat. "Howdy!"

She looked amused. "The Igbo man has a Texan side."

He grinned. "I can pull one out when needed."

Jovita slid her hand through the crook of his arm. "What are we watching?" she asked.

"Your choice," he said.

The cinema offered old movies on the second Saturday of every month. *Grease* was that day's offering.

Eziafa remembered the days of wearing faux leather jackets and posing as a T-Bird. After watching the movie, he and his friends strutted around with black combs tucked in their trouser pockets.

"My big sis loves this movie."

"I'm sure you weren't even alive when the movie came out," he said.

Jovita gave him a half-smile. "How old do you think I am?"

He studied her fresh face. "Twenty-six?"

"Those cold Buffalo winters preserve things well. I'm thirty-four."

He was older by four years. "You're still a young one."

Jovita chuckled. "The right words to say to a vain woman."

They headed for the concession stand. "You? Vain? Impossible."

Jovita nudged him with her elbow. "I truly don't feel my age."

He felt the presence of each grey hair. "This confirms that I should stay close to bask in your youthful glow." Eziafa puffed out his chest. "I have the necessary resources."

"My glow is not for sale," Jovita said.

They walked into a half-empty theatre.

"If only those kids lined up for their next slasher flick knew what they're missing," Jovita said.

Eziafa nodded. "They'll get the importance of watching classic movies one day."

Stifling a fake yawn during the previews, he stretched his arm across Jovita's back. She leaned close and whispered into his ear: "I'm onto you."

A resounding drum roll introduced the main feature and handily drowned out his chuckle. There was nothing wrong with him tapping a little current.

After the movie, Jovita insisted she didn't want to have dinner with him. Eziafa was disappointed. "How about Wednesday night?" he asked.

Jovita fiddled with her car keys. "Can't do. I'm meeting with some potential clients."

"How about next Saturday?" he asked.

She shook her head. "That won't work either."

Eziafa clenched his jaw. He could read between the lines. "I guess I'll see you around," he said.

Jovita raised an eyebrow. "That's it?"

"I don't force my presence on people."

She laughed. "Man, you're uptight."

"That's uncalled for."

Her look was apologetic. "Sorry. I tend to say the first thing that pops into my head."

Eziafa took a deep breath. He knew he sounded uptight. "Do you want me to ask you out again?"

"Yeah. But you have to understand I had a life and plans before you came along."

"Fair enough. When are you free?"

"Next weekend, I'm going to Buffalo to handle some personal business. How about I connect with you when I get back? I have your number."

"You're going to see your parents?" he asked.

Jovita fiddled with her purse strap. "I'll see them while I'm there."

He knew enough to slow it down. "Safe travels."

Jovita bent and gave him a chaste kiss on the cheek. "Thanks for a lovely evening."

He waved Jovita off before walking to his car. The next move was hers.

Jovita's telephone call came a month later. By then, Eziafa had concluded he wasn't her type. Jovita asked if he could meet her for an early dinner. He agreed eagerly.

Eziafa dropped off his customer, rushed home, took a shower, changed into a dressier shirt, and headed to the downtown café.

Jovita was out on the patio. "Thanks for coming," she said.

He sat, took off his hat, and placed it on his lap. "You sounded as if you have something important to say."

Jovita nodded. "I do."

The conversation stalled as the waitress took their soup and sandwich combo order.

"I owe you an explanation for dropping off the radar," Jovita said when they were alone.

He took in Jovita's earnest expression. During the drive to the café, he'd told himself the best way to handle things was not to make a big fuss. "You don't owe me any-thing. But if you don't mind, I'd love to hear what you've been up to."

"Well, the main reason I went to Buffalo was that my ex and I needed to settle some real estate affairs."

"You're divorced?"

Jovita shook her head. "We weren't married. We only bought a house together."

Eziafa sat up. He expected past romantic relation-ships. But this brazen property-buying and living with a boyfriend business was a different story. "How long did you live together?"

Jovita's fingers drummed a beat on the wooden table. "About three years," she said.

"What happened?"

Jovita shrugged. "Stuff."

"What does that mean?" he asked.

"I'm not a fan of relationship post-mortems. By the time it's over, I try to focus on the things I don't want to deal with in the next one. "

He decided not to force the issue. "What's your num-ber one relationship killer?"

"Dishonesty. I've dished it, received it, now it sucks the marrow from my bones."

Eziafa blinked. "Noted."

Jovita ran her fingers through her micro braids. "I stayed away because I needed to tie up loose ends."

"Are they all tied up?"

She nodded.

While he liked his women to be more submissive, he didn't want to walk away from her. "I've updated my resumé."

"Hmm. What a coincidence. I have an opening."

Eziafa smiled. "Luck is what happens when preparation meets opportunity."

Jovita looked impressed. "That sounds profound."

"I read the quote in a book. A philosopher guy said it."

"You read?"

Eziafa wanted to flash his dog-eared library card. Since he was on a budget, he needed free or low-cost entertainment. "I try not to. It would be a shame to ruin my hard-won ignorance."

The waiter walked up to the table with the bill. They both reached for it. Eziafa was faster.

"I should pay," Jovita said. "I invited you."

Eziafa brought out his wallet. "In my world, a man pays for his date's meals. It doesn't matter who did the inviting. Since this won't be our last outing, will this be an ongoing problem?"

"To be fair, we should split the bill."

Fairness is a myth. "No."

Jovita frowned. "There's no room for a conversation?"

He placed an open palm on the table. "There's always room for a conversation. I just think it's time you let someone with some solid international experience take good care of you."

"I'm quite capable of taking care of myself," Jovita said.

"*Please.* A trial will convince you."

Jovita hesitated before she placed her hand on his. "I guess I can let you show me what you've got."

Eziafa laced their fingers. "Now you're speaking my language."

Chapter Four

THE TOP OF Jovita's lime green Mustang convertible was down when she came to pick him up. The car stopped inches from his feet. Jovita pushed up her large sunglasses. "Hello, Mr. Okereke," she said.

Eziafa dropped his duffle bag on the back seat. "You're late."

"Sorry. The caterer lady was super busy," Jovita said, pulling out of the parking lot.

"What did she put in the basket?"

Jovita glanced at him. "An assortment of sandwiches, salad, fruit tray, beverage, and dessert."

Eziafa scrunched his nose. Bread and leaves. "When you said you were getting finger food, I thought you meant the original kings of finger foods like *fufu* or pounded yam."

She laughed. "*Naija* man. I told you to eat a man-sized breakfast."

He rubbed his beer belly. "I did. It takes a lot of food to maintain this figure."

"I can imagine."

Eziafa reclined his car seat. A mild sun warmed his

scalp. The day trip to Galveston Island was Jovita's idea. It would be his first visit. With smooth traffic on I–45, it took them about an hour to get to the island. Eziafa had never seen such a crowded beach.

They found a spot close enough to the water. He stood guard over their things while Jovita used the changing room.

As she approached him, Eziafa gulped. The white bikini left nothing to even the most mundane imagination. Two rows of *jigida* adorned the top of the bikini bottom. The gems on the coral bead string sparkled in the sun.

Eziafa's fingers clenched against the urge to touch the beads.

Jovita gave him a playful push when she reached his side. "That look on your face ... men!" she said.

Eziafa exhaled. "Where did you get those waist beads?" he asked.

"A cousin of mine sells them at her African store in Brooklyn."

Eziafa picked up his duffle bag. "Women back home don't display them to everyone," he said.

Jovita gyrated her waist. "By now, you should have noticed this isn't back home."

Sadly, Eziafa thought. "Why do you wear them?" he asked.

"They let me know when I need to hit the gym on a more regular basis." Jovita grinned. "I thought my mother was going to have a heart attack when she saw them for the first time."

"She didn't insist you take them off?"

Jovita frowned. "I'm no longer a child."

Eziafa felt a flicker of jealousy. His own mother either ignored or hadn't gotten the 'your boy is now a man' memo.

Jovita reached for her tote. "You should put on some sunscreen before we go into the water," she said.

Eziafa shook his head. "I don't need it. African cocoa doesn't melt in the sun."

Jovita laughed as she brought out a sunscreen container. "Brotha, here in the good ol' USA, chocolate burns. I won't go near water without an SPF 30."

"You see why those women call you ABN? They have no business with sunscreen. But since you need the protection, I'll help with your back."

Jovita handed over the bottle. "Don't say I didn't warn you."

He squeezed a generous amount of cream in his palm. "Woman, bring ya back."

Jovita gave him a coy look. "That leer makes me question your intentions."

"Ms. Asika, for the record, all my intentions towards you are bad. Extra bad."

Jovita giggled as she stretched out face down on her yellow beach towel.

When they finally came out of the water, Eziafa felt some tingling on his forearms and face. "I feel funny," he said.

Jovita frowned. "What is it?"

"I don't know. I have never felt this way before."

Her eyes widened. "It sounds like cocoa pod has some burn spots."

Eziafa looked at his arms. He couldn't see any red patches. "Are you sure?"

"Yup. I have a tube of aloe vera gel in my bag."

Eziafa cursed his stubborn streak as a snickering Jovita played nurse.

They left the beach to get some ice cream. Jovita took him to her favourite shop on Strand Street. Eziafa nearly choked on his saliva when he saw the price of a sundae. "This is highway robbery," he said.

Jovita looked annoyed. "You're not paying for the product. You're paying for the experience."

He didn't care for overpriced experiences. "Pure *oyibo wayo*. Tell me. Do you get a bonus for bringing people here?"

Jovita muttered some words under her breath. "Fine. We'll share one."

The dessert was creamy French vanilla topped with pecan nuts, caramel, and chocolate fudge. Eziafa took a spoonful and shook his head. "Hmm! They should have named this thing decadence."

"That's why I love it."

Jovita's eyes softened as they focussed on something or someone behind him. Eziafa turned. It was a family with little ones. "You like children?" he asked.

"Oh, yes. I especially enjoy spending time with my five nieces and nephews. They're as hilarious as their favourite aunt."

Eziafa looked forward to having children. All he wanted was two. "Are you planning to have your own?" he asked.

Jovita ate another spoon of ice cream before answering his question. "One day. When I'm ready for the long-term commitment."

Eyes fixed on her plump lips; he yearned to kiss them. *Eziafa, softly, softly.*

"Do I have something on my face?" Jovita asked.

Eziafa leaned back in his seat. "I'm only admiring God's craftsmanship."

They ended the day at a free bluegrass concert at Saengerfest Park. It was Eziafa's first time hearing that kind of music. To him, it sounded just like country music. Arms around each other, they sat on a blanket under a star-sprinkled sky.

Eziafa fell asleep during the drive to his place. Jovita parked in front of his building and tapped him on the shoulder. "You're home," she announced.

He kept his eyes closed. "Where's my wake-up kiss?"

Jovita leaned over and brushed her lips against his. "Don't forget to take the aloe vera gel with you. Put it in the fridge. It will feel better when you apply it. The burned areas will peel tomorrow."

"Have I said thank you for saving me?"

"No. And you're welcome, stubborn man."

He stepped out and closed the car door. "Call me when you get home."

Jovita's smile was warm. "Will do. Thanks for today. We made a great memory."

Eziafa stood and watched until Jovita's taillights disappeared. He should have told her he needed help with applying the gel. He brought out his cell phone and dialled her number.

Jovita took his call through Bluetooth. "Hey, cocoa pod."

Eziafa shuffled his feet on the cracked concrete. "You forgot something," he said.

"What?" Jovita asked.

He whispered the word. "Me."

Jovita's voice softened. "Do you want to come back to my place? I can use a little distraction."

Eziafa scratched his head. His needs and wants were clashing. "I have to work in the morning."

"You're one mixed-up man," Jovita said.

"Call me when you get home."

"I will."

Chapter Five

EZIAFA QUICKENED HIS steps. It was reveal time. After Jovita gave herself the job of sprucing up his apartment as part of her "adding colour to Eziafa's life" campaign, she persuaded him to stay away for a night at a nearby motel so she could finish up.

He couldn't wait to see the miracle performed on a two-hundred-dollar budget.

Jovita opened her purse and brought out a black scarf. "You have to turn around," she said.

Eziafa gave her a suspicious look. "For what?"

"A blindfold will increase your sense of anticipation."

Eziafa eyed the scarf. "By now you should know that I'm a paranoid *Naija* man. How am I sure you don't have a diabolical plan?"

Jovita snorted. "Yeah. I'm going to wrap this chloroform-soaked scarf around your nose. When you pass out, I'll toss you into my trunk and drive you over to a body parts dealer. I hear there's a world shortage of healthy kidneys and livers."

"Jovita!"

She cocked her head. "Do you trust me?"

Eziafa hesitated. "Well, trust is a spectrum."

She placed a hand on her waist. "Ain't nobody got time for your hallway TED talk. Yes or no?"

God help him with this woman and her antics. "Yes."

Jovita twirled the scarf. "Then step forward like a strong, fearless African warrior."

"Madam Sweet Lips." He gave a slight bow.

Jovita snickered as she wrapped the material around his eyes. Eziafa pushed it away from his nose. Wisdom was key. No man should ever forget Delilah's role in Samson's downfall.

Eziafa tensed as Jovita dug out the keys from his trouser pocket. She reached for his hand to guide him into the sitting room. He sneezed at a fresh paint scent.

"*Abeg*, untie your scarf," he said.

Jovita squeezed his hand. "Relax. I want you seated so you can take it all in."

She gently pushed him down into an unfamiliar chair. "I'm ready."

Jovita untied the knot and pulled the scarf. Eziafa blinked at the bright lights.

He was speechless. The brightness in the room came from two standing lamps placed at the ends of his loveseat. His worn chairs had shiny brown brocade covers, and oversized, orange pillows. There were new drapes and a long coffee table. Underneath the table was a beige rug with a patterned brown border.

"Do you like what you see?" Jovita asked.

Eziafa pulled himself up from the wingback chair. "How did you do all this?"

"You haven't answered my question."

"I love it. You did perform a miracle."

Jovita's hands went up in the air. "Yes! I found the wing-back chair and coffee table at an estate sale in River Oaks. Guess what? I only paid forty bucks."

Eziafa ran his fingers across the leather. River Oaks was one of the priciest neighbourhoods in Houston. "They look brand new."

Jovita nodded. "When you have many rooms, some furniture gets minimal use. The other things came from two of my favourite thrift stores."

Eziafa exhaled. "With this, woman, you have upgraded me."

Jovita gave him a soft smile. "It's how I love."

He pulled her into an embrace, followed by a heated kiss. Lip-locked, they shuffled their way to the couch. Eziafa's cell phone rang. He ignored it. The phone kept ringing.

Jovita pulled away from him. "Take the call. It could be something important."

Eziafa sucked his teeth. Some people were blessed with horrible timing.

It was his younger sister. "Brother, good evening," Evelyn said.

Eziafa's voice was gruff. "*Kedu?*"

"*Odinma*. Nne asked me to call. Let me give the phone to her."

Eziafa scratched his head. He was in big trouble. He had planned to save some money before giving his mother a definite answer to the request in her letter. His preoccupation with Jovita had pushed the matter to the back of his mind.

He covered the receiver. "Sorry, it's my mother. I need to take the call outside."

Jovita gave him an understanding look. "Sure."

"Thank you."

Eziafa stepped out on the balcony and closed the sliding door. Jovita didn't need to hear him grovel.

Nne's angry voice boomed in his ear. "Eziafakaego, why have I not heard from you?"

He leaned against the balcony wall. "Nne, I sent your monthly money."

"Did I ask you for money?"

His mother rarely made explicit requests. She only mentioned their needs and expected him to connect the necessary financial dots.

"You did not get my letter?"

"I did. I'm sorry. I only wanted to put certain things in order before responding."

"So, when are you coming home?" Nne asked.

"It has to be next year. Right now, things are not easy."

Nne gave a dismissive hiss. "When have things ever been easy? It may be time for you to move back to Nigeria."

She had to be joking. "Move back to Nigeria to do what? Farm? Tap palm trees?"

"See this foolish child. The farmers and palm wine tappers you are looking down on have built their own houses."

The insult stung. "I wasn't looking down on them," he said.

Nne ignored his words. "Some young men in the village have become fish farmers. They feed their families from the profits."

"You talk as if I'm a lazy man," he grumbled.

"*Nwa m*, I know you're not. Laziness does not run in

your lineage. But the abroad does not offer its riches to everyone."

Eziafa rapped his knuckles on the wall. He wasn't moving back to Nigeria, not before he made something of himself. "Things are turning around for me," he said.

"Are you telling me the truth? You people over there are good at keeping things from your people at home."

"Yes, Nne. My taxicab business is doing well. You will soon see my face."

"Are you sure?"

"I'm not lying. How are you?"

"My son, we are fine. We will be finer when we see your face."

"Nne, I have to go. My visitor is waiting. I'll call you later."

"Before you go, I should let you know that some wicked people tried to sell off your land. If not for your uncle, we would have lost everything. The earlier you build on that land, the better."

Eziafa's frustration boiled over. "House or wife—Nne, pick one."

Her voice rose. "Why are you talking as if it is impossible to do two good things at the same time?"

"You want me to rob a bank?"

Nne hissed. "There are no armed robbers in your lineage."

He groaned his frustration. "Nne."

"Wife. I choose a wife. It is time for you to be fully responsible."

Eziafa scowled. "I still need to save before I can marry."

"Please, don't send us any money until you come home. We will manage."

Thanks to his mother's inability to block her ears to sob stories, most of her customers got their cassava on credit. "How will you feed?"

"If I must sell my *wrappas* at the market, I will."

The words ignited his anger. Would she tie banana leaves until his arrival? "Nne, you know I can't let you do that."

"Then come home before all the girls from respectable families are married off."

Eziafa rubbed the side of his neck. Each day, the noose fashioned from Nne's expectations tightened around it. "I will."

Her relieved sigh only fuelled his fury. "*Nwa m*, thank you."

"I have to go."

"*Chukwu gozie gi.*"

Eziafa clenched his teeth. He certainly needed some divine intervention. Shoving the phone deep into his pocket, he plopped down on the couch.

"Are things okay?" Jovita asked.

He should not have taken the call. "Yes."

Jovita peered at his face. "But your face says otherwise."

He pulled her close. "We had to hash out some minor family drama."

"That is no fun." Jovita wrapped her arms around his neck and brought her lips close to his. "A liberal dose of sugar and spice will make you feel better."

Chapter Six

EZIAFA WHISTLED AS he took the elevator up to the tenth-floor apartment. Jovita, a die-hard Texans fan, had season tickets. He was picking her up for a home game.

Jovita was dressed in a pantsuit. "Hey you," she said.

Eziafa walked in. "You're not ready?"

"I'm sorry. My last home showing ran later than I'd planned."

Eziafa glanced at his watch. "You have time to change."

"Is it okay if we don't go to the game?"

He peered at her face. "You look tired."

"It's been a long week."

Eziafa leaned against a wall as he kicked off his shoes. "If that's what you want."

"Thanks. For being so accommodating, I'll make you some *ogbono* soup."

Jovita was yet to cook for him. "Are you talking about something from a can? If so, let's order Chinese."

"Nah. Chinese food can't top condensed *ogbono* soup," Jovita said. "The Campbell's version is superb."

Eziafa's stomach turned at the thought. "Tell me you're joking."

Jovita chuckled. "I need to change out of these clothes. I'll be right back."

Eziafa ambled around the loft apartment. Since his last visit, Jovita had made some changes. The crisp, white accent wall behind the mounted television now had splatters of black and red paint. Eziafa cocked his head. From every angle, it looked like something an angry two-year-old had done.

"*Na wah.*"

"Are you complaining about my new décor?" Jovita asked.

He swung around. She had changed into a loose black t-shirt and a pair of tight denim shorts.

"I wouldn't dare. It suits you. The messy wall and that wicked pair of shorts."

Jovita snorted. "Please, wash your hands at the sink. Let's get cooking."

He frowned. "Who says I'm cooking?"

"Me. The spinach for the soup won't chop itself."

"Aha. I forgot to tell you. I'm allergic to cutting vegetables."

Jovita gave him a side-eye. "Oh, yeah? How come you're not allergic to eating them?"

Eziafa snapped a finger over his head. "Allergic to food? God forbid bad thing."

Jovita opened a drawer and pulled out a yellow apron. "You'll need something to protect your clothes," she said.

The image on the apron was a Speedo-wearing thermometer in a chef hat. Eziafa read out the bold inscription: "Real men heat up the kitchen?"

"They sure do. I keep the apron for my guests. I find men who can cook super attractive."

Eziafa slipped the apron over his head. The thing hung halfway down his calves. There was no point in thinking about the tall man or men who'd worn the apron before him.

"Woman, this meal better be worth this degradation," he said.

Jovita handed him a knife and chopping board. "You show these spinach leaves who's the boss."

Eziafa eyed the vegetables. The things a man had to do to get into a woman's underwear.

After their meal, he and Jovita stacked the dishwasher and moved on to the living room with a bottle of red wine and goblets.

Eziafa sat on the loveseat. "Beautiful one, I must say the *ogbono* soup was exceptional."

Jovita placed the items on the coffee table. "That's some high praise," she said.

"It is well deserved. Honestly, the sweetness of that soup would make any child steal fried meat from their mother's cooking pot."

Jovita pulled the cork and filled his goblet. "I don't think I've ever seen you this excited."

Eziafa accepted the wine. "A combination of you and Nigerian food has a magical effect on all my senses."

Jovita sat next to him. "I can't believe this is our seventh date," she said.

He had been counting, too. "Actually, it is our eighth."

Jovita looked pleased. "The man has excellent mathematical skills."

"You forget I count money on a regular basis." He reached for Jovita's free hand. "Do you find me attractive?"

"I don't French kiss random guys," Jovita said.

"That knowledge is comforting."

"Why are you asking?"

Eziafa was tired of waiting for a spontaneous sexual encounter. "If you would be kind to a lonely man living far away from his ancestral lands, I'll love to spend the night with you."

"You're lonely?"

"I've been crying myself to sleep."

Jovita cocked her head. "You're being pretty straightforward about what you want."

Eziafa nodded. "I'm too old for games."

"It's hard to say no to such a heartfelt plea." She moved away from him. "I'm going to my room. Give me ten minutes."

Eight minutes later, he knocked on Jovita's bedroom door. It shouldn't take her that long to undress.

Jovita sat on the four-poster bed with the duvet held against her bare chest. "Do you have to go?" she asked.

Eziafa slid the belt through his trouser loops. He should have left at dawn. "Woman, I told you I must work. Bills don't pay themselves."

"I also have bills," she said.

Eziafa scanned the room for his shirt. In his haste to take it off, he had popped a button. "We don't have the same family expectations."

"I get the Nigerian first-born thing. Still, you need a life. You don't want your tombstone to say: Here lies our loving son and brother Eziafa who worked his way to a massive heart attack."

The words struck Eziafa. His father became bedridden after having one. "You have a blunt way of getting your point across," he said.

"I don't believe in wasting time. Are you staying?"

Eziafa groaned. "This woman, you're not helping."

Jovita dropped the duvet.

Eziafa gulped as he yanked out his belt. The unzipped trousers pooled around his ankles.

Jovita did a fist pump. "The amazing Jovita, one. The malleable Eziafa, zero."

"*Chei*. See my life."

"Don't be hard on yourself. I promise to make it worth your while."

Eziafa wagged his index finger. "You're bad."

Jovita's body shook with laughter as she bent her fingers into the "rock on" sign. "I'm rocking and rolling. That's why you can't get enough of me."

He'd come to realize that Jovita worked hard at shocking people. When he'd mentioned this observation to her, she'd said that, when people expected her to act that way, she became that way. He held out his hands and dove into her bed. "At your service."

Jovita gave a contented sigh. "Now we're going to cuddle."

"*Abeg*, cuddling is for learners."

"Who said you're a pro?"

After all his hard work? "This is not what you promised me," Eziafa said with a pout.

"All I said was, stay. Your raunchy imagination filled in the blanks."

"And your imagination is chaste?"

"Unlike you, I don't drape myself in a moral upright-ness toga."

Eziafa groaned. "How is this worth my while? I'm not good at this cuddling business."

Jovita batted her eyelashes. "Give it your best shot. We'll see what the rest of the day brings."

Eziafa stared at Jovita's oily face. It seemed like she wasn't one of those women who ran for the bathroom mirror as soon as they opened their eyes. Her permed hair was matted to one side of her head. She had crust around her left eye. Her morning breath would make an effective mosquito spray. Yet the confidence imprinted in her smile made Jovita even more attractive. God help him.

Chapter Seven

FELIX LEANED BACK in the chair and crossed his legs. "*Na wah* for you o. These days one has to get a Schengen visa to see your face."

With his free time reserved for Jovita, Eziafa no longer spent Sunday evenings at Felix's home. "Bros, you're on the wrong continent," he said.

Felix rolled his eyes. "*Na you sabi.*"

Eziafa placed an opened bottle of malt liquor on the small table beside Felix. "I told you I've been busy."

"Busy doing what?" Felix asked.

He grinned. "Enjoying life."

Felix looked around the living room. "Jovita must be responsible for this change."

"She is. The woman has many talents."

"What exactly is going on between you two?" Felix asked.

Eziafa stared at his friend. There weren't any no-go topics between them. Yet he felt a sudden reluctance to discuss Jovita with Felix. He chose his words. "Jovita and I are helping each other get through this stressful life."

Felix guffawed and slapped his thigh. "The Black Mamba!"

Eziafa smiled at his old nickname. During their university days, he'd kept an official girlfriend, an assistant girlfriend, and a third for emergency situations. "You're still the grand master," he said.

"I'm happily retired. Nkolika locked me down nineteen years ago."

"I can't get tired of saying this. Felix, your wife is a strong woman."

"*Wayo* man, get back to the topic. This your *waka* with Jovita is more than a stress-relieving activity. From what I've heard in many circles, you're close to carrying wine to her family house."

He had no time for gossip. "Did the basket mouths tell you the date and time of this wedding ceremony?"

"Eziafa, you're talking to me."

He shrugged. "And so?"

"Did I not see the two of you dancing blues at Kola's party?" Felix said. "Those greedy hands of yours were latched on to the woman's behind."

Eziafa held up his hands. "In their defense, they were inches below Jovita's waist."

Felix's eyes twinkled. "*Negodu* this man. I also sang 'head, shoulders, knees and toes' in primary school. There is a difference between the waist and the buttocks."

"This is the twenty-first century. Human bodies have evolved."

"Such scandalous behaviour in the presence of innocent people such as myself."

"You? Innocent?"

Felix did a sign of the cross. "I served five years as an altar boy."

"I did six years," Eziafa said. "Please, tell me, how does dancing blues with a woman translate into a marriage proposal?"

"Stop pretending. Obikwelu saw both of you at the mall. Holding hands and giggling like teenagers."

Jovita signed them up for dance lessons at a studio in the mall. The salsa moves had definitely improved his flexibility. "Mr. Telephone without Wire. Must Obikwelu talk about everything his big eyes see?"

"Why are you trying to change the subject? I have to say that Jovita is a lovely woman. When Nkolika was in the hospital, she brought us meals."

Jovita admired Nkolika's candid personality. To a degree, Eziafa did too. Nkolika wasn't one to call a snake a slithering rope. If Nkolika liked you, it was obvious to everyone around her. And if she didn't, God help you. "Jovita has a kind heart," he said.

Felix's expression sobered. "You have deep feelings for her?"

"I do." He had yet to share them with Jovita.

"That makes what I have to say harder. But I would be a bad friend if I didn't let you know about Jovita's colourful past."

Eziafa frowned. "What do you mean?"

"Did Jovita tell you about the men she had lived with? I know of three. There may be others."

Eziafa's hand shook as he picked non-existent lint off his trousers. "Who told you?"

"Presido's wife. They're family friends. She said Jovita

moved to Houston after the last man impregnated another woman."

That must have been the Buffalo man. Eziafa kept his tone casual. "Jovita told me about them."

Felix looked relieved. "She did well. When it comes to any relationship, having adequate information helps with making the best decisions."

Eziafa forced a smile. What else did other people know that he didn't?

The digital clock on the cab's dashboard read 3:11 am when Beulah, the independent cab company's dispatcher, radioed him. Beulah told him a request came in from the gas station at the intersection of Airline Drive and North Main. Eziafa headed to the destination.

To keep awake, he chewed on pork rinds from the snack pack in his lap. Out on the dimly lit streets, all he saw was the odd person staggering home from a Friday night outing.

He cranked up the radio and nodded along to The Black-Eyed Peas' "I Gotta Feeling."

Jovita had introduced him to the song. A smile tugged at the side of his mouth. The woman made life sweet.

Eziafa slowly pulled up to the gas station. Two people waited outside the building. He kept the engine running as the scowling young man helped the pregnant teen into the back seat. Her moan alarmed Eziafa. She looked very pregnant. He reached for his radio. "Should I call for an ambulance?" he asked.

"No man. She's alright. Keep driving. East 40th Street."

Eziafa hesitated. He didn't like the young man's tone.

The girl grabbed the back of Eziafa's headrest. "I wanna get home. Please."

Eziafa lifted his foot off the brake. Halfway through the drive, he flinched when the young woman's long nails scratched the back of his neck as she gripped the headrest even harder. He couldn't wait for the ride to be over.

The young woman made a retching sound. "Oh my God. I'm gonna puke."

Eziafa's heart sank. The car had been steam-cleaned two days earlier. "I have a plastic bag under my seat—"

"Forget that. Pull over!" the young man barked.

Eziafa struggled to keep his eyes on the road. "What?"

"I said pull over!"

As Eziafa debated his next action, the young man gave a loud shout. "Damn it! Her water just broke."

Eziafa's eyes flew to the rear-view mirror. "Eh, which water?"

The girl gave an ear-piercing scream. "Stop this car now!"

The tires screeched as Eziafa swerved the car into a nearby alley. As he pulled the parking brake, cold metal pressed hard into the base of his skull. Eziafa didn't have to turn around to tell it was a gun. His hands flew up. "*Nne'm o!*"

Spittle sprayed the back of his head. "What the hell is he saying?" the young man said.

The girl broke into a wild giggle. "I think he's speaking Spanish."

Eziafa gagged. His life was in the hands of two idiots. "*Ewo!*"

The gun barrel dug deep into his skull. "Shut your pie hole!" the young man said.

"Please, don't shoot me. Don't shoot o!"

"Then you'd better shut the fuck up!"

Eziafa clamped his lips. It wasn't his bullet-ridden body they would ship back to Nigeria.

"Where's the money?" the girl asked.

"It's in my glove box," Eziafa said. "The key is in my back pocket."

The girl hopped out of her car. Her pregnancy bump was now at her side. She walked around, dug a hand into Eziafa's back pocket and pulled out the key. She opened the glove box and whistled. "Payday!"

The young man barked at him. "Get out."

Eziafa opened the driver's side door and fell to the ground. He buried his face deep in the dirt and braced for the impact of a bullet.

Something dug into the middle of his back. "Listen, I got people watching. You make any noise, I'll be back."

Eziafa heard a metal clink as something dropped into the nearby drain. The sound of their running footsteps receded down the alley.

After what felt like hours, Eziafa lifted his head. He was alone. He scrambled to his feet, leapt into the car, slammed the door and pressed the locks. His key was missing from the ignition.

Eziafa reached into his thick sock and yanked out the key taped above his ankle. Thanks to Mr. Osas' safety class, he always carried a concealed spare key. The tires raised dust as he accelerated out of the alley.

He ended up at Jovita's condo building. She buzzed him up. Dressed in an oversized leopard print housecoat, Jovita's eyes were wide with worry. "What happened?"

"A robbery. I almost got shot."

She held on to his arm. "Oh my God! Are you hurt? Did you call the police?"

Eziafa shook his head. "All I could think of was getting to you."

Jovita stroked his cheek. "Let's go take a shower."

Eziafa was silent as Jovita walked him to her bedroom. She stripped his clothes and led him to the bathroom. His tears finally came when he stood under the pulsating jets. Eziafa muffled his cries as the teardrops mixed with the warm water. *Na so person dey die?*

He forced himself to drink the cup of sweet tea Jovita put in his hands. They snuggled in her bed. "I'm so grateful nothing happened to you."

Eziafa closed his eyes. Piece by piece, Jovita had managed to strip away his protective sheath. He whispered the words he'd been reluctant to say into her lavender-scented skin. "I love you."

He felt Jovita's chest rise and fall as she took a deep breath. "I love you, too."

Chapter Eight

EZIAFA COULDN'T WAIT until he got home to call his mother. He parked his car on the roadside. The connection was spotty. After several minutes of trying her number, he got through. "Nne, I have good news," he said.

Her voice brightened. "You have bought your airplane ticket?"

"No. I met a beautiful woman here. Her name is Jovita Asika."

"She is an Igbo woman?" Nne asked.

The joy in his mother's voice was palpable. "Yes. One hundred and one percent."

Nne called for his sister. "Evelyn, come and hear o. Your brother has found us a wife."

Eziafa heard Evelyn's excited chatter in the background.

"Where are her parents? What is the name of their village?"

Eziafa had prepared for his mother's questions. "Jovita's parents also live here in America. They're from Umuonyeori."

For several minutes, all Eziafa heard was silence. "Nne, are you still there?"

"Did I hear you say Umuonyeori?"

The warmth in his mother's voice was gone. "Yes. Is there any problem?" he asked.

"*Tufiakwa*. You have not found your wife," she said.

Eziafa rested his head against the steering wheel. "Nne, what did you say?"

"Is something wrong with your ears? I said you are yet to find your wife."

Eziafa ran a hand over his face. "Nne, why?"

She spat her words. "Everyone from that cursed village is a thief."

His furrowed brow cleared. "That is statistically impossible."

Nne's hiss was long and loud. "Be speaking English. Listen, her ancestors were slave traders. They raided our village."

His heart rate settled. "All that was in the past."

"Spoken like a child. Once a thief, always a thief. Eziafakaego, why would you want to tie yourself to people who caused your people pain?"

"It's not right to punish people for something their ancestors did," he said.

"They're still farming on the lands they bought with blood money."

He would not inherit the hate. "Nne, Jovita is a woman of integrity. When you meet her, you'll see that I'm right."

"I have no intention of meeting this Jovita. You tell me when you are coming home and I will hasten our search for a proper woman."

"Please listen to me," he said.

"*Bia*, did this thing bewitch you?"

"Jovita is not a thing. I love her. And I know that you will—"

"I told you this woman is from a lineage of thieves and killers. How do you expect me to love such a person?"

"Jovita makes me happy."

"She makes you happier than your mother makes you?"

Eziafa clenched his teeth. Jovita's love nurtured him. He knew his mother would be heartbroken if he told her how his love for her had acquired a taint from the duties she imposed. "There's room for both of you in my life."

"Why is your voice hard?" Nne asked.

"My voice is fine."

A wail filled his ear. "*Chi m*! This morning, as I prayed, my spirit told me danger laid ahead. So, this is how the devil wants to destroy our family?"

"Nne, you're overreacting. We have to let the past stay in the past."

She continued to cry. "*Ewo*! I have lost my son, my crown. *Chineke*, why have you kept me alive to watch my only son commit suicide?"

He gritted his teeth. "Nne, *ozugo nu*. There's no need to cry."

"Let me cry. People are already laughing at us. Imagine how loud their cackling would get when they hear about this woman."

"I'm not living my life for the village people."

"Who else will truly celebrate your success? Ezi-afakaego, those who left for America after you have come back to do bigger, more important things. All I'm asking for is a bride. Is that too much?"

He slouched in his seat. "I am trying my best."

Her voice caught. "If your father were alive, he would have forced you home. Is it because it is me, a mere woman, doing the asking?"

"You have never been a mere woman to me. Please, stop crying."

She continued to sniffle. "You will come back home to find someone else?"

"I will do whatever you need me to do."

"Nwa m, I only want your happiness."

Overcome by a wave of weariness, Eziafa closed his eyes.

It was close to dawn when Eziafa rolled off the bed and pulled on his pajama bottoms. He couldn't sleep. To avoid waking Jovita, he tiptoed his way out of the dark room. He watched the sunrise from the balcony.

As the sun broke the horizon, vibrant shades of red, orange, and yellow lit up the dark blue sky. The days were flying. He wasn't any closer to finding a solution to his dilemma. Perhaps it was time for him to accept that a woman whose introduction into the family would bring enmity between him and his mother was not the right choice for a wife.

"Morning."

He turned. Jovita stood behind him. "You're out here again. What's going on?"

He offered her a half-smile. "I have a lot on my mind."

Jovita rubbed her eyes. "I've got two dollars and twenty-five cents in my purse," she said. "At the penny rate, I can pay you a good chunk."

Eziafa exhaled. Despite Nne's opposition, he continued to entertain thoughts of marrying Jovita. He was ready to plead with Nne until she changed her mind. However, he needed full disclosure about Jovita's past. "There is something I need to know," he said.

Jovita sat across from him. "What is it?"

Eziafa picked his words. "How many men have you ... been with?"

Jovita's face darkened as she pulled her robe closer. "We've already talked about this. It's none of your damn business."

Eziafa bristled at the dismissive tone. "I'm not interested in playing sexual roulette."

"Now, you care about getting STDs?"

He had to know. "Jovita, this a valid concern. What are you hiding?"

"Nothing."

"Then tell me."

Jovita shrugged. "As you wish. Do you need the stats for this quarter or the whole year? If I'd known there would be an interrogation, I would have prepared documentation."

Eziafa sat up. "What?"

Jovita ran fingers through her weave. "I'll start from my first experience."

He fought the urge to shout at her. "Jovita ..."

She held up her hand. "You asked for the information,

so you need to listen. There was Benny Boy in my kindergarten class. I tell you, that love affair had many ups and downs. Even though he found my kinky hair quite attractive, some days, he pulled on it for fun."

Eziafa groaned. "This is ridiculous."

Jovita held up a hand. "I'm not done. In grade four, after a much-needed hiatus from the dating scene, I moved on to a more sophisticated boy. His was my first kiss. He did miss my mouth by several inches."

Eziafa paced the small space. "Why are you acting as if this isn't a valid question?"

"I don't get why this is so important to you," she said.

"For one, it would be nice to take you somewhere and not wonder how many men there have seen you naked."

Jovita's eyes narrowed into slits. "That is a you problem."

"You don't understand. I've been thinking of marrying you."

After gaping at him, Jovita began to laugh. "Man, you're killing me."

"This is not funny."

"Well, it's a good thing you're still at the thinking stage," Jovita said.

"What do you mean?"

Jovita straightened her shoulders. "For the record, just in case I never made it clear, I don't need your or anyone's wedding band to cast a sheen of respectability on me."

Eziafa scowled. "Is it true you've lived with three men?"

"You missed one. *And*?"

The flippant response made him clench his teeth. "Why aren't you married?"

"If I were, you do realize I wouldn't be here with you?"

"Why didn't you just go to their houses on the weekends like other women do? Why did you have to advertise it to everybody?"

Jovita frowned. *"Advertise?* I lived with my exes because I wanted to, because in one situation pooling our resources saved me money. Because living with them worked until it stopped working."

"Do you still think about these men?" he asked.

"Occasionally."

The response made his blood boil. "Why?"

She gave him a hard stare. "Because, good or bad, they were a part of my life. I'm not pining for them. But I certainly can't wipe out my memories because they make you feel insecure."

Eziafa hung his head. He loved Jovita. His feelings were the strongest he'd ever had for any woman. Still, it was impossible for him to parade a queen many in their community would consider a second-hand woman. He imagined Nne's horror if she discovered Jovita's past.

Jovita stood. "I should go."

It was best she did since he needed space to think. "I'll drive you."

She moved away from him. "No thanks. I can find my way home."

Chapter Nine

AFTER THREE DAYS of intense internal debate, Eziafa made his decision.

During one of their man to man conversations, Papa told him there were two types of women. There were ones who were suitable for marriage and there were enchantresses who wise men kept as cherished lovers. If one was lucky, one married a woman who commanded one's full attention. While Jovita certainly did that, Eziafa couldn't convince himself that she fell into the former group.

Nne sounded weary when she took his call. "Eziafa-kego, *kedu?*"

"*Odinma.*" He rested against the wingback chair. "How was your day?"

"It is better now that I have heard your voice," she said.

"Your prayers worked. I'm coming to Nigeria this December."

Her voice trembled. "You are coming home?"

"Yes. Before I return to Houston, you will have a new daughter."

Nne broke into one of her church songs. "*Kpo ya Chukwu no gaza ...*"

Eziafa could not sing along.

Nkolika answered their door. "*Oga* Eziafa, your face has been scarce around here. Were you fighting with us?"

He gave Nkolika a warm smile. "*Nwanyi oma,* I can never fight with you. Blame your husband. Felix told me to stay away since he no longer wants to share your cooking."

Nkolika chuckled. "Is that so?"

Eziafa followed her into the living room. "Yes o."

"*Yeye man,* I can hear your wicked lies," Felix shouted from the couch. "Tell Nkolika what you have been busy doing. Shameless woman *wrappa.*"

"You tell your wife the truth and shame the devil," he said.

Nkolika shook her head. "You two have always been trouble."

He and Felix met Nkolika when she was about fourteen. Nkolika's older cousin was their village playmate. Eziafa was the lookout for Nkolika's parents during the times Felix visited her home.

Felix turned to his wife. "My queen, don't mind him o. The man wants to add sand grains to our excellent *gari.*"

"My own king, it is not possible," Nkolika said.

Felix's eyes twinkled. "Eziafa, *ntorr.* Your plan to destabilize our love has failed."

"Because Nkolika called you king, your head is swelling. Thank your *chi* you married a paragon of virtue."

Nkolika and Felix exchanged a look and the couple

burst into laughter. Felix stood from the couch and patted Eziafa on the back. "Welcome."

He took a nearby seat while Nkolika sat next to her husband.

"Is everything okay?" Felix asked.

As close as they were, he rarely made unannounced visits to their home. "I had to let you know that I've asked Nne to find me a wife."

Felix slapped his thigh. "Yes! Soon, you'll have a personal hot water bottle."

"With this Houston heat, a human Popsicle would be best." Eziafa noted Nkolika's stoic expression. "*Nwanyi oma*, I'm sure you'll be happy to have another Oji woman around."

Nkolika's response was a tight-lipped smile. After he'd declined her offer of food and drinks, Nkolika turned to her husband. "I'll leave you to entertain your friend while I finish the laundry."

Felix waited until his wife was out of earshot. "Are your finances in order?" he asked.

Eziafa knew that, because of his American resident status, the whole village would expect an invitation to a grand feast. They would also judge him on the quality of food and entertainment provided. "I get chest pain every time I think about the money I have to spend. They act as if dollar bills float in the air here."

"Some people at home still think they do," Felix said. "Thank God Nkolika's people were so understanding. The traditional marriage item list they gave us didn't break our backs."

With his history, Eziafa couldn't count on such luck. "My brother, I only have two months to save."

Felix gave him a sympathetic look. "I had to max out my credit cards to pay for our wedding. *Nna*, the amount ballooned after three years of minimum payments. In hindsight, I should have put a limit on my spending. No matter how many cows you kill, our people will still complain about a meat shortage."

Eziafa had created an Excel spreadsheet to track his expenses. "I can't do this without taking out cash advances."

"A man must do what he has to do," Felix said.

"I swear. These women have easier lives."

"They would disagree. Don't worry. The ceremonies will come and go. And when your wife joins you, it will all be worth it. Please know that Nkolika and I are willing to help out in any way we can."

Their oldest child would soon be leaving for college. "You have done enough for me."

Felix lowered his voice as he moved to the edge of his seat. "What happened with Jovita? Have you told her about your decision?"

Eziafa squirmed. "Not yet."

"Tell her. Please, try to end things well. While I like Jovita, I understand your reservations. If she couldn't make those relationships work, how can you be sure you won't end up in divorce court?"

Eziafa relaxed in his seat. "I knew you would understand. I also want a woman committed to our traditional values. A woman who won't complain when you send money back home because she accepts that, when you marry a man, you marry his people."

"My brother, these days, few women want to live by all our traditional values. They want to pick and choose."

As far as Eziafa was concerned, most of the traditional

ways of living worked. In an à la carte life, access to a myr-
iad of choices only led to irrational decision-making.

"Nne has promised to find a young woman I can
mold to my taste," he said.

Felix's laughter rang through the room. "What is it with
men like you and your fantasies about moldable women?"

Eziafa didn't think it was a fantasy. "Tell me, which
man does not want a woman who reflects him?"

Felix shook his head. "I don't. My Nkolika has a mind
of her own."

Eziafa lowered his voice. "Because you failed in that
area doesn't mean I will. We all have our fields of expertise."

"My friend, shine your eyes. It's no longer wise to travel
back home to marry a woman whose character you don't
know."

Eziafa waved aside the warning. His mother would not
let him down. "I know what I'm doing."

"I have said my own." Felix stood. "Well, this news of
yours calls for a celebration. Since Nkolika has molded me
to her fantastic taste, I need to ask her if I can go out for
drinks."

On the way to Jovita's place, Eziafa convinced himself it
was premature to tell her about his decision. Yes telling
her was the honourable thing to do. However, he was yet
to buy his plane ticket. Things could change. He silenced
the admonishing voice in his head. Yes, they could.

Eziafa made a quick detour to the grocery store. At
his request, the baker used sliced raspberries to write
SORRY on a ready-made cake. He should have called to

make sure Jovita made it safely home after she left his place in a taxi.

Her car was in the parking lot. Eziafa stood by the entrance and waited for someone to let him into the secured building. A teenaged girl did after he told her he was making a surprise birthday delivery.

Jovita was in the hall locking her front door when he arrived at her floor. "Hello, sunshine," he said.

Her face was anything but sunny. "What are you doing here?"

Eziafa held out the cake box. "I brought you a little present."

Jovita folded her arms. "How nice of you."

"I'm sorry I didn't call," he said. "I thought you needed some time to cool off."

She hitched her purse strap up her shoulder. "Anger sucks up too much of my energy. I don't have any to waste."

He balanced the cake box in his hands. "May I come in?"

Jovita stepped away from the door. "As you can see, I'm on my way out."

"Please. Give me five minutes."

Jovita turned around, unlocked her door and held it open. "The clock's ticking."

Eziafa licked his dry lips. "I'm truly sorry for what I said to you. It was rude and hurtful."

"It was. But I'm glad the conversation happened. You clearly want something that I'm not."

Eziafa knew it was the right moment for him to say to her, you're right, thanks for everything and have a good life. "Jovita, I do want you," he said.

"My body or my heart?"

Eziafa forced a smile. "It is not a package deal?"

Jovita sighed. "I can't do this right now. Let's finish this conversation tomorrow evening."

Eziafa held out the box. "It's a triple chocolate cake with a raspberry sauce filling."

Jovita's face softened. "You remembered?"

It was her favourite dessert. "I don't forget anything you tell me."

She accepted the box. "Thank you."

Eziafa stood by the kitchen island and watched Jovita place the cake box in the fridge. "Where are you off to?" he asked.

"My mom's in town. We're meeting up at a restaurant for her birthday dinner."

Eziafa recalled an earlier conversation. "I thought she was going to stay with you?"

"There was a change of plans. Sometimes, space makes for a healthy mother-daughter relationship. I've got to go."

"Tomorrow evening, your place or mine?" he asked.

"I'll let you know in the morning."

"You're going to make me suffer until then?"

"Not my style," Jovita said. "My place. Six pm. Come with an empty stomach. I'm not eating that huge cake all by myself."

Chapter Ten

JOVITA PLACED THE dessert plate on the little table beside him. "Would you like some coffee?"

Eziafa shook his head. It was too late in the day for caffeine. "Water is fine."

Jovita brought back glasses and a pitcher of water infused with cucumber, mint, and lemon. She swore by its health benefits. He drank it to please her.

She sat cross-legged with a dessert plate balanced on her lap. "I've been waiting for this."

Eziafa picked up his fork and took a bite of the chocolate cake. The excessive sugar made his teeth hurt. He took a drink of his water to wash away the taste. "How did the birthday dinner go?"

"It went well. My mom told me to pass on her thanks."

"For what?" Eziafa asked.

"She wondered about my improvement in Igbo. I told her a man I know gave me lessons."

"I've become a random man?"

"Eziafa, you acted like a chauvinistic bully."

Eziafa fought the urge to defend himself. "I'm sorry. You did not have to answer my questions."

Jovita gave a heavy sigh. "I can't help thinking that Cupid has a lousy sense of humour."

"Why would you say that?"

"Because we're so fundamentally different, it's mad scary. Yet here I am, eating an apology cake while actually trying to mentally skew things so I can see more pros than cons with continuing with this relationship."

"Am I all bad?"

"It would be easier if you were. I love the way you pamper me. The way you support the things important to me. So, if you still want the numbers, we can talk about them."

The sincerity on her face made Eziafa uncomfortable. "It's fine. I no longer need the information."

She whipped her head back. "You don't?"

"No."

Jovita held his gaze. "Before we wrap up this conversation, there is something I need to know."

Eziafa shifted in his seat. "What is it?"

"Are you sure this relationship is enough for you?" she asked. "Although I want you in my life, I'm not afraid of being alone."

The assurance that Jovita was strong enough to move on eased the tightness in Eziafa's chest. "You're enough," he said.

For now.

Jovita came out of the bathroom and climbed back into bed with him. Eziafa placed a hand behind his head. "Have I told you I'm going to Nigeria?"

Jovita shook her head. "What's going on?"

"Family business. It was kind of last-minute. Thankfully, I found a ticket deal on a discount travel site."

Jovita looked excited. "When do you leave?"

He played with her braids. "The first week of December. I'll be back in the new year."

"Can I come with you?" Jovita asked. "I could use a tropical vacation."

"This isn't a trip to the Islands," he said with a short laugh.

"I'm serious. My parents took us to Nigeria when I was nine. I don't remember much of the visit. This trip would be the perfect opportunity for me to experience it again."

"I'm sorry. You can't."

"Why not?"

"This is my first trip back to Nigeria since I left in 2000. There would be many people to visit and unresolved family matters to address."

"I certainly don't want to get in your way," Jovita said. "I'll stay at a nearby hotel, and you can take me around for the touristy stuff. If you can't, I'm sure my parents can tap some relatives to help out when you're busy."

"I can't hide you. What do you think my mother would say if I were to show up at the village with a woman hanging on my arm?"

Jovita gave him a cheeky smile. "First of all, I'm not doing any hanging. And your mom will take one look at me and say, son, dang it, you've got great taste."

Nne would wield a large raffia broom and chase Jovita out of their compound. She would then sanctify the place with copious amounts of holy water.

"What my mother wants is a woman ready to have my children," he said. "About ten of them. If you're fine with those expectations, sure, I'll take you with me."

"Forget it. I'll plan my own trip. If I can't go, at the least I can help you get ready. Have you sorted out your clothes?"

Eziafa was thankful for the change of topic. "It's on my to-do list."

Jovita untangled their legs and scooted off the bed. She opened the closet doors and took an inventory of his mostly frayed, bargain-store clothing. "From what I see, you have a lot of shopping to do."

"Are they all bad?"

Jovita planted a hand on her waist. "To put it nicely, they'd make a fantastic bonfire."

He gaped at her. "How come you never said anything?"

She shrugged. "You didn't ask."

"Jovita, how could you have done this to me?"

"What? I haven't been hanging with you because of how well you dress," she said.

"You should have said something."

Jovita shrugged. "You own a full-length mirror."

Eziafa glanced at his closet. "I guess I'll donate the clothes to Goodwill."

"Please don't. If you're feeling charitable, write them a check."

He groaned. "See me see trouble. I didn't plan for this extra expense."

"Relax. We'll get bargains at the holiday sales."

"Sale does not mean free."

Jovita winked. "I'm sure you want to impress the village beauties."

"You endorse other women ogling me?"

"Guys check me out all the time. It doesn't mean there has to be follow-through. I've told you my deal-breaker. If you want to be with someone else, tell me, and I'm out of here."

"Life is not always that straightforward."

Jovita frowned. "What does that mean?"

"Nothing. Back to the matter at hand, when do you want to go shopping?"

Jovita crossed her arms. "Is there something you need to tell me?"

He should have kept his mouth shut. "The only thing I have to say is you look amazing this morning."

Jovita gave him a long, hard look, and then shrugged. "I need a pen and paper. Let's make that shopping list."

The following Saturday, they drove to the Premium Outlet Mall at Cypress. Jovita cringed when Eziafa insisted on designer clothing with big, bright logos. "I need to do some personal branding," he said.

"Boy, they're tacky. Have you never heard the phrase less is more?"

The phrase meant nothing to him. "What's the point of wearing expensive designer clothes if no one can tell?"

"I thought my good taste would rub off on you. I'll have to work harder when you get back from your trip."

He would return to Houston as a married man. Eziafa

gave a hollow laugh. "Why do I have the feeling a particular woman is envious of how good I'm going to look in these clothes?"

Jovita smirked. "I'm not sure which is bigger: your head or your ego."

"Envy's a bad thing," he said.

"We all have our vices."

They left the clothing store and sat on a bench while Jovita went through the shopping mall brochure. Grateful for the break, Eziafa dropped the heavy bags at his feet.

"We should find a pair of sunglasses to complete your makeover."

"It wasn't on our list."

"This woman messes with lists." Jovita stood. "Let's go find you a pair."

They strolled to the Ray-Ban store on the other side of the mall. Eziafa tried on a couple. Their price tags made them unattractive. "I'll buy a pair at the dollar store."

"That would ruin the GQ look I'm trying to create." After searching through the display, she handed him a pair. "Try these."

Eziafa stood in front of the mirror and checked himself out. "These are nice."

Jovita took the sunglasses from him. "I'm buying them for you. Consider it an early Christmas present."

He hadn't bought her one. "You don't need to buy me a gift."

"I want to. Just say thank you."

He reached out and squeezed her hand. "Thanks."

"You're welcome."

Eziafa ran a list of possible gifts through his mind. He remembered something that would make Jovita happy.

She paid for the sunglasses and slid the case into one of his bags. "You're all set."

"What do you say to a photo session?"

Her face lit up. "Are you serious?"

"Yes."

She gave him a suspicious look. "Why the sudden change of mind?"

"You don't want to take pictures with me?"

"I do."

"There's a portrait studio in the mall."

"You want us to go now?"

"Yes."

Jovita's hand went to her hair. "I'm not dressed for pictures. Let's go back to my place so I can change. The mall closes late."

"You don't need to. You're beautiful this way."

She nudged him with her elbow. "For a grouchy, unromantic guy, you say the sweetest things at the right time."

He reached for her hand and squeezed it. "Don't start crying. You can't afford to tarnish your badass reputation."

Jovita smiled. "Look at you talk like me."

"You're a good teacher."

While Jovita chatted with the photographer, Eziafa bought a voice recordable picture frame and hid it inside one of his shopping bags. He would record an apology and have the frame mailed to Jovita. It wasn't the best way to handle things. However, it was better than standing at the end of a church aisle with a corrupt conscience.

The evening before he left for Nigeria Eziafa picked up the photographs from the studio and took Jovita's copies to her place.

The glossy photos lay scattered in Jovita's lap. She gave him a pleased smile. "They turned out great."

Eziafa blinked back unexpected tears. Jovita made him happy. He could imagine her giving him the same joy for the rest of his life. He pictured the non-refundable plane ticket in his drawer. The suitcases packed with new clothes and gifts. It was too late for regrets.

Jovita gave a soft sigh. "I didn't think I was going to feel this sad about you leaving. I keep telling myself you're not going off to war."

He couldn't meet her eyes.

"Are you spending the night?" she asked.

The way he felt, he might wake Jovita up at midnight to confess. After two long hours, all he had recorded into the picture frame were the words, "I'm sorry for my weakness. Please forgive me."

"No." Eziafa stood from the couch. "I have a few things I need to do."

Jovita rose to her feet. "You still want me to drive you to the airport?"

He nodded before drawing her into a tight hug. "Please take care of yourself."

As Jovita burrowed her face in his neck, Eziafa told himself that, with all he had to be and do for his people back home, he could not afford the luxury of emotions.

Chapter Eleven

To avoid the long road trip from Lagos to the village, Eziafa bought a Houston-to-Port Harcourt plane ticket. As the plane landed at Port Harcourt International Airport, Eziafa heaved a sigh of relief. After travelling for two days, he was ready to plant his feet on solid ground.

At the arrivals lounge, he scanned the crowd for Evelyn's face. She saw him first. "Brother Eziafa!"

He stared at the fair-skinned young lady walking toward him with open arms. Evelyn was a younger version of their mother.

They wrapped each other in a tight hug. "You're a proper madam now," Eziafa said.

His chest expanded at the familiar sound of Evelyn's rich laughter. It made him smile. "Brother, we are both aging."

They stepped outside the air-conditioned building. The still air was steeped in fog and humidity. Eziafa drew a deep breath. During his Minnesota days, someone had asked him if the air in Nigeria felt different. He could not explain the sense of belonging it evoked.

Eziafa's eyes swam in tears. He blinked them away before Evelyn could see. He was back in the world of real men.

Eziafa was silent as she negotiated the price for their hired car. Any hint of a foreign accent would jack up the price. He had a vague recollection of the areas they drove through. Towering buildings elbowed each other, garish signs advertised businesses new to him. Decades of oil money had left an indelible mark.

Once out of Port Harcourt they headed north for Oji. Four-lane expressways replaced the two-lane tarred roads he had left behind. He turned to his sister. "Things look better than I thought."

Evelyn shrugged. "We're experts at keeping up appearances. Even as everything around us turns to ashes."

"How is our mother?"

Evelyn's expression softened. "Nne is delirious with happiness. She didn't sleep last night."

"I'm surprised she didn't come with you."

"She wanted to. I told her you would want to eat her fresh okra soup."

"It's all I've been dreaming about," he said.

Eziafa's heart pounded when the driver pulled up to a small bungalow with red roof tiles. The home he knew was a rented flat in Ehiri.

A big nanny goat and her kids crowded the car door as he stepped out. Eziafa smiled at the loud bleats of protest. A perfect welcoming committee.

"Nne, I'm home!" Eziafa announced.

Their mother rose from a chair placed on the verandah. She pressed a hand to her chest as if afraid her heart would leap out. "Eziafakaego. *Nwa m.*"

Eziafa experienced a floating sensation as his body moved through the space between them. Their bodies collided, instantly closing the twelve-year gap of separation.

He hugged his mother's fragile frame. Her head nestled under his chin. Eziafa did not remember her being that small. Her body shook as she rubbed her face in his shirt. Nne looked up and trailed her fingers down his cheek. "I am not dreaming. You are here."

The sight of deep wrinkles and the stoop in her back saddened him. Nne was not yet sixty. No doubt his father's illness and death had aged her.

She tugged on his arm. "Come, let us go inside. Your sister will bring in your things."

He glanced at Evelyn. "The suitcases are heavy."

"Leave them. We women carry heavier things."

Eziafa hesitated before taking his shoes off by the front door. The first thing he saw after he stepped into the room was his father's large armchair. In front of it were the fuzzy house slippers he had sent home to Papa on his first Christmas abroad. They could have been waiting for their owner.

Nne had sent him a copy of the large picture of his parents that hung on the wall. The photo marked their thirtieth wedding anniversary. As his eyes followed the row of pictures, he wished he'd come home for that celebration. His father died before their thirty-fifth wedding anniversary.

Nne hurried ahead of him. "Your bedroom is down this corridor."

When Eziafa opened the door, his jaw dropped. The bedroom was a replica of his old one in Ehiri.

Two wooden bookshelves crammed with dog-eared

university textbooks rested against a rough wall. Eziafa ran his fingers across one of the academic achievement plaques hung above the bed. Nne had kept them all.

A minor civil servant, Papa often told him and Evelyn an education was the only lasting inheritance he could offer them. While at university, Eziafa studied as if his life depended on it. Who knew that his first-class degree in computer science would count for nothing in his new home?

Eziafa turned away. He had to stop tormenting himself with unproductive thoughts.

Spiced palm oil coated his fingers. Eziafa licked it off. He hadn't eaten authentic *abacha* and *ugba* since leaving home. In America, the *abacha* he had tried to make from imported cassava tubers was a failure.

After his meal, Eziafa took a walk around the fenced compound. His father's massive heart attack happened in the middle of the building project. A rushed finish was part of the funeral preparation.

Eziafa stopped at the cracked outer wall. It looked like it was sinking. He would have to get someone skilled to check it out before he left Oji.

As Eziafa examined the rough-hewn wooden shutters, a piece of crumbling window ledge fell. He dusted the cement particles off his trousers. Time and cheap building materials were unkind to the structure. He would have to tackle the new home construction project sooner than planned. It seemed like it was always a case of one step forward, three steps back.

Eziafa sat at the back of the house and watched as two

Agama lizards flitted along the fence. He envied their freedom.

Nne came looking for him. "There you are."

He offered her the wooden stool and sat on the ground beside her. "I needed some fresh air."

"It is good medicine," she said.

As she stared ahead, he glanced at her face. He wasn't sure how to ask her about the location of his father's grave.

She turned to him. "We have to go and see my husband. I told him you were coming home."

"Nne, I'm sorry. I should have come for Papa's funeral."

A shadow passed over his mother's face. "Your father understands."

He hoped so. On the day Eziafa got his American Green Card Lottery winner notification letter, he went to his father. Papa's gaze lifted from the letter to Eziafa's face. "Are you prepared to go?" Papa asked.

"I'm tired of being jobless. There'll be more opportunities for me there."

"It is good for a young man to come out from under his mother's *wrappa* and leave home. Otherwise, he may think his father's farm is the largest in the world. I hear your friend Felix is doing well in America. However, when Mazi Ogbuefi visited America, he came back home as an unhappy man. He told me things in distant lands are not always what they seem."

Papa conveyed his confusion in the look he gave Eziafa that day.

"Not only was his doctor son fishing in Alaska, he lived in a house with five other men. If all the boy wanted in life was to be a fisherman, why didn't he tell his father?

My friend would have sent him to his brother living in Onitsha. There are fish in the River Niger. He would not have worked himself almost to death paying those exorbitant school fees. My son, our people say knowing the truth and not telling it is what kills old men. And hearing the truth and not heeding it is what kills young men. Do you understand me?"

"Yes, Papa."

"When you get there, *biko*, don't forget the meaning of the name we gave you. *Eziafa ka ego*. Indeed, a good name is worth more than money. If you find that their life is not for you, come back home. Your father's door is always wide open."

The vivid memory brought tears to Eziafa's eyes. He wiped them before facing his mother. "Papa was a great man."

"Your father was. *Ngwa*, let us go."

Eziafa's inherited piece of land was on the way to the cemetery. Attached to the barbed wire fence was a white wooden sign with "This Land Is Not for Sale" handwritten with bright red paint.

Eziafa noted the harvested corn stalks. "I trust you got a good crop this year?"

Nne shook her head. "The lack of rain affected the plants. Most of the husks had scattered kernels."

"That is too bad."

"*Nwa m*, your uncle has tried for you on this land matter. In all things, he has stayed close and faithful to us."

Nne gave him regular updates about the care and support provided by his father's older brother. "I will visit him tomorrow."

She walked with him to the edge of the cemetery and described the grave's location. "I will let you men talk in peace."

Eziafa walked through creeping undershrub until he found his father's grave. He was pleased to see the simple granite stone slab he had requested. Despite his larger-than-life personality, in all things, his father loathed extravagance.

He sat on a pile of fresh-cut grass and gave the headstone a gentle rub. "Papa, it's me, Eziafakaego. I came home today. Nne says you're not angry with me. Please, don't be. I should have come to see you one last time."

Eziafa wished he told his father when he was alive how much he appreciated his guidance. In the throes of grief, one forgets that the dead can't hear accolades.

He closed his eyes to pull his thoughts together. "You remember the factory job I told you about? I'm no longer working there. I now drive a taxi. You were right, Papa. America is not what I thought it would be. Maybe I expected too much, or it was not the place for me. You did say I could come back home. On many nights, I thought about it. But shame kept me away. And the right time passed. I never thought you would go so soon. I promise that, for as long as I live, Nne and Evelyn will lack for nothing. I won't fail you, Papa. Not again."

Eziafa rested his head against the headstone and sobbed.

Chapter Twelve

"**N**WA M, ARE YOU awake?"

Eziafa pulled himself up. "I am."

Nne entered the bedroom and sat next to him on the bed. "I hope you slept well?"

He covered a loud yawn. Back in Houston, there were days when the wailing police sirens and ambulances kept him up. The previous night, it was the sound of a chirping cricket. He had searched the room and could not find the vagabond. "I'm getting reacquainted with the night noises."

She gave him a sympathetic look. "*Ndo o.*"

He slipped his arm around her shoulders. "How was your sleep?"

"Thanks to God, it was restful. I wanted to remind you about the visit to your uncle. He is expecting you. I hope you brought him a present?"

"I got him some dress shirts. I also have a small monetary gift."

Nne nodded. "Those items should do for this visit. We all know you came to spend money."

"I've come home. What are our next steps?"

"Evelyn wrote a list of all the eligible young women in the village. I spoke to their mothers. As of yesterday, we have twelve girls to consider."

Eziafa scratched his head. It was a high number. "That will mean a lot of meetings," he said.

"One does not rush the choosing of a wife. You will see each of them before you make up your mind."

After a breakfast of bean cake balls and millet pap, he and Evelyn set out for Dede Matthias's house. *Okadas* zipped by them on the narrow untarred roads. The motorcycles were still the fastest means of transportation.

Eziafa was pleased to see signs of progress. There were newer homes and a sizeable community clinic. The primary school compound had doubled in size and there were fewer mud huts. Evelyn told him that a group of indigenes living abroad funded the clinic. One day, he too would be in the position to contribute something to his people.

He gave his sister a teasing look. "Is there any young man I need to threaten with fire and brimstone before I return to Houston?"

Evelyn scowled at him. "Brother, I'm almost thirty o. Don't you want me to marry?"

In his head, Evelyn was much younger. "I only want to make sure potential husbands don't mess with my sister."

"When the time is right, I will tell you."

He narrowed his eyes. "There is someone?"

Evelyn's eyes twinkled as she put her fingers to her mouth, zipped her lips, and turned an imaginary key.

Eziafa hoped this man wasn't looking to do a hit and run on his sister. "I'll be patient."

"The big brother I knew wasn't a patient man," Evelyn said. "You have changed."

Eziafa smiled. He was just better at hiding his feelings. It struck him that Nne would be all alone when Evelyn married. Even if he were in the position to file immigration papers for her, Nne would never leave her world.

He realized Evelyn was still talking to him. "Sorry, what did you say?"

"I hope you've not forgotten about the master's program. It will help me get a better job."

Evelyn's anxious look made him weigh his words. He didn't have a column for graduate school tuition on his spreadsheet. "I've not forgotten. Just know it may not happen right away. Please, try and find a job. No matter how small."

"Brother, I keep submitting applications. I don't get interviews."

Eziafa remembered the days of waking up to nothing. His mistake was not looking around for something he could do with his hands. "I know you've been helping Nne on the farm. What else are you doing?"

"I make hair and supply *zobo* drinks at parties."

Eziafa nodded his approval. It is easier to help people who work hard at helping themselves. "*Jisie ike.*"

"Thank you. If you're still gathering the money for graduate school, maybe you can give me something little to build an earth oven? I know how to bake bread. People must eat."

"That is a good plan," he said.

Evelyn sighed. "Brother, too many young people are jobless and hopeless. How will this country move forward?"

"My sister, I don't know the answer."

"That's who we need as leaders," Evelyn said. "Those who understand the questions and can provide the right answers."

With conflicting national needs and ethnic identities, it was hard to determine the right answers. "I will support anyone who can move us beyond the empty rhetoric."

Evelyn was sharing family news when they ran into a large crowd at the village square. The tops of the evergreen *obeche* trees formed a canopy over the space. "Is there a village event today?"

Evelyn looked around. "I don't think so."

Eziafa's eyes widened when he saw the young woman standing in the circle tear off her clothes. Several young men hooted when she took off her bra and threw it. "Is she a mad woman?"

Evelyn's hand went to her mouth. "*Ewo!*"

"You know her?"

Tears formed in Evelyn's eyes. "My friend's younger sister. I attended her wedding in October."

Eziafa frowned. "What could be wrong with her?"

The old woman standing beside them volunteered the information. "The useless girl committed adultery with an old boyfriend." She cleared her throat and spat a thick blob of phlegm into the red soil. "Tueh!"

A shiver ran up Eziafa's spine. Their village got its name from the founding ancestor Oji. One of Oji's duties was enforcing community laws. Adulterous women from their village often ran mad. Without cleansing rituals, they also died terrible deaths.

He turned to his sister. "Why didn't she marry this boyfriend?"

Evelyn wiped her eyes. "Her parents withheld their approval. Several people in the boyfriend's family have hunchbacks. They were afraid her children would have them too."

Eziafa understood the need for strict community laws. The lack thereof would lead to a state of anarchy. But, because he'd also experienced the conflict between compliance and desire, a part of him felt sorry for the new bride. It was good that her parents would not be exempt from the public ridicule.

As he looked around, Eziafa noticed a girl at the edge of the crowd. Short and lean, she stood on her tiptoes, her neck arched as she tried to get a clear view.

There was something attractive about the way her pink tongue peeked out between parted lips. Eziafa's eyes kept wandering back to her. Her small, pointed breasts rose and fell as she clasped her hands in apparent distress.

He nudged Evelyn with his shoulder. "Who is that girl?"

Evelyn followed Eziafa's gaze. "Her name is Zinachidi. Why are you asking?"

It was a good question. The young lady was not his usual type. "Don't worry. Let's go."

Ten minutes later, they arrived at their uncle's compound. A minivan and a sedan were parked under a massive oak tree.

According to family lore, the brothers had two choices; farming or an education. As the eldest, Dede Matthias picked first. He took the farm. Eziafa's father went to school.

Dede Matthias was seated in the lower verandah. Dressed in a red *isiagu* shirt, complete with a fez cap, he looked every bit the prosperous farmer.

After greeting their uncle, Evelyn went into the house. Eziafa bowed his head. "Good evening, Sir."

The old man stood and gave him a hug and a pat on the back. "Welcome, my son."

Eziafa addressed his uncle by his titled name. "The steady hand that bends the iron."

His uncle smiled. "I see you have not forgotten our ways."

Eziafa nodded. "How can I forget my roots?"

The sight of his uncle's face brought a lump to Eziafa's throat. He hadn't realized how much Papa looked like his older brother. "It is so good to see you."

"*Nwa m*, we must celebrate your arrival."

One of his cousins placed a small keg of palm wine on the table. His uncle said a quick prayer of thanks to the ancestors and God before Eziafa poured their drinks.

"How is America? I hope life is good?"

Eziafa stared at the foam in his glass. "Things could be better. I'm making progress."

"Have you gone back to school?"

As a young boy, Dede Matthias used to tease him about his constant reading. Eziafa forced a smile. "I now have a Ph.D. in Transportation Studies."

Dede Matthias looked puzzled. "*Biko*, which one is Transportation Studies?"

Eziafa averted his eyes. "I'm a taxi driver."

"It is an honest living."

His uncle's approval felt like a balm. "When I have enough savings, I will explore other business opportunities."

"Well done. Remember, the hunger that has hope for its satisfaction does not kill."

"I will try not to lose hope."

"Your mother said that you are here to find a wife. I was happy to hear this news. Children who were born when you left home are in Secondary School. The bright ones who got double-promotion are close to finishing."

"I had to wait until I could afford a wife," he said.

"I understand. Women respect men who take good care of them. It is a sign of strength. Money also supports the necessary discipline."

"In what way?" Eziafa asked.

Dede Matthias smiled. "Have you ever met a woman who does not like gifts? With one hand, you chastise when needed, with the other, you give imported lace and gold."

"These modern women are not easily pacified," Eziafa said.

"I have heard so. That is why you must tread softly. The woman you bring into your house can make or break you. *I ghotara m?*"

"Yes, Sir."

"When you have found the woman you want to marry, come and tell me."

Dede Matthias would represent his father during the visits to his in-laws. "Thank you."

"When you leave this time, I beg you, do not stay away for too long. Your mother is not getting younger. For her mind to be at rest, she needs to see your face regularly."

"I have heard."

Dede Matthias smiled. "You also need to build a house on your land. Old age is closer than you think. One cannot use all ten fingers to eat. You must save for the raining season."

Eziafa was sure Nne had asked his uncle to have this conversation with him. "What does one do when life is full of rainy days?"

"One roasts one's corn and *ube* under a leaking umbrella," Dede Matthias said. "Life does not always give us the luxury of waiting for the sun."

"I have to thank you for taking care of Nne and Evelyn."

"They are mine too," his uncle said.

Eziafa smiled. "Yes, they are."

Dede Matthias patted him on the back. "My brother was proud of you. We all are."

When they returned home, Eziafa went looking for Nne. She was peeling a pile of cassava tubers at the back of the house. "I thought you were going to rest while we were gone?"

Nne added a peeled tuber to those in the basin of water. "My hands needed something small to do."

There was nothing small about the task. Eziafa went to the kitchen and brought back a knife and a wooden stool.

Nne smiled her appreciation. "Was your uncle home?"

"Yes. He sends greetings."

"When I fry this batch of *gari*, I will take some to him."

Eziafa cleared his throat. "Nne, I saw this girl on our way to Dede Matthias's house."

Nne raised an eyebrow. "What did she look like?"

He recalled the girl's features. "She's slim and dark-skinned. Evelyn said her name's Zinachidi."

"Oh. I know Zina. She is Mrs. Nwoye's first daughter."

"She's beautiful."

Nne nudged him with her shoulder. "I already spoke to Zina's mother about a possible match between the two of you. She is not opposed to it."

A warm feeling went through Eziafa. They had to move fast. He was not the only man back home this Christmas to find a wife. "When can I meet Zina?" he asked.

"I will visit Mrs. Nwoye later this evening to arrange a meeting."

Eziafa remembered the mad young woman stripping at the village square. Nne's expression grew somber as he recounted the incident.

"That wayward child has killed her mother," Nne said.

"It was not the mother's fault."

"You have been away for too long. Who do you think gets the blame for a daughter's wayward behaviour?"

Eziafa cocked his head as a question popped into his mind for the first time. "Nne, what happens to Oji men who cheat on their wives?"

"Nothing."

Her answer surprised him. "I thought our ancestor Oji frowns on adultery?"

"Nothing happens to the men from this village because they do not commit adultery."

He gaped at her. "You believe that?"

"My beliefs do not matter. Oji decides. We women commit adultery. You men are only unfortunate victims of your excesses."

Lips pursed, Nne flung a peeled cassava tuber into the basin. Eziafa flinched as droplets of water splashed his face.

Chapter Thirteen

GRATEFUL FOR THE solitude, Eziafa rubbed weary eyes. After living alone for so long, it was hard adjusting to the women's constant chatter.

Over the past forty-eight hours, he had seen seven young women. They came to the house under the guise of retrieving random items. One even left with a live chicken. They were mostly pretty and voluptuous, but they were not Zina.

He scrolled through the Excel sheet. Some family members also came to visit. Due to the unexpected monetary gifts, it was vital for him to keep a close eye on his expenses.

Nne found him talking to himself. "Mr. Calculator, you are still on this matter?"

He closed the laptop lid. "I have to make sure I don't run out of money."

She narrowed her eyes. "Are you telling me you came home unprepared?"

"If I brought all the money I have, what would we eat after the wedding?"

Nne pulled out a dining chair. "Others have married wives before you. They didn't starve. My son, there's something I need to discuss with you."

He forced himself to sit still at the serious expression that always made him squirm. "I'm listening."

"Did you send a message to that Umuonyeori woman?" Nne asked.

Eziafa shifted in his seat. Before they left the airport, he'd used Evelyn's cell phone to send an arrival status text to Jovita. He didn't want her worrying. "I did."

"Tell me the truth. Are you married to this woman?" she asked.

"How can I marry her without your approval?"

Nne clucked her tongue. "Many sons in the abroad have given themselves wives without consulting their parents."

"You raised me better than that."

Nne placed her elbows on the dining table and rested her chin on laced fingers. "I know you were angry with me when I said you could not marry that woman. *Nwa m*, I would rather live with your displeasure than watch you carry fire on your head."

"If I was married to Jovita, why would I come home to find another woman?"

Nne shrugged. "A young bride from this village lived with her in-laws for five years before finding out why her husband could not take her to Italy. His secret European wife would not give him a divorce."

Eziafa had heard similar stories. "I'm not married to Jovita or any other woman. Zina will be my first and only wife."

For a few fraught moments, Nne's anxious eyes searched his face. "You are telling me the truth?"

"Yes."

Nne pushed herself from the chair. "I am going to the parsonage to meet with Father Ide. We have to consider the dates for your wedding mass."

Eziafa rebooted his computer after she left the room. He could no longer concentrate on the numbers. His mouth dried out as he imagined Jovita's confusion when she received his photo frame. He should have followed Felix's advice to break the news in person.

He went to the bedroom. He made sure the door was locked before he brought out his temporary cell phone. He mouthed the digits as he dialled Jovita's number. A part of him prayed that she wouldn't pick up. She did.

"Hello?"

Eziafa cleared his throat. "It's me."

"What do you want?"

There could only be one explanation for the cold reception. Jovita now knew what he was doing in Nigeria. "I'm sorry."

"You're pathetic."

"I didn't mean to hurt you."

He heard a sharp intake of breath. "Don't ever call me again."

A loud click. Eziafa pitched the cell phone at the pillows on the bed and cradled his head. He should not have taken the easy way. He fantasized about abandoning his mission and returning to Houston to grovel. His fantasies disintegrated as he remembered the graveside promise to his father. The shock would kill his mother.

"Eziafakaego, where are you?" Nne called.

"I'm coming." Eziafa's hand shook as he slid the telephone under his pillow. After composing himself, he met her at the passage.

She gave him a look over. "Go and change into some nice clothes. Your Zina is on her way."

The loud knock on the front door made Eziafa jump.

"Good evening," a soft, female voice called out.

Nne gave him a thumbs-up sign before answering. "Ada, *nnoo*. Come in. The door is not locked."

Zina stopped at the doorway when she saw him. Nne beckoned her forward. "My dear, good evening. How is your mother?"

"Mama's fine," Zina said. "She sent me to collect the agenda book for the women's council."

"Ha, yes. Zina, this is my son Eziafakaego. He is visiting from America."

Zina gave him a shy smile. "Good evening, Uncle. Welcome home."

They had to work on getting rid of the uncle title. Eziafa inclined his head. "Thank you."

At Nne's request, Evelyn had arranged clothes on the other chairs so the only empty one was beside him. "Sit, my daughter. Let me go and get the book for you."

Nne left the room with a spring in her steps. Zina sat with hands folded in her lap. They would be left alone for a few minutes.

Eziafa opened his mouth and said the first thing which came to his mind. "Will you like to live in America?"

Zina lifted her head. "Live in America?"

He gave himself a mental kick. "Yes. A beautiful girl like you should live in God's own country. I'm sure people think you're a model."

As she laughed, Zina's hand hovered over her bucked front teeth. "Uncle, you're funny."

"Please call me Eziafa. I'm not that much older than you."

Zina gave him a disbelieving look.

Recently out of secondary school, Zina would be eighteen, which meant there was a twenty-year age gap between them. "I know that was a little exaggeration," Eziafa said. "Still, I would prefer you to call me Eziafa."

"My mother will be angry with me."

"She won't be if you tell her that I insisted."

Zina's hands twisted in her lap. "Yes, unc ... I mean Eziafa."

"I like the beautiful way you say my name."

Zina giggled.

Nne coughed three times before she parted the corridor curtain. She handed the agenda book to Zina. "My daughter, thank you for waiting. Please greet your mother for me."

After Zina left, Nne gave him an expectant look. "Now that you've spent some time with her, what do you think?"

"When can we go to her father's house?"

Nne laughed. "Patience."

"I don't want to see any more girls."

"We only have a few names left on the list. Their mothers will be offended if I cancel the meetings."

Their feelings were inconsequential to him. "Isn't it better to end this now?"

"No. See all the girls before you make up your mind."

"To speed things up, we should invite the girls for a joint interview."

"*Negodu* this foolish child."

Eziafa frowned. It was a good idea. "I'm no longer a child. I'm a grown man with a big beard."

Nne extended an arm in his direction. "Bring that beard of yours here. I will twist it into dreadlocks."

Eziafa hurried to the other side of the room. "That will be physical assault."

Nne clapped her hands. "*Onye Bekee.* I said come here. *Osiso.*"

Eziafa stayed behind the couch. He was still there when Evelyn walked into the sitting room with hands planted on her waist.

Evelyn stood in front of him. "Brother, I'm angry with you."

Grateful for the interruption, Eziafa feigned annoyance. "Can't you see we're in the middle of an important conversation?"

"How come you've never told me I should live in America?"

Eziafa narrowed his eyes. "It's because you're not beautiful enough to get a visa."

Evelyn gasped. "Nne, did you hear what Brother Eziafa said to me?"

"Don't call my name. I told you not to listen to your brother's conversation."

Evelyn pouted. "But we were both listening," she said.

"It's my job as a mother to listen," Nne said.

"And as a good daughter, I was supporting you."

Eziafa gaped at the women. The thought that they heard what he said to Zina made him want to sink into the ground. "This isn't fair," he said.

Nne tugged on her clothes and straightened her back. "You talk about fairness. I carried you in this stomach for nine months. You even did extra time. Why have you not said beautiful old models, like me, deserve to live in God's own country?"

Eziafa felt his face go warm. "Nne."

"Brother, can I call you by your first name too?" Evelyn asked.

"Oh. You now think it's okay to disrespect me?"

"I was just clarifying."

Laughing, Evelyn hid behind their mother as he marched in her direction.

To please his mother, Eziafa met with the remaining girls. The meetings were a blur. After the last one, Eziafa said firmly: "The girl's legs are too straight."

Nne frowned. "When did straight legs become a problem? Is that not what you young men want?"

"I'm a man with different tastes."

"How about Adaora? She's a good girl."

Eziafa shook his head. "Adaora's hips are too slim. We don't want any birth complications."

"Zina's hips are slimmer," Nne said.

"It's all in the bones. I'm sure Zina would give you ten grandsons."

"You want to kill her?"

He grinned. "How else will we start a chapter of the Okereke clan in America?"

"Listen, before you start counting your American chicks, we better visit your uncle to tell him of your choice."

"What if Zina's people say no?"

"Her father and yours were childhood friends. It would be an honour for our families to become one."

He hoped so. Since he could not retrace his steps, it was time he gave full attention to the future.

Chapter Fourteen

ZINACHIDI NWOYE LIFTED the wide-brimmed straw hat and scratched a nagging itch on her scalp. She had arrived at their family farm shortly after dawn. In the hours since then, she had weeded the yam and cassava ridges and watered their vegetable patch.

As she walked through the short, leafy cassava plants to the other side of the farm, her rain boots left crack marks in the dry, clay soil. If things did not change, they would end up harvesting rotten tubers.

Zina flexed her aching fingers. Each year, the sun grew hotter, the rains took longer to arrive. Farming communities like theirs suffered the most. That year's drought was the worst Zina had ever seen. The irony was that, while they were crying out for rain, other parts of the country were facing floods that swallowed everything in their path.

Her mother said the innocent blood being spilled all over the land by Boko Haram, armed robbers and kidnappers, was making it cry out in vain for vengeance.

At school, one of her teachers said global warming

was to blame for the erratic weather patterns. Zina felt it was a mixture of both.

As she picked some *ugu* for that evening's soup, Zina frowned at the shrivelled-up leaves. There were days when she wished she knew how to do a rain dance. According to family stories, her great-grandfather was a renowned rain-maker.

Zina stood to stretch her back. In the distance, she saw her younger sister, Ebele.

"Mama wants you," Ebele called.

Their mother rarely sent for her when she was at the farm. "Did something happen?"

Ebele shrugged. "I was sweeping the compound when she called me."

Zina packed up her things and they headed home. She found Mama in her bedroom.

Mama patted the spot next to her on the bed. "Come."

Zina hesitated. She was still in her farming clothes. "I'm dirty."

"Sit."

Zina did as she was told. Her heart raced as she waited for her mother's words.

"*Ada m*, congratulations."

Zina's heart skipped. She had applied to the Business Studies program at the state university. "My admission letter came?"

Her mother's excitement was palpable. "This is greater news."

What could be greater, Zina wondered.

"Mrs. Okereke's son, Eziafa, has expressed an interest in you for marriage."

Zina's eyes widened. "Marriage?"

"Yes."

"But I'm supposed to go to school."

"My daughter, one does not have to stand in the way of the other. Some women go to school after having children."

It wasn't what she wanted. "Mama, I'm too young—"

"Ta! Did I not marry when I was your age? Your father was forty years old, a grown man who knew his left from right. Eziafa is like him, older and wiser. The best kind of man for you. He does not need a mother to help him wash his back."

Zina pictured Eziafa's face. The man's massive head bobbled on a short, thick neck. His waist seemed nonexistent under a rounded stomach. She knew Eziafa didn't create himself, but the thought of him touching her in an intimate way made her stomach turn. "I have no interest in his proposal," she said.

"Sweet One, listen to me. You know how your father and I struggle to take care of you and your sister." Mama tugged on her blouse. "People say cut your coat according to your size. My daughter, we are half-naked because we do not have money to buy enough material."

Despite their challenges, her parents made sure they never went to bed with empty stomachs. "I see all you do. It is time for me to help. I'll work while I go to school. You won't have to worry about me."

Mama snorted. "A mother always worries."

"I will be fine," she said.

"Since the day you were born, I have prayed your life would be easier than mine. There is dignity in hard work. But when one's life is full of endless toil and uncertainty, fulfilment is scarce. Look at the families who have children living in the abroad. They do not struggle the way we do. Please. Do not let us waste this opportunity."

Zina acknowledged that her parents' arranged marriage worked for them. But she wanted the freedom to choose. "Mama, the man is a stranger."

"We know Eziafa's family and they know us. I do not doubt that he will make a good husband." Mama patted her on the shoulder. "Go and rest. We will talk about this at another time."

Zina was in a daze as she walked to the bedroom shared with Ebele. There were many other girls in Oji. Girls who were prettier than her. Clutching her rosary, she prayed that Eziafa's attention would shift to one of them.

Four days after their conversation, Mama woke her up before dawn. "Come, let us not disturb your sister," she whispered.

Zina stifled a yawn as she followed Mama back to her bedroom. "Yesterday, your father sent word to Eziafa's people. Our first meeting is next week."

Her hands went to her throat. "So soon?"

Mama nodded. "Eziafa is going back to America in January. We do not have plenty of time."

"But I don't want to marry Eziafa. I want to go to school."

Her mother's eyes flashed. "Did you not hear me say your father told them to come?"

"What did I do wrong? Why are you punishing me?"

"*Nwa m*, this is not punishment. When you are enjoying life in America, you will thank me."

Zina choked on a sob. "I don't want Eziafa. He is ugly."

"That is foolish talk. Can one eat good looks? They say Eziafa is a hard worker. Remember, he chose you out of all the girls in this village."

Zina placed a hand on her head. "Why do I have such bad luck?"

Mama glared at her. "Shut your mouth! Do you want to make me a liar before your father's people?"

The words weighed her down. "No."

"Then you must accept that this marriage is for your good."

After their evening meal, Zina slipped out of the house to break the news to her friend Immaculata. Together, they finished up Immaculata's chores, then left the house and sat on a bench in the backyard.

Immaculata gave her a puzzled look. "What is wrong with you?"

"I'm getting married."

Her friend's jaw dropped. "You're marrying Ndu?"

Zina's heart skipped at the name. Ndu was her first and only boyfriend. The kissing partner unknown to her mother. "No. Mrs. Okereke's son."

Immaculata scooted closer. "The Americana?" she asked gently.

"You've heard of him?"

Immaculata nodded. "I overheard my mother say he was back in the village to find a wife."

"His people are coming next week to see my parents."

Immaculata looked around before lowering her voice. "What did Ndu say when you told him?"

"We have not spoken."

"If I were you, I will tell Ndu that you two are no longer on the same social level."

"Those words will hurt him."

"Zina, why are you worried about a small boy with an uncertain future when a big man wants to make you his queen?"

"Ndu may not have much money, but he has potential," she said.

Immaculata held on to her sides. Her hoarse laughter frightened two birds out of a nearby palm tree. "*Po gini*? My dear friend, potential can't buy you one spoon of *gari* at the market." She nudged Zina with her shoulder. "Does your Americana have friends also looking for wives?"

Zina frowned. "Didn't you say all these *obodo oyibo* men are heartless frauds? Anyway, what does that have to do with Ndu?"

Immaculata crossed her arms over her chest. "You girls with two-man problems must have special powers. I worked hard to lock down my Fredo."

Zina had assumed Fredo did the chasing. "You went after him?"

"*Gbam*. Chase well and you will catch."

"Ah, Immaculata."

"*Abeg*, free me. Holy Sister Mary Zina." Immaculata tugged on her right earlobe. "Listen, when you get to America, don't forget about me. We all saw Chioma Emezi when she came home last Christmas. Her skin shimmered like imported *akwa oche*."

It was true that Chioma's ebony skin had acquired a lovely sheen. Someone said it was the effects of winter.

What did she know? "Of course, I won't forget you. We're best friends."

Immaculata smiled. "So, tell me. Is this Eziafa as fine as Ndu?"

Zina cocked her head as she pictured the two men in her mind. The comparison did Eziafa no favours. "Eziafa is short and old," she said.

Immaculata frowned. "Old like forty?"

"No. He looks like he's fifty."

"*Ewo*. Your mother is younger than that."

Zina sighed. "I know."

"Don't worry your head too much about Eziafa's appearance. When a man is too handsome, he's ninety-nine percent trouble." Immaculata grinned. "That is why I like my Fredo. Who else would want him with his body odour?"

Zina stood and dusted the seat of her skirt. "I have to go. I will see you tomorrow."

"Let me go and tell my mother I'm walking the new Yankee Noodle home."

She gave Immaculata a weak smile. "Stop it. And they say doodle."

"See? You are already talking like them."

Zina held back a yawn as she walked down the narrow footpath leading to the village stream. To give herself enough time to water all the crops, she'd left her bed after the first cockcrow.

She gripped the handle of her metal bucket when she saw a blurry image ahead. The dark shade and weak light made it difficult for her to make out any distinct feature. As she debated on whether to keep walking or run, Zina heard her name. The voice belonged to Ndu.

As she took slow steps toward him, Ndu stepped out of the shade of a large boulder and blocked her way. Zina wanted to throw herself into his arms.

Ndu's frustration was visible on his face. "Baby m, what is going on?"

His younger sister brought her Ndu's messages. Without knowing how to break the news to him, Zina refused to see him.

"Nothing. It's just time for us to end this relationship."

"Come again?"

Guilt raised her voice. "Ndu Mbogu, please, free me. After all, you haven't asked for my hand in marriage."

He gave a short, mirthless laugh. "So, it is true. When Immaculata said you were getting married to that old man, I told her to shut her big mouth."

Immaculata would have enjoyed throwing the news in Ndu's face. "Yes, I'm marrying Eziafa."

Ndu's eyes blazed. "I heard about the old fool. He must think he's the Pied Piper of Oji. Strolling through the village and charming hungry girls with the promise of one-dollar bills."

The words made her feel cheap. "This isn't about Eziafa's money."

Ndu's grip on Zina's arm was so strong she dropped her bucket. He pulled her close, his hot breath fanning her face. "Tell me. What is it about?"

There was no easy answer to Ndu's question. At the hairdresser's, Zina often glanced through piles of old *Ebony* and *Essence* magazines. As her fingers flipped the glossy pages, Zina imagined the lives of the beautiful black girls captured in photos. Although they looked like her, they would never spend long hours working on a farm or worry about their parents' ability to pay school fees on time.

On the evening she broke her news to Immaculata, the envy in her friend's eyes made Zina realize that she too could have something that others wanted. The knowledge was intoxicating. If she married Eziafa, the other girls would gossip about her fresh skin during visits back to the village.

She pulled away from Ndu. "I'm not the master of myself. I have to do what my parents want."

Ndu had tears in his eyes. "What about us? Baby, please. Give me one more year to finish university. I will get a good job."

Zina took a deep breath. It would be kinder to take away any hope. "I can't wait around for that. I'm going to America. Don't worry. There are girls in this village who will manage what you can offer."

Ndu's agonized expression made her chest hurt. He backed away. "Zina, me?"

"I have to tell you the truth," she said.

Ndu lifted his chin. "I won't be the stubborn fly who followed a dead body into the grave. I may only have these hands. They won't fail me."

Zina picked up her metal bucket and ran. It was a good thing her feet remembered the way to the stream. She couldn't see through the veil of tears.

Chapter Fifteen

To Eziafa's delight, the Nwoye family accepted his marriage proposal. He had three weeks to plan both the traditional *igba nkwu* and church ceremonies.

Eziafa was under the backyard tree when Nne found him and handed over the traditional item list from Zina's family. "You have to give me back my five thousand o. I had to pay to get the list."

Eziafa scratched his head. "We have to pay for the list?"

"It is not a new thing," Nne said.

The practice was new to him. Eziafa's eyes bugged out as he scanned the list. "We're expected to buy all these things?"

Nne planted her hands on her waist as she drawled the answer. "Yes."

The two hundred-plus items didn't include monetary gifts for his future in-laws. He read the list aloud. "Five female goats, twenty litres of kerosene, ten litres of palm oil, four Singer sewing machines, ten sets of Dutch wax material, ten gallons of palm wine, twelve cartons of Star beer. Nne, these gifts are too much."

"*Nwa m*, is a wife a good thing?"

"Yes. Still ..."

Nne held up her hand. "Stop there. Are good things cheap to get?"

"Marriage should be affordable. After all, the best things in life are free."

"Nonsense. Go to the General Hospital and tell the doctor you want him to give you free health care. He will ask if you contributed to his school fees."

"Honestly, with things the way they are in this country, they should have a recession period list."

"My son, this one is not too bad o. You should see the list for university graduates."

"They have different lists?"

"We have specific lists for those who are primary school certificate holders, those who are secondary school certificate holders, undergraduate students and university graduates."

"*Na wa*. Can we not ask Zina's family to reduce the number of items? This kind of list can chase away a suitor o."

Nne snatched the list from his hand. "Reduce what? Have you forgotten that I'm the Secretary for the *Umu Nwanyi*? You will not embarrass me in this village."

Eziafa knew it was unwise to mess with the women's association. He would have to call Felix to see if he could send some money through Western Union. If Felix was low on funds, he might have no choice but to ask Dede Matthias. It was the last thing he wanted to do.

Nne's voice interrupted his thoughts. "Did you buy the wedding and engagement rings?" she asked.

"I did."

He'd picked a size seven. The jeweller assured him it

was the average size for women. If necessary, the rings could always be re-fitted later.

Nne nodded her approval. "Tomorrow, you and I will go and see the priest to confirm the date. Then Evelyn and I will go to the market. The earlier we start buying the list items, the better."

He wanted to see Zina. Their eyes had met only for a moment while she served them drinks at her father's house. "Can I visit Zina at home?"

"You may visit for short periods. Remember we have not yet paid Zina's bride price. Keep your hands to yourself."

He grinned. "Don't you trust me?"

She snorted. "You are your father's son."

Eziafa grimaced as he dusted off the seat of his trousers. There were certain things one did not want to know about one's parents.

At the Nwoye house, Zina's mother welcomed him with a warm smile. He could see where Zina got her good looks. Both women had the same slim physique.

"You should have given us adequate notice," Mrs. Nwoye said. "Zina would have cooked a nice meal for you."

"I didn't want to cause her any trouble."

"That is what you men say before the marriage. After you bring the woman home, all you give her is plenty trouble."

He laughed. "I'm not like that. I'm a gentleman."

Mrs. Nwoye clucked her tongue. "I hear you."

She left him in the sitting room and went to get Zina. Eziafa looked around. The mismatched furniture pieces reminded him of his apartment before Jovita's make-over.

He turned at the sound of footsteps. Dressed in a simple blue gown, Zina smiled shyly. "Good afternoon."

Eziafa stood. "Afternoon." He turned to Zina's mother. "Please, can we take a little walk down the street?"

"Zina must be back in one hour," she said.

He inclined his head. "She will. Thank you."

Zina was quiet as they left the house. Eziafa glanced at her pensive face. It seemed unreal that, before the end of the month, she would become a fundamental part of his future. "Since we have limited time, where do you think we should go?"

"Wherever you want," she said.

He wanted to go somewhere they could sit and talk with little distraction. "I'm sure you and your friends have a place where you hide from the adults."

Zina blinked. "We don't hide from the adults."

Eziafa smiled. "I was your age once. We all did it."

Zina fought a smile. "There is a place near the stream."

"Let's go there."

Zina turned off the main road and took him past the cemetery. When he saw the headstones, Eziafa thought about his father. After the wedding, he would bring Zina for an introduction.

Zina's steps halted when she saw two young men walking towards them. "Are those your friends?"

She gave him a desperate look. "They're friends of a friend."

Why was Zina scared of them? He pulled on her arm. "Let's go."

The young men blocked their path. "What are you two doing?" Eziafa asked. "Move."

They gave Zina scornful looks before stepping aside. As they walked on, Eziafa could feel their eyes boring into the back of his head.

Zina was quiet as she led them down a well-trodden path. Dense trees provided a shield as they stepped into a small clearing.

Eziafa looked around. The boulders were in a half-moon formation. He sat on the biggest one and patted the space beside him. Zina hesitated. "I'm not going to bite you."

Zina sat, leaving plenty of space between them.

"Are you okay?"

She nodded.

"Is there anything you want to know about me?"

Zina stared at her hands. "No."

Hoping to pique her curiosity, Eziafa talked about his life in Houston. The strategy worked.

"Is the city bigger than Lagos?"

He'd done some research about the population before his move from Minnesota. "It's much bigger. The state of Texas is about the same size as Nigeria."

"America must be big."

It was a shame that he'd never travelled around the country. "From what I've heard, New York and Los Angeles are more major cities."

"When people from America visit the village, they all talk about New York," Zina said.

"When you join me, we'll visit New York."

Her delighted expression made him feel about a foot taller. "Is it far from Houston?"

"We'll have to travel there by plane."

"I've never been on a plane."

Eziafa smiled to himself. Zina's limited life experiences made for lots of teaching opportunities. "There'll be many plane rides in your future. I promise."

He leaned forward to steal a kiss. Nne hadn't put any restrictions on his lips.

Zina stretched away from him. "Please, no. Mama won't like it."

Her reaction pleased him. "I didn't mean to scare you. Looking at your beautiful face, I couldn't help myself."

Zina kept her eyes down.

"My mother said you're happy about our upcoming marriage. I'm happy, too."

Zina glanced at him. What he saw in her eyes was resignation, not happiness. "I do what my parents tell me."

"You don't want to marry me?"

Zina hung her head.

He remembered the sour looks on the faces of the two young men. "Tell me the truth. Do you have a boyfriend?"

"No."

The quick response roused his suspicions. "You're lying."

"I don't have a boyfriend. I'm ... I'm grateful you chose me."

As he stared at the sweat beads gathering on Zina's forehead, Eziafa told himself gratitude could turn to love. "I visited today because I want to get to know you better," he said.

Zina shrugged. "My life is simple."

"You must have dreams. Tell me about them."

She looked unsure.

"Go on."

Zina stared off into the distance. "I wanted to attend

university. While in school, I would have started a recharge card business. After graduation, I was going to move to a big city where I can start a poultry business." She turned to look at him. "I know how to raise chickens and turkeys."

There was pride in Zina's voice. There was also a familiarity to the despair in her eyes. Eziafa could understand feeling trapped.

"You'll still go to school," he said in a gentle tone. "And you can have a small business in America."

Zina gave him an uncertain look. "I will go to school?"

"Yes." As he reached for her hand, Zina pulled away. "My palms are rough," she said.

"Any man would be proud to have such a hardworking wife."

Zina was about to place her hand in his when she noticed his missing finger. Zina was unable to mask the repulsion that flitted across her face.

Eziafa was working mandatory overtime hours the day of the incident. Exhausted, his hand slipped while he was feeding pork shoulders into a spinning saw. He could still picture his blood spraying the stainless-steel surface. "I lost the finger at work."

She gave him a pitying look. "Sorry o."

"It's in the past."

Zina stood. "My chores are waiting."

They were both silent walking back to Zina's. He stopped by the door and stared at her sweaty face. It wasn't a hot afternoon. "Can I come back to see you tomorrow? We have to see the priest about our marital counselling classes."

Zina lifted her shoulder in a half-shrug. "If Mama says it's okay."

As Eziafa stared at her sad face, his head ached. The resignation in her eyes bothered him. Did he choose the wrong woman?

He remembered Zina's quick denial about having a boyfriend. Could it be that his village virgin wasn't so innocent after all?

Chapter Sixteen

EZIAFA WAITED UNTIL he was alone before calling Houston. Felix listened as he ranted about the list Zina's family gave them. "I'm not against giving gifts to my in-laws. But the whole thing has turned into a money-grabbing scheme."

"It sounds like they adjusted for inflation. Who makes these lists?"

"Nne said it's the community women."

"I guess they're using it as a community wealth-building strategy. If only they would focus on making sure our people have successful marriages."

Eziafa scratched his head. "I'm about to lose my mind," he said.

"You take things too seriously."

"It is a serious matter. I don't have enough money to buy all the gift items."

"You need me to send you some?"

"As a loan. And only if you don't need it for the next six months."

"I'll send you what I can spare."

Eziafa heaved a sigh of relief. "Thank you."

"You're welcome. Make sure you bring plenty *gari* with you."

He couldn't travel with a whole sack. And back in Houston, if push came to shove, he would get groceries from the food bank. Eziafa forced some lightness into his voice. "Forget that. I intend to eat at your house until my bank account balances."

"You had better make other eating arrangements," Felix snapped.

Eziafa frowned. "Are we fighting?"

"We should be," Felix said. "You told me you would inform Jovita about your plans."

"I tried to tell Jovita the truth. I couldn't."

Felix's tone was anything but sympathetic. "You wanted to keep enjoying the benefits of your relationship."

Felix knew him too well. "I can't deny that."

His friend sighed. "I wish you had done the right thing. The way Jovita found out about your marriage plans was not good."

"Who told Jovita?"

"Nkolika and Presido's wife did. Nkolika ran into Jovita on the day you left. Jovita told Nkolika she was looking forward to your return. They couldn't let her wait in vain. Nkolika said Jovita didn't cry. If she had, they would have known how to comfort her. She just thanked them and left."

"Jovita's not good at showing her vulnerable side," he said.

"I don't blame her. You should call her to apologize."

Eziafa knew he sounded like a whiny teen. "I tried. She hung up on me."

"Do you blame her? Eziafa, if that woman curses you, it will catch you o."

His heart skipped. "Jovita is not that kind of person."

"I pray you're right."

Eziafa was on his laptop at the dining table when Evelyn and Nne walked into the house. He eyed their large shopping bags. "Nne, welcome."

She shook her head. "Eh. Leave that thing alone. Come and sit with your mother. Please. Don't give yourself high blood pressure."

He closed the laptop. There was no point telling Nne he was already hypertensive.

"Brother, the tailor was making eyes at your mother," Evelyn said.

Eziafa frowned. "That young man?"

Evelyn nodded. "You should have seen the blouse design he chose for our mother. It was sleeveless."

"Sleeveless?" Eziafa asked.

Nne wagged her finger. "The young man was joking."

"The tailor meant business," Evelyn said.

"Is he one of those dangerous young men who prey on older women?" Eziafa said.

Evelyn snapped her fingers. "Yes, brother. He had a dangerous gleam in his eyes."

Eziafa turned to his mother. "Nne, did the tailor touch you?"

His mother looked puzzled. "Touch me?"

"While you were at the tailor, did he touch you?"

His mother's forehead furrowed. "Our hands touched while he took my measurements."

Eziafa stamped his foot on the linoleum tiles. "I knew it. Nne, the tailor was flirting with you. If he asks for your hand in marriage, we're demanding a high bride price."

Evelyn clapped her hands. "Yes! I need plenty money for graduate school."

The confused expression on Nne's face cleared. "See these children. I'm collecting and spending my bride price. Nonsense and ingredients."

Eziafa rubbed his palms together. "As your children, we're entitled to a percentage."

Nne snorted. "I'm sure my young husband will protect me from the both of you. Greedy people."

The women began a conversation about catering arrangements. Eziafa's gaze wandered around the room, finally settling on his father's record player. Papa, a *highlife* connoisseur, created a tradition of listening to the music on Sunday afternoons.

Eziafa turned to his sister. "Does the record player still work?"

Evelyn shrugged. "We haven't touched it since …" Her voice trailed off.

He stood. "Let's find out."

Nne and Evelyn were quiet as he walked to the player, reached behind it and pulled out a frayed cord. Lifting the dusty cover, he wasn't surprised to see Nelly Uchendu's album on the turntable.

Eziafa glanced at his mother's face. He remembered the many times his parents danced to Uchendu's "Love Nwantinti." To Eziafa, Uchendu's voice was unforgettable.

Eziafa nodded when the vinyl record began to spin. Back in the day, electronics lasted a lifetime. He lifted the arm and gently placed the needle on the vinyl.

As the music filled the room, Eziafa stood before Nne. "Madam Model, excuse me dance."

Nne's eyes were bright as Eziafa helped her to her feet.

"You have to be careful with her," Evelyn said with genuine concern. Evelyn hadn't forgotten Eziafa's uncoordinated moves on the dance floor.

"Your brother can now dance," he said to her.

He and Nne took slow steps around the room. He would miss her and Evelyn when he returned home. With some sadness, he realized it was the first time he'd thought of America as home.

"What are you thinking of?" Nne asked.

He stared at her face. She'd told him she wanted him to move back to Oji one day. "I was thinking of how lucky I am to have you."

The night before their traditional wedding ceremony, Eziafa decided to go for a walk. The house was full of overexcited relatives and he needed some time to himself. The conversation with Felix continued to weigh on his mind. He hoped he had not damaged their friendship.

On his way back home, Eziafa took a different route. He found himself in front of the local beer parlour. Little had changed since his last visit. With its corrugated iron roof, it still looked like an open picnic shelter. Named Ejima Cool Spot, the establishment belonged to twin brothers. The older twin, Livinus, moved to Germany months before Eziafa left Nigeria. As far as he knew, the other twin Hyginus still ran the beer parlour.

Eziafa stared at the Christmas lights wrapped around the structure's wooden poles. He had not eaten since lunchtime. He could get some food.

Hyginus saw him and hurried outside. "The Black Mamba. Na your face I see so?"

Eziafa smiled. "Hygienic Hyginus. Original chairman of enjoyment services."

Hyginus gave his hand a vigorous shake. "I am honoured that you came to my establishment. My wife made some fresh fish pepper soup."

They walked inside. "I still remember Amaka's excellent cooking," Eziafa said. "I'll take a big bowl."

Hyginus motioned for a server to clear a nearby table. "Our special guest, Dede Foreign Currency, is in the house."

The perception that you had money would allow your peers to elevate you to "uncle" status. Eziafa laughed. "*Abeg*, na only local currency I get."

Hyginus dismissed his objection. "You must share this wealth."

Eziafa was grateful for the silver upright fan placed next to him. Houston heat was a joke compared to what he had been experiencing. Eziafa relaxed and hummed along to Oliver De Coque's music playing quietly. Several people stopped by his table to congratulate him on his upcoming wedding.

"If you entertain us with one bottle of beer each, it's not a crime o," one of his well-wishers said.

Eziafa remembered the garrulous man from his past visits to the village. The man was usually seen involved in a brawl. "Mr. Cause Trouble, na your face be dis?"

The man laughed. "I don gentle o."

"For where? A leopard can't change its spots."

Cause Trouble laughed. "This is Nigeria. In this land, anything is possible."

Eziafa silently agreed. The leopard would probably find another animal willing to exchange its spotless hide for a price. The consequences of disrupting order or structure be damned.

Hyginus, a savvy businessman, did not miss the opportunity to increase his sales. "My brother, we should add some fried meat to those bottles of beer. He who gets much must share much."

Eziafa fixed a smile on his face as he scanned the space and did some mental math. He should have kept walking. "Go ahead. Don't worry, I'll come back with some money."

Hyginus snorted. "You are one of our celebrated goldfishes. You have no hiding place in this village."

To get his customers' attention, Hyginus clapped his hands. "My people, our brother has decided to start the wedding celebration early. One more bottle for the road."

The roar of approval was deafening. "Dede Foreign Currency!"

A raised voice from a nearby table drew Eziafa's attention. He looked over his shoulder.

"I swear, if any of you accepts his crumbs, it will be the end of our friendship."

The speaker sat amid a group of young men. From the number of empty beer bottles on their table, they'd been there for a while.

"Ndu, take it easy. It is only free food."

The scowl the young man named Ndu gave his friend

turned his handsome face ugly. "Have you no shame? He already turned Zina's head with his cheap promises."

Eziafa's ears perked up. Which Zina? When their eyes met, the hatred in Ndu's eyes scorched him.

Another young man at the table laid a hand on Ndu's shoulder. "My guy, patience. It is these old people's time. When our time comes, their daughters will pay the penalty for their sins."

Eziafa recognized this face. It was one of the young men he and Zina had run into during their walk. He remembered Zina's words. They were friends of a friend. Was Ndu the unnamed friend?

Ndu shook off the hand placed on his shoulder. "*Abeg.* As soon as small alcohol enters your bloodstream, your ignorance starts showing." Ndu pounded on the table. "Our time is now! We must seize our destiny from these greedy old men. *Wetin* we do them? They won't let us lead this country; they won't let our women be."

"Ignorance? So, because they asked me to leave the university over some little cheating, you think there's nothing inside this head?"

Ndu scoffed. "*Mumu.* You carried a whole textbook into the examination hall."

"This is what Mr. Ubanozie taught us in biology class. Remember the survival of the fittest? The men with the means marry the beautiful girls. When you think of the cost of maintaining a family, it makes sense."

Ndu spat the insult. "*Ewu.*"

"This is why I like simple girls," the young man on Ndu's left said. "You won't hear that one man from America came and carried away my Immaculata."

Ndu pointed a finger in his friend's face. "Fredo, you're a confirmed fool. Which man, in his right mind, would carry your loudmouth girlfriend past the village boundary?"

Fredo rose to his feet. "Say what you want. This fool still has his woman. I am going to my house."

"Go!" Ndu said.

Fredo ignored the pleas from the other men as he stormed out of the beer parlour.

Eziafa dropped his spoon. Ndu was talking about his Zina. He was trying to gather his thoughts when a server approached Ndu's table and asked what type of beer they wanted.

Ndu exploded. "Gerrout! Do we look like beggars?"

Cause Trouble raised his hand. "Ndu, if you don't want the drinks, *biko*, send them this way. My throat is still thirsty."

Ndu shot Cause Trouble a dirty look. "Shameless man. When will you stop begging for crumbs?"

Hyginus walked over to Ndu's table. "What is going on here?"

"Ask your thieving relative," Ndu said.

Hyginus's face darkened. "Ndu Mbogu, if you cannot behave yourself, leave."

A man near Eziafa's table looked in his direction and spoke in a calm voice. "No mind those young boys. They don't want to accept that heaven, in its great wisdom, reserved some cuts of meat for adult teeth."

Eziafa gave his supporter a close-lipped smile. He agreed that Zina was out of Ndu's league.

On his way out, Ndu stopped at Eziafa's table to glare at him. Eziafa craned his neck at an uncomfortable angle so that he could look the young man right in the face.

"*Agadi nwoke*, you seem to have forgotten that *ashawo wey go marry, na holiday e go*. You're not man enough to keep Zina happy."

Ndu touched a finger to the tip of his tongue and raised it in the air. "You will both regret this humiliation you've subjected me to. I swear it."

Everywhere went silent as the whole bar watched. Eziafa forced himself to take a casual sip from his glass. The little boy was not going to make him bare his formidable fangs.

From the corner of his eye, Eziafa saw Hyginus marching in their direction. He looked at Hyginus and shook his head.

After some coaxing, Ndu's friends dragged him away into the night.

Before Eziafa left the beer parlour, Hyginus had a private conversation with him. "I'm sorry for what happened with that young fool," Hyginus said. "Make we brush am for you?"

It had been a while since Eziafa heard the slang for a beating. Back in his university days, many people suffered serious brushing for lesser offences. Eziafa smiled. "One does not display the extent of one's might before a child."

Hyginus cleared his throat. "You know that if a snake fails to show its venom, little children will use it in tying firewood."

Eziafa was not interested in seeking revenge. "Nna, old things have passed away."

Hyginus laid a hand on Eziafa's shoulder. "The hen does not forget the person who plucked its tail feathers during the rainy season. Please. Let me repay your kindness to me."

Eziafa couldn't remember the debt Hyginus wished to repay. "You don't owe me anything."

"My brother, if we let Ndu get away with this behaviour, how would he learn some manners? Let me discipline him."

Eziafa tapped his foot. In Oji, they took care of their own. Perhaps it wasn't a bad thing for the young man to receive an in-house lesson on the importance of respecting one's elders. There would be no limits if outsiders taught Ndu the lessons he needed. He gave Hyginus an approving nod. "As you wish."

Chapter Seventeen

EZIAFA WALKED THROUGH the open door of his mother's bedroom. "Nne, I'm going to Zina's house."

Nne placed the folded *wrappa* on top of a pile of clean clothes. "I am sure they are busy with last-minute preparations. Tomorrow, you will see Zina at the church."

What he had to say to Zina could not wait. "Is there a tradition which says I can't see her today?"

Nne paused from her task. "No. Is Zina not your wife?"

According to their traditions, she was. The ceremony took place earlier in the week. The village people ate, drank, and ate some more. Nauseous from thinking about the money he had spent, to Eziafa the whole ceremony was a blur. Afterwards, he had wanted to bring Zina home. It would have been the best reward. Nne insisted Zina couldn't move to their house until after the church wedding. In her eyes, God's blessing trumped tradition. Zina's staunchly Catholic parents shared the same sentiment. Eziafa had to go along with their wishes.

"I'll be back right after our conversation."

"*Nwa m*, what is the matter? You have not been your-self."

Eziafa shuffled his feet on the concrete floor as he thought of the best way to respond. He couldn't stop thinking about the beer parlour encounter with Ndu.

"What are you going to discuss?" Nne asked.

It was best he didn't say anything that would tarnish Zina's image before Nne's eyes. The two had to live togeth-er until Zina joined him in Houston. It would be a waste of money for Zina to attend a Nigerian university. Until she received her immigration papers, she would help at the family cassava farm.

Eziafa forced a smile. "This is a husband and wife matter."

"Then this old woman will mind her business. Please, leave their house on time."

"Yes, Nne."

Mrs. Nwoye told him Zina was at the beauty salon. When Eziafa insisted on seeing her, his little sister-in-law, Ebele, took him to the salon. He waited outside the small bungalow.

Zina looked alarmed when she came out with a partly braided head.

"Is there somewhere private we can talk?"

She looked around before pointing to a cluster of trees nearby. "We can stand over there."

They were quiet during the short walk. Zina's eyes flitted about, her gaze landing everywhere except his face.

"Who is Ndu Mbogu?"

Zina looked as if she'd been cornered by a horde of masquerades. "Ah."

"I said, who is Ndu Mbogu?"

Zina lowered her eyes. "My ex-boyfriend."

"You told me you didn't have a boyfriend."

"I didn't when you asked me. I'd already told Ndu that we could no longer be ..." Zina's voice caught.

Eziafa's mind spun. He remembered the half-naked bride at the village square. Was he about to make the biggest mistake of his life? "Tell me the truth. Do you still love Ndu?"

"You're my husband,' Zina whispered.

"That is not the appropriate response to my question. Yes or no?"

Zina's tear-filled eyes spoke for her. The thought of having to cancel the church wedding made Eziafa feel sick to his stomach. How would Nne handle the whispers? "What do you want me to do?"

"Nothing. Ndu is my past. You are my future."

A sense of calm came over Eziafa as he weighed her words. Zina was right. There was no need for them to look back.

Eziafa held out the polyethylene bag in his hand. "I brought you a special gift."

"You already gave me a suitcase full of beautiful things."

"This gift is between us."

Zina took the bag from him. Her eyes widened when she opened the gift box and saw the colourful *jigida* set he had ordered. She stared at the strings of beads for a while before speaking. "They are beautiful. *Imeela.*"

He had planned to give Zina the gift the following night. To ensure some privacy, he booked a suite at a hotel in Ehiri for a couple of days. He didn't need Nne and Evelyn listening at his bedroom door.

"Tomorrow, I want you to wear the beads under your

wedding gown. When I hold you during our first dance, I want to feel them."

Zina's eyes widened. "Mama doesn't like them. She says they're fetish things."

"I'm your husband. And you will wear what I want."

She took a deep breath. "I will."

He reached out and stroked Zina's cheek. "I can't wait for tomorrow night."

The following morning, Eziafa stood in front of the full-length mirror in Nne's bedroom and gave himself a proper inspection while his mother watched from her dressing table.

He looked darn good in his three-piece black suit, a red cravat, and shiny lace-up shoes. "Nne, your son is hand-some o," he said in a sing-song voice.

"Eziafakaego."

The way she said his name, soft and sweet, captured everything she was feeling. "Yes, Nne."

"*Nwa m, daalu. Chukwu ga gozie gi*. Thank you for honouring your mother. Thank you for not letting me endure the ridicule of my peers." She gave him an apologetic look. "I know I have been pushing you. It's a mother's duty to push a reluctant child into the right path."

Eziafa scratched his jaw. The words were the closest thing he would get to an apology. "Are you ready for your new daughter?"

Nne smiled. "I have been ready since the day you were born. When Zina gets to America, you will call to tell me that my baby is on the way." She cupped hands behind her to indicate a child balanced on her back.

He gave her an indulgent look. It would be years before that grandchild arrived. He was not leaving behind a pregnant wife or starting a family as soon as Zina landed in Houston.

After a final look at his outfit, he moved away from the mirror. "Remember, the priest said we could not be late for the service."

Wide-eyed, Nne called for his sister. "Evelyn, *bia*! I need help with my head tie."

The women were still working on a masterpiece when Eziafa walked out of the house. Nne had kept insisting it wasn't the day for her to tie a modest one. She wanted her head tie to scream mother-of-the-groom.

Outside the house, Dede Matthias's driver was waiting to take him to the church. Eziafa jumped into the car. He was ready to bring his wife home.

Zina's entrance with her father made Eziafa clear his throat. Some of his friends told him their hearts skipped when they saw their brides walking down the aisle. What Eziafa's heart did was a combination of break dancing and flying.

The snug lace dress Zina wore complemented her slim figure. In flat silver sandals, she held the fresh flower bouquet he'd asked Evelyn to drop off at their house.

To match his red cravat, the tailor had added a red satin sash to Zina's dress. Fresh-faced with only a hint of pink lipstick and face powder, she looked like the woman of his dreams, and more. His only concern was Zina's serious expression. It would have been more appropriate at a funeral.

"Smile," he whispered to her when she reached his side.

As Zina said her vows, he realized it was the first time she'd given him a direct look. He was glad there wasn't any hesitation in her voice.

Eziafa took his vows and pushed his ring down Zina's trembling finger. It was a perfect fit. He saw it as a good omen. For the rest of his life, there would be no other woman for him.

He drew Zina close and felt the *jigida* beads under her lace dress. For a moment, Eziafa deepened his kiss. As long as Zina continued to give him the respect he deserved, they would live in peace until the inevitable arrival of the kind of love one needs to build a home.

Zina burst into tears as their car pulled out of the church compound. Because he wasn't sure of how to console her, he left her alone. She didn't speak to him throughout the one-hour drive from Oji to Ehiri.

Dede Matthias' driver dropped them in front of the self-advertised five-star hotel. From what Eziafa could see, a three-star rating would be generous. He held on to their suitcase as they stood on the front steps. "Are you feeling better?"

Zina nodded. "Yes."

Eziafa stroked her cheek. "No more tears." He held her hand as they walked into the reception area.

Zina had changed out of her wedding dress by the

time Eziafa came back to the room. He placed the bottle on the side table. "Why didn't you wait for us to take a shower together?"

She looked embarrassed as she tugged on the bottom of the teddy nightgown he'd packed in their suitcase. "The gown is not my size," she said.

Eziafa smiled. "That's the style."

Zina turned her face away when he began to strip off his clothes. Before they got into bed, she insisted on switching off the lights.

Eziafa wanted to see everything. "We're now husband and wife."

Her voice shook. "Please."

Eziafa pushed down his frustration. "You can switch it off."

The bed creaked when Zina finally joined him. Eziafa tried to calm himself. He didn't want to hurt her. When he stuck his hand under the lace teddy, he could feel Zina's body trembling. The warmth eroded some of Eziafa's control. "You're so beautiful," he said.

Zina sighed as his hands roamed over her body. "I'm afraid."

"I promise, I'll be gentle," Eziafa said in an urgent tone as he searched for her lips. Their moist softness was his undoing. Focused on achieving his climax, he didn't wait for her to be ready for him. And even though he knew Zina's moans were more from pain rather than pleasure, Eziafa didn't stop or slow himself down.

Afterward, Zina's body shook as he held on to her. It wasn't how he had planned to start their marriage. "I'm sorry," he whispered into Zina's ear. "I could not control myself."

Zina cried in his arms until she fell asleep.

The rest of Eziafa's days at Oji flew. The night before he left for Houston, he sat in front of the house and gazed at the twinkling stars. They looked like the same ones he'd seen as a little boy seated at his father's feet during visits to the village.

He closed his eyes and whispered the plea under his breath. "Papa, I'm leaving again. Please, bless me."

Moments later, a passing breeze caressed Eziafa's face. The sensation calmed his heart. His father had heard him.

Eziafa stretched his arms. The two most important women in his life sat on either side of him. Nne lifted her head from his shoulder as he turned to look at her. "*Nwa m*, thank you," she said.

This Nne was different from the woman he'd met on his arrival. Zina's presence in the home had brought new life to everything.

Eziafa glanced at Zina's face. She also gazed at the stars. He swallowed hard. Despite his earlier doubts, he made the right choice.

Nne's voice thickened as she began one of her favourite songs. "*Come and join me sing Hallelujah. Jehovah Nissi has done me well.*"

Eziafa noticed that Zina wasn't singing along. He gave her a gentle tap on the shoulder. Zina's eyes were sad when she looked at him. Her melancholic disposition was beginning to irritate him. She had been quiet for most of the day.

To make up for his wife's silence, Eziafa raised his voice. If only Zina knew the most exciting years of their lives were on the way.

PART TWO

*No one gets a mouthful of food by picking
between another person's teeth*

Chapter Eighteen

ZINA RUBBED BLOOD-SHOT eyes. Her whole face felt as though she'd washed it with sand. She looked for the mint-flavoured toothpaste in her bag of toiletries. Eziafa hadn't told her about the terrible thing the flight attendant called turbulence. While Zina held the brown paper bag to her mouth, she thought their plane would fall right out of the sky.

She rinsed out her mouth with warm water and washed her face. The cool water brought some relief. Five more hours at the airport and she would be on her way to her new life.

Zina held on to her little suitcase as she went in search of her departure gate. Her legs grew tired when she missed the directions to her terminal and ended up in the wrong place.

Unsure of what to do, Zina stood in the middle of the big airport. Desperate, she sought directions from a woman in a uniform. Zina joined a line of people stepping onto a moving conveyor belt. The problem was getting off. She tripped when the wheels of her suitcase got caught on the edge of the walkway.

Zina smiled when she finally saw her departure gate. If not for the long stopover, she would have missed her Amsterdam to Houston flight. Eziafa would have been angry with her.

She found a seat and took a drink from the bottle of water given to her during the flight from Lagos. Refreshed, she placed her feet on her suitcase. She then brought out the Mills and Boon romance novel she'd been reading on the plane.

Her fingers flipped to the folded page. Zina liked this part of being a married woman. Away from her mother's probing gaze, she finally had the freedom of choosing what she wanted to read.

Right in the middle of an intense first date scene, Zina's stomach began to rumble. The real food she ate in Lagos was long gone. She ignored it until the increasing loudness made her look around. She hoped no one else heard the sound.

Her eyes met with those of a woman seated on the opposite bench. She gave Zina an understanding smile.

Moments later, Zina lowered her gaze at the sound of another loud rumble. The nonsense stomach was disgracing her in front of strangers.

Zina looked up when the woman's stomach rumbled a response to hers. She covered a laugh.

The woman shrugged. "We can't control their protests. I think they want us to get some food."

Eziafa told her not to act familiar with anyone during her journey. That airport security was always watching. The woman's slight African accent helped to put her mind at ease. "That is a good idea," she said.

Before they left the gate area, her new friend stuck out her hand. "I'm Titilope Ojo."

Zina shook the offered hand. She recognized the Yoruba names. "You're a Nigerian?"

Titilope smiled. "The green passport peeking from your purse tells me you are one too."

"I'm Zina Nwo ... I mean Okereke." She was still getting used to her new name.

"Nice to meet you," Titilope said.

They stopped at a café around the corner. Zina was afraid to eat anything that would further upset her stomach. She ordered a cup of tea and a toasted wheat bagel.

Titilope ordered black coffee and something called a croissant. Zina stared at it. Even though it didn't look like a doughnut, it had strawberry jam inside.

They sat on a pair of silver bar stools. "Where are you going?" Titilope said.

She told Titilope about Eziafa and explained that she was joining him in Houston. "It took almost one year for them to give me a visa."

Titilope shook her head. "The processing wait times for immigrant visas are horrendous."

Zina agreed. After several months, people had stopped asking her when she was leaving Oji. "Do you live in Houston?" she asked Titilope.

"No. Maryland. I'm on my way to Houston for a job interview. Afterward, I'm going home to my son."

"Eeyah. How old is he?"

"Seven. An energetic, curious, seven-year-old." Titilope pulled a picture from her wallet. "Here's my T.J."

Zina examined the boy's face and looked at Titilope's scarred face. "He must look like your husband."

"I'm divorced. And yes, T.J. does look like his father."

Zina had noticed the band of paler skin on Titilope's ring finger and assumed Titilope forgot to wear her rings.

They returned to one of the benches at the departure gate. Zina felt comfortable enough with Titilope to share her dilemma. "Sister, I have a problem," she said.

"What is it?"

"I forgot to put our wedding album in my hand luggage. It's in the suitcase I checked in. Do you think the immigration people will send me home since I don't have it on me?"

"Don't worry. They won't send you back to Lagos because of that."

"I heard that before they deport people, they shave their heads. I can't return to Oji with a bald head."

"I've never heard of such a thing," Titilope said. "Who told you that?"

"It's common knowledge in Oji."

Titilope gave her a reassuring smile. "It's not true. When my ex's cousin came to join her husband, she didn't present her wedding album at the airport."

"Thank you."

"You're welcome. So, are you excited about starting your new life?"

Even though the year apart gave her time to adjust to her new status, Zina still struggled with mixed feelings. "I've never left my mother before. I miss her."

"You should be able to call her on a regular basis."

She hoped so. "My husband gave me money to buy her a cell phone before I left."

"You have nothing to worry about."

"Thank you, Sister."

"You can call me by my first name." Titilope pointed to Zina's novel. "I haven't read one of those in a while. Is your husband, tall, dark and handsome?"

"Eziafa is dark," she said. "But he's not tall."

"It does not matter. Trust me, a man's looks are no guarantee of romantic behaviour."

"My mother said a husband's strength is more important than his physical appearance."

Titilope shook her head. "In my book, a man's kindness is his best feature."

Zina squirmed. Eziafa had tried to be kind to her. Still angry over what happened during their first night together, she made things difficult for him.

"You look worried," Titilope said.

It was easier for Zina to admit her feelings to a stranger. "I am scared about our marriage."

"I know how doubts about having a successful marriage can induce fear. But, if you stay on the same page about important things, things should be fine."

"Thank you."

Titilope opened her purse and brought out a business card. "Balancing the expectations of our old and new worlds can be challenging. If you need to talk about anything, please give me a call."

Zina took the card. "Thank you, Sis ... Titilope."

"That wasn't difficult, was it?"

She gave Titilope a shy smile. "No, it wasn't."

Titilope glanced at her wristwatch. "I need to have a chat with the airline people about changing my seat before we start boarding. I'll be right back."

Zina watched as Titilope walked over to the customer care counter. She was glad to have defied Eziafa's orders.

The captain's announcement interrupted the in-flight movie. Zina's bloodshot eyes looked up from the small screen.

"Ladies and gentlemen, we're now approaching the George Bush Intercontinental Airport. Local time is 5 pm Central Daylight Time. The temperature on this beautiful January day is welcoming at 75 degrees Fahrenheit. On behalf of Alpha Airlines and the entire flight crew, thank you for joining us on this trip. We look forward to seeing you onboard again soon."

Zina secured the screen and adjusted her seat belt as the cabin crew prepared for landing. She held on to the armrests and braced herself as the plane tires touched down on the tarmac. When the plane came to a complete stop, people began clapping. Zina joined in.

Zina jumped to her feet and retrieved her little suitcase from the overhead bin. She couldn't wait to get off the plane.

After passing through Immigration and Customs, she caught up with Titilope.

"How did it go?" Titilope asked.

Zina's heart rate hadn't quite returned to normal. "They didn't ask me for the photo albums," she said.

Titilope smiled. "Welcome to America."

Swept up by the crowd, the women hurried down the corridor leading to the luggage carousel. All Zina could see were faces in varying shades of white and pink. She took a deep breath as her head spun from the bright lights. "The incitement is getting to me," she said to Titilope as they arrived at the baggage claim area.

Titilope's eyes twinkled. "The incitement's affecting me, too."

When she realized her mistake, Zina's hand flew to her mouth. Titilope must think she was an uneducated village girl. "I meant to say excitement."

"I know. I was teasing."

They retrieved their suitcases and piled them on silver trolleys. "I'm sure your husband can't wait to see you," Titilope said.

Zina gave her a half-smile. During their last telephone call, Eziafa kept telling her how much he missed her. She'd mumbled the same words back because she knew Eziafa expected to hear them. It was hard to long for him when Ndu was still king of her heart.

Chapter Nineteen

EZIAFA BROWSED THE airline's website for Zina's flight information. The estimated time of arrival was unchanged. The long journey would have exhausted Zina.

Distracted, he took the wrong highway exit. It took several minutes before he could turn around. At the airport, he hurried out of the car and headed toward the vending machine to get a parking ticket.

Eziafa almost ran into a woman as she stepped out of the elevator. A quick apology was on his lips when he heard his name. "You still haven't learned to slow down," she said.

He stepped back. "Jovita?"

Jovita gave him her sassy grin. "The one and only."

Her protruding midriff made him take a second look. "You're pregnant!"

Jovita gave her stomach a slow rub. "Well, Daddy, this wasn't how I planned to tell you the good news."

Eziafa's car key dropped to the floor. The ringing in his ears cleared as he remembered when they last had sex. To be sure, Eziafa counted the months in his head. "I haven't seen you in over a year. I can't … I can't be the father."

"Ding, ding, ding. Someone, please, get this smart man a prize."

His heart was still racing as he bent to pick up his key. "That was not funny."

"I figured you would appreciate the opportunity to use those famous money counting skills."

Eziafa exhaled. "I thought you left Houston."

She raised an eyebrow. "Were you hoping I would leave town for you?"

Eziafa glanced at her stomach. "Congratulations on the baby. I'm sure you and your husband are ..." His eyes went to her ring finger. It was bare. "I mean, you and the father must be happy."

"I'm happy," Jovita said. "I can't speak for the sperm bank donor."

He gaped at her. "Sperm bank donor?"

"Donor Number 007AJB. A six-foot polyglot with interests in martial arts and conspiracy theories."

Eziafa laughed. "How I've missed your craziness."

"I can't say the same for your deceit."

He couldn't meet Jovita's eyes. "I'm sorry for what happened between us."

"That is a non-apology. Things didn't just happen. Your actions were deliberate."

He scratched his scalp. "Did you get the picture frame I sent?"

"Yeah. I dumped it and the things you left at my house in the trash."

"I know I should have told you before I left."

Jovita snickered. "If you're looking for a pardon, I don't have any to offer. I do hope you have a happy life."

Eziafa's heart pounded as he watched Jovita walk away.

By the time he walked into the arrival lounge, Eziafa had composed himself. He couldn't let Zina think he wasn't happy to see her.

He expected to find Zina looking a little lost as she waited for him. Instead, she was in the middle of an animated conversation with a strange woman. She didn't even see him walk up to her. Irritated, Eziafa called her name. "Mrs. Zina Okereke."

Zina turned around. "Eziafa!"

He pulled Zina into a tight embrace and gave her a deep kiss. She pulled away from him. "You look beautiful."

Zina appeared dazed. "Thank … thank you. How are you?"

"I'm fine. Who were you talking to?" Eziafa asked. The woman had moved her trolley away from them.

Zina glanced at the woman. "Her name is Titilope. We met in Amsterdam, Netherlands. She was coming from Paris of France."

He smiled at the way Zina emphasized the place names. "International Zina."

Zina lowered her eyes. "I know you said I should not talk to strangers. Titilope was nice to me."

"I should thank her." He pushed Zina's trolley in the woman's direction. Zina followed.

"Hello, my name's Eziafa."

"Titilope. Nice to meet you." She shook his hand before smiling at Zina. "Time to go. I have to pick up my rental car."

Zina looked sad. "I may never see you again."

"We can talk on the phone. And if I get the job I'm

interviewing for, I'll be back to Texas before the end of the year."

Eziafa lifted the camera slung over his shoulder. "Do you ladies want me to take your picture?"

Zina gave him a grateful smile. "Yes, please."

"I'm sure Zina would love to have a record of the day she began her journey as an American wife," Titilope said.

Eziafa shook his head. "The picture would symbolize the day Zina became a Nigerian-American wife." To him it was a subtle yet vital distinction.

Titilope snorted. "God forbid Zina forgets her Nigerian-ness."

He gave Titilope a closer look. He knew her type. The Nigerian woman who left home as a teenager to study in the U.S. After acquiring an accent, they worked hard to transform themselves into something even more American than an apple pie.

Eziafa checked to make sure the date stamp on his camera was accurate. 01/15/2014. "I'm ready to take the picture," he said.

Oblivious to the undercurrents, Zina placed her arm around Titilope's shoulder. The click of his camera captured their tired faces.

"Please make sure you send me copies. I'll call when I get back to Maryland."

Eziafa was happy to hear Titilope lived on the other side of the country. She would be trouble for his impressionable wife.

"I'll make sure Zina sends them. I appreciate your help."

"My pleasure."

Eziafa turned to his wife. "We have to go."

After she and Titilope said their goodbyes, Eziafa

took the trolley from Zina. He stopped his brisk walk when he realized Zina had fallen behind. "I'm tired," she said when she caught up with him.

"Life here is fast-paced," Eziafa said as they continued their walk. "You have to keep up." He was forced to slow his stride as Zina continued to look around her.

Before they walked through the sliding door of the gangway leading to the parking garage, she gave him a sad look. "I'm already saying goodbye."

"The goodbyes you said in Nigeria would be the hardest. Trust me."

Eziafa glanced at his watch. "We don't want to get caught up in the rush hour traffic."

Inside the car, Zina turned to him as he closed his seat belt. "Is your house far from here?"

He corrected her. "Our house."

Zina gave him a tired smile. "Is our house far from here?"

"No. We should be there in about an hour."

Zina covered a yawn. "I've not slept much since I left Oji."

He reached over and gave Zina's warm thigh a gentle squeeze. "I'm happy you're here."

"I've been dreaming about this day," Zina said.

The words were what he wanted to hear. "My dear, your dream has finally come true."

Chapter Twenty

DETERMINED TO TAKE in all the new sights, Zina stayed awake. She held on to the dashboard. The six-lane freeway made her dizzy. Some drivers wove through the lanes and several times she was afraid someone would hit them.

"Ten more minutes," Eziafa said in a cheerful tone as he glanced her way. "Tonight, I will make sure you sleep like a baby."

Zina gulped at the thought of what Eziafa's words implied. Did men not think about other things?

The first sight of her new home was disappointing. A drab brown apartment building with peeling paint wasn't what she had imagined.

They stepped into an empty lobby. The mouldy smell made Zina sneeze. The walls were dingy, the carpeted stairs marked with dark stains. Zina told herself Eziafa did not promise her a mansion.

At his apartment door, Eziafa insisted on carrying her inside. "It's the *ndi ocha* way of welcoming a new bride," he said.

Zina backed away from him. "You can't carry me."

"My friend, come here."

"Eh, if you break your back at your age, your bones won't heal on time."

Eziafa puffed his chest. "What do you mean by at my age? I'm a man in his prime."

Zina prayed that her enemies in the village would not have the last laugh as Eziafa pushed the front door open with his foot. She sighed her relief when Eziafa dumped her on the couch. The decorative pillows bounced to the floor.

Eziafa dusted his hands. "Here you are, ye little woman of minuscule faith."

"Thank you for not sending me to the hospital on my first day in America."

He sat beside her. "You're welcome."

Zina looked around the room. The tasteful décor surprised her. From the way Eziafa studied his Excel sheets, she'd thought he wouldn't spend money on any frivolity. "This is nice," she said.

"I'm glad you like it. Do you want something to drink?"

Zina shook her head as she swung her feet off the couch. She wanted to see the rest of her new home.

After the short tour, Eziafa left her in the bedroom. He'd told her a hot shower would help her to sleep better. Zina almost scalded herself when she fiddled with the shower lever. She had not expected the quick transition from cold to hot.

Before joining Eziafa in the living room, Zina put on one of the colourful, Senegalese *boubous* Nne's tailor sewed for her.

Eziafa smiled at her. "The dress looks good on you."

"*Daalu*. It is one of Nne's parting gifts."

Eziafa ushered her to the table. He pulled out a dining chair. "You must be hungry."

Her last meal was at the Amsterdam café. "Yes."

Eziafa served her some rice and stew. The spicy tomato stew comforted her with the distinct taste of home. She washed a mouthful down with a sip of her cold fruit juice. "You cooked this?"

Eziafa dabbed at his mouth with a napkin. "Of course."

"This must be the result of Nne's training," she said.

"I'm joking. I ordered this food from a Nigerian caterer." Eziafa picked up his glass of water. "How are Nne and Evelyn?"

"They're fine. Sister Evelyn came with me to the airport."

"Good. And your people?"

Her mother cried throughout their last visit. "Mama was sad."

"That's expected. At least you lived near your parents for a year. Most brides don't get to enjoy that. We'll call Oji in the morning."

Zina dropped her spoon to cover a yawn. "My eyelids are heavy."

"Try and stay up for a couple of hours. The earlier your body gets used to the local time, the better you'll feel."

Zina stifled another yawn. After their meal, she went to the bedroom and brought out the wedding albums from her suitcase. The pictures weren't ready by the time Eziafa had left for Houston.

Eziafa smiled when they came across a picture of Dede Matthias. "Did you see him before you left?" he asked.

Zina nodded. "Nne and I visited. He sends his greetings."

Eziafa closed the album and placed it on the coffee table. "Enough for tonight."

She stiffened as Eziafa pulled her close and nuzzled his nose into the side of her neck. "I have missed you. Are you still afraid?"

Zina dropped her gaze. Mama's voice played in her head.

"Eziafa left all the women in America, came home and chose you. If you do not want him to stray back into their arms, you must respect him, learn what he wants. Make yourself available. Then, no matter what these outside women offer him, he will always come back to you. My daughter, a good name is all we have. Don't bring shame to it."

Eziafa stood and pulled on her hand. She lifted her head. "I'm going to go as slow as you need me to."

Zina stared at him. If the ancestors were kind to her, it would be over soon.

Chapter Twenty-One

ZINA HELD EZIAFA'S lunch box while he put on his shoes. She wanted to go with him. Two months in America and she still wasn't allowed to walk down the street on her own. When she reminded Eziafa about his travel promises, he told her to exercise patience. Annoyed by the memory, she kissed her teeth.

Eziafa picked up his bunch of keys from the dining table. "What is it?"

She'd not intended for her feelings to show on her face. "Nothing."

Eziafa gave her another questioning look when she walked him to the door and handed over his lunch box. "You're not walking me to the car?"

She grimaced. "I have back pain."

Eziafa's forehead furrowed. "Do you need painkillers?"

"I'll take some."

He patted her shoulder. "Take care of the house."

Zina clenched her jaw. As if there was anything else to do.

After Eziafa left, she locked the door, took the pain

medication, and went back to her spot on the couch. In her short time in America, she'd done more sitting than all through her years at Oji. Who knew boredom could create physical pain?

Her mind wandered back to Eziafa. The man she reunited with in Houston was different from the man who came home to marry her. This Eziafa always seemed to have something on his mind. He laughed less. But to be honest, not everything was bad. Unlike her father, Eziafa did not demand freshly-made soups. He also helped around the house.

The main thing she did not like about Eziafa was the way he spoke to her in a "Papa and Pikin" manner. She kept reminding him that she was his wife, not his child. She also did not like his attitude when he became angry. He would act as if a painful boil festered inside his anus.

Zina's hearty laughter stopped short when her eyes landed on the statue of the Virgin Mary she brought from home. Its plastic face conveyed gentle rebuke.

She was shocked to discover Eziafa no longer attended mass. The increased demand for rides on the weekend made Sundays profitable. Her only choice was to stay home and watch mass on television.

Zina never thought that she would miss having many people around her. In Oji, people were always there. Even on the days you didn't even want them to be.

She stretched out the kinks in her body. It would have been nice to knock on a neighbour's door for a chat. Eziafa had instructed her to leave them alone. People mind their own business here, he'd said. Zina did not understand that kind of life.

During their first grocery shopping trip, Zina added

five containers of salt to their cart. Eziafa did not respond when she asked him how one was supposed to borrow salt from people she did not talk to.

Zina glanced sideways at the sound of a flushing toilet. She was accustomed to the sounds of her neighbours' lives through the thin walls. Most evenings, strange cooking smells wafted in through her kitchen vent. No doubt they had the same opinion about the palm-oil based soups she cooked to remind herself of home.

She dragged herself up. There were chores to do.

By midday, Zina was even more bored. Tired of pacing through the rooms, she picked up the telephone and dialled Titilope's number.

With Eziafa's long work hours, conversations with Titilope were the highlights of her week.

The previous day, Titilope had told her she would be home for a couple of days. Her son T.J. was sick with the stomach flu.

T.J. picked up the phone. "Hi. Who is this?"

"My name is Zina. I want to speak to your mom."

"Are you in Nigeria?" T.J. asked.

"No. I'm calling from Houston."

"My mom's in the bathroom. I think she's pooping. Do you want to leave a message?"

Zina smiled. Children and the things they share. "Please tell her that I called."

"Okay. Bye."

Before she could say thank you, Zina heard a click. She shook her head. These *obodo oyibo* children. She walked over to the wall and placed the cordless phone on the charger.

On her way back to the couch, Zina stood by the living

room window, and stared at the apartment buildings around them. They stretched as far as her eyes could see. Since Eziafa has refused to take her out, she would have to discover America all on her own.

The next day, Zina waited for Eziafa to leave for work before changing into one of her new blouses and a pair of blue jeans. She tucked the ten-dollar bill Eziafa let her keep after a grocery store trip in her pocket. She may see something nice to buy.

Outside the building, Zina stood for a few minutes. Eziafa usually drove to the right. She would go left.

Ten electric poles from their apartment building, Zins saw a small, red brick building. The big white sign had the words "Piggy Market" written on it in bold, brown lettering.

Zina mouthed the words. It seemed like a strange place to sell live pigs. Curious, she headed for the store. The front door chimed as she stepped in. The woman behind the counter glanced her way and went back to arranging cigarette packs in a glass case.

Zina strolled up and down the aisles. The pig market was a small grocery store. Why didn't they just say that?

"Maybe I can help you find what you're looking for?"

Zina shook her head. "I'm only looking."

The woman raised an eyebrow. "You're looking at food?"

"I have ten dollars."

The woman smirked. "You may find more interesting things to look at the dollar store across the road."

Zina held her head up high as she walked out. *Onye Ezi.*

To get to the other side, she had to use a crosswalk. Zina stood by the busy road. Couldn't the drivers see the white lines?

Zina clutched her purse as she looked both ways. If she timed it right, she should be able to run across the road without getting hit.

Zina was halfway across the road when one of her sandals slipped off. She stooped to pick it. Lifting her head, Zina found herself staring into a car's headlights.

The driver blasted his horn. "Are you crazy?" he shouted, as Zina ran back to the roadside.

She leaned against the metal pole and tried to catch her breath. The sensible part of her brain told her to turn around and head back home before something terrible happened. Her stubborn part wanted to cross the road. She was debating what to do when a boy younger than her sister Ebele rode up on a bicycle.

"Excuse me," he said.

Zina glared at him. "I'm not blocking your way."

"I need to push the button," he said.

Someone had failed to teach the child some respect. "Which button?"

He smirked. "The one you're leaning against."

Zina moved. The boy reached for the yellow box on the pole and pressed the silver button.

"What does that do?" she asked.

He gave Zina a puzzled look. "You don't know that's how you get a walk signal?"

If I knew, I would not have asked you. Her face burned from the embarrassment.

The pedestrian crossing light changed to a walk signal. The fast cars stopped. The boy gave Zina a little wave before riding across the road. She stared at his back. Wonders shall never end. No wonder that man said she was crazy. Angry with herself, Zina turned around and headed home.

There was nothing to suggest Eziafa stopped by in her absence. She changed back into her house kaftan and resumed her chores.

It was dark when Eziafa returned home. He sprawled beside Zina on the couch. "So, what did you do today?" he asked.

Mama had told her men need limited information because many of them could not handle the truth. "I ironed all your clothes." Zina stood. "Food is ready. I made yam pottage with dried fish."

Eziafa covered a yawn. "Don't give me a large portion o."

Zina scowled as she dished Eziafa's food. If she had not left their apartment and met that boy, how would she have learned how to cross a busy road? Every time she disobeyed Eziafa's instructions, she became wiser.

She took a paper towel and wiped the edge of the dinner plate. Tomorrow, as soon as Eziafa left, she was going back to push the silver button.

Chapter Twenty-Two

EZIAFA STOOD IN front of the closet mirror and gave himself a critical look-over. Zina's good cooking had expanded his waist. He turned to the side and sucked in his gut. The shirt was still snug. Resigned, he put on his baseball cap, headed to the living room and stood behind the couch. Zina was watching another episode of her favourite tabloid talk show, *Daddies on the Lam*.

The red-faced guest screamed obscenities as she ran off the stage. A new guest came on. The young white woman popped her chewing gum as she balanced a beautiful baby boy on her lap. The host assured her that all the ten men contacted by the show took DNA tests.

A crew member paraded the baby before the entranced audience before leaving the stage.

Photos were displayed. Zina remarked on the close resemblance between potential father number four and six. When the host mentioned that the men were cousins, Zina's hands flew to her head. "*Tufiakwa!*"

Eziafa laughed heartily at her reaction. "*Abeg*, stop acting like a village girl. There's nothing new under the sun."

Zina ignored him. By the time the host called out the tenth man, and there was still no DNA match, she sank back into the couch. "How can a woman parade ten people in broad daylight and not one of them is the father?"

"I've told you. The networks stage these shows for ratings."

He got Zina's full attention. "Ratings?"

"Yes. Television ratings measure how many people are watching a program and the advertisements."

"Why do they do that?"

"The companies paying for the ads you see during the program need those statistics to determine the best return on their investment." He smiled. "Isn't it a good thing you have me to teach you all these things?"

Zina gave him a sullen look. "I am not an idiot."

"I didn't say you were. Anyway, I'm going to see Felix. When I leave his house, I'm off to work."

She gave him a hopeful look. "Please, let me come with you. I can help you collect money."

He knew the sedentary life affected Zina's mood. Their apartment sparkled. However, the activity could not match the rigours of regular farm work.

"I'm not driving a bus. Enjoy this down time. After you start school, you will wish you had time to watch television."

Her face brightened. "I won't."

Since her arrival, he'd been researching their eligibility for various student loans. They had limited options. With the other financial demands on them, the years ahead would be lean. "Remember, I told you today's Saint Patrick's Day. I usually get lots of business. Don't wait up for me."

She stood. "I'll get your lunch box and walk you to the car."

He'd forgotten about his box. "Thank you, my dear."

From the car's rear-view mirror, Eziafa watched as Zina wrapped arms around herself. If he could, he would exchange places with her.

After Eziafa sat, he noticed the gift bag on the dining table. "Whose birthday is it?"

Felix gave him a somber look. "It's a baby gift. Jovita had a son."

The news brought a heaviness to his chest. "I didn't know you people were still in touch with Jovita."

"Nkolika likes her. And there was no point talking about it. You'd both moved on."

Eziafa glanced at the shiny blue bag. The boy could have been his. "I'm happy for her."

"You ever wonder what your life would have been like if you'd married her?"

Eziafa stared at his friend. "Thinking about it changes nothing."

Felix nodded. "You're right. I'm sorry I asked the question."

Eziafa waited until Nkolika and the girls left the house before broaching the reason for his visit. "I need your help."

Felix gave him a puzzled look. "What is the matter?"

It was crucial he do something about Zina's growing restlessness. He didn't want her to become one of those women who came to America and lost their heads.

Their friend Obikwelu's fighting words were never far away from Eziafa's mind.

"Once these women hear land of the free, they think it means freedom to use hamburger-fattened fingers to poke their husbands in the eye. I have told my madam, not only am I free to dictate what happens in my home, I am brave enough to enforce the rules."

He blinked away the memory. "Zina needs an older woman to mentor her. Please, help me talk to Nkolika about taking on this role."

Felix smirked. "I thought you were going home to find a woman *you* would mould to your taste. You shouldn't be outsourcing your job."

"You're going to make me beg?"

"You'll be begging the wrong person. Nkolika is still angry about the way you treated Jovita."

Eziafa sighed. Nkolika's aloofness clearly communicated her anger. He'd hoped that, with enough time, Nkolika would let the matter go.

"As long as there's life, it's never too late to make amends. I'm sure Presido's wife can get you Jovita's current phone number."

"I already apologized," he said.

"When?"

"On the day Zina arrived in America. Jovita was at the airport."

Felix's eyes widened. "The women saw each other?"

"No."

"What happened?" Felix asked.

"We spoke. I said I was sorry. After that, Jovita went on her way."

Felix nodded. "I'm glad you apologized to her. I'll let

Nkolika know. I will also talk to her about taking Zina under her wing."

"Thank you."

"It can't be a one-way street. Zina has to be open to Nkolika's advice."

He was sure the more time Zina spent with Nkolika, the more she would learn to be like her. "Zina can come over to make your daughter's hair. She's quite good."

"Nkolika may still say no."

A sensible woman wouldn't work so hard to alienate her husband's best friend. From all he knew of Nkolika, she had sense. "All I need is for you to ask."

Felix nodded. "I will let you know what she says."

Chapter Twenty-Three

ZINA WHISTLED AS she lined her emptied dresser drawers with pages from grocery store flyers. She moved on to Eziafa's side. Underneath the layer of old grocery pages lay a large manila envelope.

Curious, Zina opened it. Inside were several photographs of Eziafa and a woman. They both wore Father Christmas hats. The woman sat on Eziafa's lap.

Zina's eyes grew big as she flipped through the collection. If someone told her Eziafa would engage in such playful poses, she would have said: "*Mba*, not my husband."

She studied the woman's face. If pictures always told true stories, it was clear this woman made Eziafa happy.

Her feet tapped on the worn carpet. Eziafa never looked at her with such tenderness. Nor had she ever seen him look as happy as he did in the photographs.

Zina dropped them on the bed. She couldn't disregard them, not when she was familiar with Okafor's Law.

The widely known law rested on the time-tested belief that once a man has great sex with a woman, it will be easy for him to get her to have sex with him again. The woman in the pictures looked like someone who was satisfied.

Zina's lips curled. All she had left of Ndu were bittersweet memories. It would be unfair for Eziafa to have something he could touch. At the sound of heavy footsteps, Zina stuffed the pictures back into the envelope. She hid it under the mattress.

As soon as Eziafa left for his Saturday shift, she called Titilope.

"Madam Zina, I thought you were going to call me last week?" Titilope asked.

Zina sat on the couch with the telephone receiver wedged between her cheek and shoulder. "Your son didn't tell you I called?"

Titilope clicked her tongue. "No. I've told that boy not to pick up the phone. The way he rushes for the phone, you would think he has people calling him at least three times a day."

There was something off about Titilope's voice. "Are you okay?" Zina said.

"No. My ex, Tomide, called to tell me he lost his job."

"What happened?"

"It's a long story. The condensed version is Tomide's criminal record affected his security clearance, and he could no longer do his primary job."

Zina was surprised. Only in America would an educated woman like Titilope marry a security guard working at a primary school. "Eziafa has said finding a job is not easy. Why didn't Tomide beg his *oga*? We all make mistakes."

Titilope gave a short laugh. "The bosses here don't listen to our Nigerian style of begging."

"I'm sorry for him o."

"I have good reason not to be, but I am too."

Zina had wondered about what happened between Titilope and her former husband. "He was the one who asked you for a divorce?"

"No. I did."

Zina frowned. "Why?"

"Tomide was using me as a punching and kicking bag."

Zina would not have felt one ounce of pity for such a man. "You are a virtuous woman," she said.

"Virtue has nothing to do with it. Tomide's pain does not bring me any pleasure. If he doesn't find another good job soon, it will impact his child support payments. I use them to pay for T.J.'s extracurricular programs. These past two years have been hard on the boy. He doesn't need any more changes."

"His father will find a job," Zina said.

"I hope so. Enough about me. How are things with you?"

Given Titilope's current dilemma, Zina felt reluctant to share the reason behind her call.

"Are you still there?" Titilope said.

"Yes. I have a problem too. I found pictures of Eziafa and a woman in our bedroom."

"What kind of pictures are you talking about?"

Zina drew up her legs on the couch. "They look like studio pictures."

"Phew. I thought the pictures were risqué."

She was too shy to ask Titilope what the word meant. "You should have seen Eziafa's smile."

"Were they recent?"

The shirt Eziafa wore in the pictures hung in their closet. "I think so."

"Are you worried that your husband is still seeing this woman?" Titilope asked.

"Hmm." Eziafa was rarely home. "It is possible."

"Since you're not going to stop thinking about it, ask him about the woman."

Zina frowned. "I should ask him?"

"Who else has the answers you need?"

Zina bit her lip. But, what would she do if Eziafa told her he was still involved with this woman?

"Please wait. Someone's at my door."

"Okay."

Titilope came back a short while later. "It's the maintenance man for the condo complex. We've been calling for days about our leaky kitchen tap. I'm sorry, I have to go."

"I'll ask Eziafa as you suggested. Thank you."

"Anytime. I'll keep my fingers crossed for you."

Eziafa talked to himself as he dumped the contents of his drawers on the top of the dresser. "Where did my envelope go?"

"What are you looking for?" Zina asked,

He kept searching through the pile of socks and underwear. "An important document."

Zina hid a smile. "What document?"

"My vehicle registration. The documents were in a brown manilla envelope. You must have seen it."

Zina crossed her arms. "No o. Maybe it's behind the dresser."

Eziafa dropped to his knees and reached under the dresser. He scowled as he pulled out a dirty sock. "Only two people live in this apartment. How does an object develop legs and walk out of this room?"

She shrugged. "Are you sure the envelope is not in the car?"

"Yes." Eziafa slammed the drawers shut. "It was here two days ago. Are you sure you didn't see it?"

"If you insist that what you're looking for is an envelope of documents, I didn't see any."

For a moment, Eziafa stood still. "Zina, where did you put the envelope?"

"I don't know what you're talking about."

"Zinachidi Okereke, where are my pictures?"

Eziafa's cold tone made her hurry to the bed. She lifted the mattress and pulled out the squashed envelope.

To her surprise, Eziafa burst into laughter. "So, you can pretend like this?"

"So, you can lie like this? You said you were looking for vehicle documents?"

He searched her face. "What do you want to know?"

"What is her name?"

"Jovita Asika."

Eziafa pronounced the name like a caress. "She's a beautiful woman."

He gave her a soft smile. "Not as beautiful as you."

Eziafa told her she couldn't wear makeup or keep long nails. In the pictures, he sat there, grinning like a foolish child as Jovita's long, painted fingers rested on his cheek.

Zina snorted. "Negro, please."

Eziafa's eyes widened. "What did you say?"

Her hand flew to her mouth. It was meant to be an internal thought.

"I'm sure you heard those words on a tabloid show. Listen, if you start acting like a woman with no home training, I will take the television cord to work."

Tears sprang to her eyes. "I can't leave the house, I can't make friends, and now I can't watch television? Did you bring me to America to punish me?"

Eziafa walked over and pulled her into an embrace. "I didn't say you can't have friends. Be patient. Building a new life takes time."

She moved away from him. "I should also be patient while you sleep with your girlfriend?"

Eziafa chuckled. "I think my wife is jealous."

"I'm not."

"Listen, you have no reason to be jealous. Those pictures happened before our marriage. The relationship is over."

"Then why did you keep the pictures?"

Eziafa was silent for a few minutes. "Do you still remember our conversation about Ndu?"

How could she forget? "Yes."

"What did you tell me that day?"

The words still tasted like charcoal bits. "I said Ndu is my past. That you're my future."

"Jovita is also my past. You're my present, my future. What do you want me to do with the pictures?"

Zina lifted her chin. "As the head of our home, I trust you to do what is right."

Eziafa picked up the pictures. Her jaw dropped when he tore them into several pieces. After he packed the pieces into the brown envelope, he handed it to her.

"You tore them?"

He raised an eyebrow. "Did you want me to keep them?"

She shook her head.

"Good. So, what are we eating this afternoon?"

Zina blinked. "Eating?"

"You have not cooked?"

"I did. I made some *ora* soup,"

"With plenty of dry fish?"

"Yes."

"Let's go and eat."

Zina's fingers clenched around the envelope. She was no fool. Eziafa tore the pictures because he had another set. She forced a smile. "Yes, my husband."

Chapter Twenty-Four

ZINA PEERED AT her watch's tiny face. Five more minutes before their guests arrived. She adjusted the cutlery by each plate and stepped away from the table to take another look. Eziafa told her where to put the cutlery pieces after he found a web site on the subject.

Besides pounded yam and *egusi* soup, Zina cooked the red snapper bought at the farmers' market. "Are you sure everything is good?" she asked.

Eziafa pushed in the last dining chair. "Why are you worried? It's Felix and Nkolika."

Felix was kind to her. It was his wife's pensive silence which made her uncomfortable. It felt as if she had done something to offend the woman. "Nkolika does not like me," she said.

Eziafa shook his head. "Nkolika takes time to warm up to new people."

Zina's intuition told her otherwise. "If you say so."

"Felix and I are like brothers. It's up to you to find a way to make Nkolika like you. She can introduce you to the other women and teach you how to adjust to this place."

She would prefer the men continued their friendship without dragging them along. "I've heard."

"Zina, I'm serious," Eziafa said.

"And I said, I've heard."

Eziafa frowned. "Zinachidi, I don't like this your tone o."

To maintain peace, she gave him an apologetic smile. "I'm sorry."

The muscles in Eziafa's jaw worked as he ground his teeth. "Let it be the last time you raise your voice at me."

Zina could have shouted a Hallelujah when the doorbell rang. She hurried to the door to welcome their guests.

"Aunty, Uncle, *nnoo*." Zina had decided not to call the older couple by their first names.

Felix's easy laugh settled her nerves. "Our beautiful wife."

"Thank you for coming," she said.

"We should have been here earlier," Felix said.

Nkolika handed Zina a wrapped parcel. "We brought you a small wedding present."

Pleasantly surprised, Zina smiled. "*Daalu.*"

Nkolika gave her a half-smile. "Thank God."

Eziafa echoed her thanks as he took the parcel from Zina and placed it on the coffee table.

Zina led their guests to the dining table. The men washed their hands in the waiting bowl of water while she and Nkolika used forks to eat their pounded yam.

"How are you adjusting to your new life?" Nkolika asked.

Zina shrugged. "It is a little lonely."

Nkolika gave her an understanding look. "I remember

my first days here. When you start school, I'm sure things will be better."

Zina hoped so. "I'm thinking of applying to Rice University. I was on their website yesterday."

Nkolika nodded. "Our daughter attends the school."

"What program is your daughter taking?" Zina asked.

Nkolika picked up her knife. "Business."

"That is what I want to do."

"Good choice. The business school application deadline is coming up fast."

To catch Eziafa's attention, Zina raised her voice. "Someone in this house keeps saying that I have to be patient."

Eziafa looked her way. "*Oginni?*"

"We were talking about my school," Zina said.

Nkolika smiled. "Since your goddaughter Dumebi is taking the same program at Rice, she can help Zina with the application."

Eziafa smacked his oily lips. "Zina is applying to the Registered Nursing Program at Houston Community College."

This decision was news to Zina. "Nursing *kwa?*"

Eziafa gestured for Zina to pass him the Pyrex dish of pounded yam. She did. Her eyes filled with tears. Zina, you cannot cry now.

Oblivious to her distress, Eziafa hummed as he heaped a mound of pounded yam on his plate. Even though Zina's thoughts raced, Eziafa's actions seemed to be in slow-motion.

Eziafa took his time moulding a morsel of pounded yam. He dipped it in the bowl of *egusi* soup. Zina's eyes followed his fingers as they made their way to his mouth, his tongue snaking out to lap up the food.

Eziafa washed the food down with a sip of water. "You will then transfer to the Bachelor of Science Nursing Program at the University of Texas. It's an excellent university."

"I don't want to do nursing," Zina said.

Eziafa frowned. "*Asa Nwa*, this is not the right time for this conversation."

Zina knew the term of endearment was a warning. She ignored it. "I don't like looking at blood or touching sick people."

"I said this is not the right time for us to talk about this!"

Nkolika gave her a discreet pat on the thigh. Zina clenched her teeth.

Felix smiled at his friend. "*Nna*, nursing is not an easy job o."

Eziafa snorted. "Which job is easy? At least, nursing is a lucrative profession. Money helps to lessen the pain."

"Money shouldn't be the only deciding factor," Nkolika said in a soft voice.

Eziafa gave Nkolika a half-smile. "*Nwanyi oma*, it's not the only deciding factor. But it is the major one."

He turned to Zina without waiting for Nkolika's response. "My dear wife, this soup is exceptional. This cooking is why I flew miles across the Atlantic Ocean to marry you."

Zina lowered her gaze. If all Eziafa wanted was someone who could make him home food, he should have asked his mother to find him a cook.

The rest of the evening passed in a blur. On their way out, Nkolika hugged her for the first time. "Thanks for the invitation. You've fed us, and we're fed up."

Zina didn't have to force a smile. "Then you must retaliate," she said.

Nkolika nodded. "Next weekend? Same day, same time, our place?"

Eziafa looked as if he had won the lottery. "We will be there."

Zina walked into the bedroom and found Eziafa awake. Angry with him, she had declined his offer to help her clean up.

He gave her a happy grin. "What a beautiful dinnerware set. Did you tell Nkolika pink was your favourite colour?"

"No."

"The woman has good taste. When we go to their house, you must offer to help Nkolika and her daughters do their hair."

Zina sat at the edge of the bed. "Eziafa, I don't want to be a nurse."

Eziafa pushed himself up. He sat with his back propped against a pillow. "Is that why you have been acting like a baby?"

It's hard not to act like one when that's how you treat me. "I don't like the job."

"Listen. The bottom line, this country has an aging population. With all the medical problems that come with that, nurses are in high demand."

The tears she'd held in all evening spilled over. "Is my happiness not important to you?"

"Of course, it is. One learns how to get used to things one must do. One's affection for it is secondary."

She lifted her chin. "I'm not going to nursing school."

Eziafa looked confused. "What is wrong with you? That Yoruba woman must be teaching you this defiance. Didn't you say she was a divorcée?"

"Titilope has nothing to do with this," she said.

"Big, fat lie. Women like her are bitter. They will do all they can to sabotage other people's marriages. My dear wife, I keep telling you. Stick to your kind."

The accusations were unfair. "You don't know Titilope."

"Oh. Because you met the woman during your only plane ride, you do?"

Zina stood from the bed, walked into the bathroom and slammed the door behind her.

Eziafa's raised voice filtered through the wall. "When you're ready to listen to the voice of reason, we will continue this discussion."

The next day Zina sat in silence as Eziafa tried to coax her into signing the college admission forms.

He flung the forms on the dining table. "We don't have time to waste. School starts in five months."

"I don't want to be a nurse."

Eziafa shook his head. "Less than a hundred days in America, and you're already making trouble for me. Listen. If you will not make any sacrifices for this family, I will no longer send any more money to your family."

One of her father's favourite sayings came to Zina's mind. When a woman makes her soup watery, the husband learns to dent his ball of *fufu* before dipping it into the soup.

Eziafa will find out that she could be as stubborn as a man.

Chapter Twenty-Five

FOR TWO WEEKS, the college admission forms sat on the dining table. The late application deadline loomed. Zina dusted around the forms. Instead of badgering her, Eziafa's dark eyes followed her around the apartment.

Zina decided to call her mother to report herself before Eziafa did. "Sweet One, how are you?" Mama asked.

"I am well."

"And your husband?"

Zina rolled her eyes. "Eziafa has gone to work. How are the people at home?"

"We all woke up this morning."

Zina shuffled her feet under the dining table. "There is something I need to discuss with you."

Her mother's voice grew alert. "What is the matter?"

"Mama, Eziafa wants me to become a nurse."

"And what is wrong with that?"

"It is not what I want."

Mama clicked her tongue. "Have you been fighting with your husband over this matter?"

Zina kept silent.

"You kept crying that you wanted to go to school. Now, your husband is ready to send you, and you are fighting with him? Zinachidi, what has come over you?"

"Can I not choose my career?"

"*Tueh.* What nonsense are you saying? Your husband has lived in that place for many years. He knows what is best for you."

Zina pursed her lips. When would she be the master of herself? "Since all I'm good for is kitchen work, let me go and cook Eziafa's food. I will call you another time."

"*Nwa m*, wait. There is something important we must discuss." Zina's heart raced as her mother cleared her throat. "Ebele has to pay her NECO and JAMB fees by the end of the month. Your father and I were gathering the money. It all disappeared after your grandmother fell sick. Remember, I have not asked you for anything since you left Oji."

"Mama, I don't have a job. And Eziafa said business has been slow. Maybe you can borrow the money for now?"

"Borrow from whom? When the whole village heard our daughter moved to America?"

"Are you able to sell some crops?"

"Nothing has changed since you left. With the weather, we can only grow enough to eat. *Biko*, tell your husband about Ebele's need. When you marry someone, their burdens become yours."

Zina's pulse quickened as she followed Eziafa into their bedroom. "Please, we need to talk," she said.

Eziafa took off his Kangol hat and placed it on the

dresser. "Can I at least sit and catch my breath before you start another argument?"

"I'm sorry. Should I get you something cold to drink?"

Eziafa held up his hand. "What I need right now is a shower. I'll drink something afterward."

"Should I set the table? I made some *ofe nsala*."

"I already ate," Eziafa said.

"Oh." Zina's shoulders slumped.

Eziafa stopped unbuttoning his shirt. "Why is your face long?"

"My mother called today."

Eziafa's tired eyes searched her face. "Did somebody at home die?"

"No."

Eziafa turned away. "Then, we'll talk after my shower."

Zina paced the room until Eziafa came out of the bathroom. He gave his body a rub down and threw the wet towel into the laundry basket. "So, why did your mother call?"

"They need money to pay for Ebele's university entrance exams."

Eziafa raised an eyebrow. "And?"

Zina mumbled her words. "They need me to send them some."

"Come again?"

Zina repeated herself in a louder voice.

"Go ahead and send them the money."

"But I don't have any," she said.

"You do not have any money?"

"Yes."

Eziafa snickered as he opened his drawer and pulled out a clean pair of white underwear. "You want me to help your people, yet, you are not willing to do the one thing I've asked of you?"

"*Biko*. This matter is not about me," she said. "Ebele needs to go to university. If she doesn't, what else would she do?"

"Ebele can work with her hands," he said. "That is what I do."

"Whatever we can send, they will manage."

Eziafa shrugged. "If you want me to send the money, you know what you need to do."

Zina glared at him and walked out of the room.

Chapter Twenty-Six

EZIAFA SAT AT an empty table under an overhead fan. Maggie, one of the regular waitresses, approached him with a big smile and a laminated menu. "Mr. Eziafa, good afternoon o," she said.

Eziafa rested against the chair. "Maggi Kitchen, how now?"

"I'm fine o. I know you won't order your food until your friend arrives. I thought you would like a chance to look at our new menu."

He and Felix met regularly for lunch at Bottom Pot, a popular destination for Nigerian drivers in the Greater Houston area. Frequented by other Africans, it was where they all caught up with news from home.

"Thank you. Don't tell me you people took away my fried yam?" Eziafa asked.

Maggie smiled. "Your precious yam is still there. We couldn't handle your one-man riot. Can I get you something to drink?"

"A bottle of malt will be fine."

Eziafa was half-way through his bottle when Felix

walked into the restaurant. The tired look on Felix's face cleared when he looked around and saw Eziafa's waving hand.

"No vex," Felix said as he pulled up a chair. "I ran into some traffic. I was tempted to carry my car on my head and walk."

Eziafa laughed. "You for try am now."

Maggie brought a pitcher of ice water with slices of lemon to the table. "Mr. Felix, welcome."

"Thank you, my sister."

Felix was still wearing his sunglasses.

"Take off your shades. It is not sunny in here."

"I'm wearing them on purpose," Felix said. "When we become too scared of the king, we wear a basket as a mask to tell him the truth."

Eziafa snorted. "You've never had a problem with telling me what I should be doing."

"These words are being spoken on behalf of your wife."

"You're now Zina's basket mouth?"

Felix took off the sunglasses and placed them on the table.

"On my way here, Zina called to ask for my help."

Eziafa had an inkling of what was coming. All week Zina had been walking around the house looking like someone died. "What did she want?"

"Zina asked me to beg you. Eziafa, she does not want to do this nursing thing."

Eziafa's mouth soured. Why was Zina looking for trouble? "Who told that woman she has the right to report me to anyone?"

"I am your best friend," Felix said.

"Mr. Bestie, how many times has your wife, Nkolika, called me to intervene in your affairs?"

Felix gave him a pacifying look. "You know I usually mind my business when it comes to the matters between a man and his wife. But Zina was crying. Remember, when an animal has an itch, it goes to a tree to scratch its body. A human being with an itch goes to a fellow human to be scratched."

He wasn't ready to listen to Felix's proverbs. "Are you telling me you've been scratching my wife's body?"

"Stop saying nonsense. Who else do you want Zina to go to?"

"Zina's eyes produce a lot of tears. Like I told her, we didn't leave Nigeria to come here, fold our hands, and watch other people prosper. The many responsibilities we have at home do not give us the liberty to indulge in frivolous pursuits."

"My brother, you are right about our responsibilities. Still, nursing is a difficult profession. I'm sure there are other programs Zina can do."

"Tell me, is cab driving easy?"

"Remember, we chose to drive a cab," Felix said.

Eziafa shook his head. Did they truly have a choice in the matter? To him, it felt as if immigrants were allowed only into certain professions.

"Look at you, fine lawyer man. Tell me you would hate sitting in an air-conditioned office where you make six-figures?"

"Several Nigerian men have gone back to school to study nursing. Why don't you go back? You finished with a first-class degree. Doing the program will not be a problem for you."

The only school Eziafa wished to attend was one where they taught people how to make quick money. "Zina is the one with the fresh, young brain," he said. "She would do better than me."

Felix sighed. "I still remember how Obikwelu and his wife fought over her going to nursing school. It nearly ended their marriage."

During one of their outings, Obikwelu told Eziafa his wife Chigo made over $90,000 a year. Imagine. If he changed a tenth of that amount into *naira*, he could do a lot for his mother.

"Now that Chigo is cruising around Houston in a brand-new BMW, I'm sure she's grateful Obikwelu put his foot down."

"Believe me, things are not as rosy as they appear," Felix said.

Eziafa wasn't interested in hearing Obikwelu and Chigo's story. This opportunity was his second chance to make something of himself. He had no intention of wasting it. "Zina should be grateful I brought her to this country. There were many other girls."

"It seems like this nursing thing was your plan before you went home."

"I thought about it."

"Then why didn't you choose someone who would have enjoyed nursing?" Felix asked.

In hindsight, he should have asked Nne to make it a search criterion. On top of their constant bickering, Zina's cantankerous nature was obscuring her beauty.

"Felix, I'm tired. I'm tired of always counting my pennies, of wondering how I can reinvent myself. Once Zina finishes school and gets a good job, I will finally have enough."

Felix's expression became pensive. "At whose expense? My brother, I've come to realize we all have to figure out what is enough and what we're willing to exchange for it. And it has nothing to do with living amid want or plenty."

"Are you done talking?" Eziafa asked.

Felix gave him an annoyed look. "Yes."

"Thank you. Let me decide what is best for my family."

Chapter Twenty-Seven

DRESSED IN A floral, ankle-length nightgown, Zina sat at the edge of the bed. The signed admission forms were in her lap. During her telephone conversation with Felix, he was clear about his limited ability to change his friend's mind. And even if her parents were able to find the money for Ebele's exams, there would always be something they needed.

She jumped up when Eziafa walked up into the room. "Welcome."

Eziafa frowned. "You're still awake?"

"I was waiting for you."

"Felix told me you called him. I don't appreciate—"

She held out the forms. "I've signed them."

Eziafa's eyes gleamed with self-satisfaction. He pulled his wallet from his trouser pocket and emptied it on the bed. The avalanche of coins from the pouch section made Zina flinch. Six worn twenty-dollar bills floated down and joined the pile of coins. Eziafa took one of the bills and slid it back in his wallet. "I need this for gas. You can send the rest to your mother."

Zina mumbled her thanks as she gathered the money.

Ebele called after they received the money transfer. "*Imeela*. I'm grateful," she said.

Her sister could not understand the cost of her gift. "The best way you can show me your gratitude is to pass with flying colours."

"I will do my best. *Eh hen*. Yesterday, I saw Immaculata. She said you've forgotten about her."

Zina pursed her lips. Her last conversation with Immaculata ended on a sour note. Immaculata became angry when Zina said she could not buy the requested designer shoes.

Even though Eziafa was not home, Zina lowered her voice. "When was the last time you saw Ndu?"

"He is currently in Oji. Something bad happened."

"What?"

"A month ago, they brought him home with two broken legs."

Zina jumped from her seat. "He was in a motor accident?"

"No. Some *confra* boys gave him a serious beating. They're saying Ndu must have offended someone."

Zina blinked back her tears. Ndu was too outspoken. It was a dangerous personality trait for someone who had no godfathers to fight his battles.

"Mama wants to talk to you," Ebele said.

"Okay."

Zina heard her mother's voice. "Why were you asking about that boy?"

"Mama, I don't understand," she said.

"See this child. I know you and your sister were talking about Ndu. How many people in Oji have two broken legs? Zinachidi, face your front. Remember Lot's wife."

She wasn't going to turn into a pillar of salt. "Is it wrong to ask after a childhood friend?"

Her mother gave a mirthless laugh. "You think I did not know about the two of you? Ndu's mother told me about his interest. I told them to wait until Ndu had finished school and had a job. Listen, you are now a married woman. Let today be the last time you ask after that boy."

"Yes, Mama."

Three days later, Eziafa came with another request. "Now that we've settled this matter, we should look at getting you some birth control."

"Birth control? The parish nuns always said contraceptives are not good for us. Why can't we continue with natural family planning? It has been working."

Eziafa shook his head. "*Mba*. If my Olympic swimmers catch your eggs, you will get pregnant with triplets. Until you finish school, we can't afford any babies."

"Mama also told me it was wrong."

"What happens in our bedroom is not your mother's business," Eziafa said. "I will let you know when we have an appointment."

At the family planning clinic, they met with the nurse for a private intake interview. Zina was silent as Eziafa completed the forms.

"We don't want pills. Zina might forget to take them," Eziafa said after the woman handed them an information pamphlet.

The nurse turned to Zina. "Honey, do you have a preference?" she asked.

Zina's preference was not to be in the room. She glanced at Eziafa. He jabbed a finger at the IUD image in the information pamphlet. "This is what she wants," he said.

Zina kept quiet.

"We need something that would last a long time," Eziafa said.

Zina looked at her pamphlet. Both types lasted between five to ten years.

The nurse gave Eziafa a tight-lipped smile. "Sir, since this is about your daughter's health, please, let me ask her what she wants."

"Zina is my wife."

The nurse's face flushed. "My apologies. She looks so young to be ..." Her voice trailed off.

Zina squirmed in her seat. The woman wasn't the first person to assume they were father and daughter.

Eziafa's voice dripped ice. "Do we have a problem here?"

"I'm not sure what you mean by that."

"I don't see how our age difference is your business. Do I need to talk to your supervisor?"

The nurse closed her file. "I have all the information I need. You can go back to the waiting room. I'll notify you when the doctor becomes available." She gave Zina a soft smile. "You'll be able to discuss your options with the doctor."

"Thank you."

Eziafa scowled. "I already told you my wife wants an IUD."

Embarrassed, Zina tugged on Eziafa's shirt. "Please. I'm sure the nurse heard you the first time."

Zina hid her trembling hands as they sat in the packed waiting room. She would have to tell the doctor something.

Minutes later, the nurse came out and told them the doctor wanted to have a private consultation with Zina.

"I want to go with her," Eziafa said.

The nurse gave him a tight-lipped smile. "I'm just following orders."

Eziafa gave Zina a warning look as he whispered: "Don't forget what's at stake. Tell them you want the ten-year IUD."

Zina gaped at him. Ten years of no children? "I will be too old."

Eziafa waved aside her concern. "Women here have children at any age they want. Ask this nurse. Don't worry. We will take it out before it expires. Remember, in five years, you would be fresh out of school and just starting your career."

The nurse placed a gentle hand on Zina's arm as she led her out of the room. "Are things okay at home?" she asked Zina when they were out of earshot.

Zina nodded. "Yes." She averted her eyes. "My husband just likes to get his way."

"I can tell."

When she met with the doctor, Zina insisted that despite what the nurse may have said, she was not a victim of domestic abuse, and the request for an IUD was her choice.

Chapter Twenty-Eight

"**N**WATA AKWUKWO, COME and see o," Eziafa called.

Zina waited until he called a third time before shuffling to the living room. She stood in front of Eziafa. "What is it?"

"Your college acceptance letter is here," he said.

"Is there anything else?"

Eziafa wrapped his arms around Zina's waist. "Mrs. Okereke, it's enough now. This much anger can't be good for you."

Zina shrugged. "I'm not angry."

"Then why won't you talk to me?"

"What is the point of talking when you don't listen?"

"*Ozugo nu*. You're blowing this matter out of proportion."

"What other choice have you left me?"

"You have more choices than I had. Listen. Start with this program. See where it takes you. When we have dealt with our needs, you can go back for a business degree."

Zina gave him a wary look. "I can?"

Eziafa was open to it, if it didn't affect his other plans. "Of course. It's never too late for a career change."

Zina's eyes welled up. "I didn't think of that. Thank you."

"You're welcome. You might end up enjoying the nursing profession."

She shook her head. "I doubt it."

Time would show who was right. Zina pulled away from him. "I should check the university bookstore website to see which books I need. I don't have a lot of time left before school starts."

"That is a good plan. You will also need to buy some new clothes." He had asked Zina to leave most of her clothes behind for her younger sister.

Zina picked up the computer and sat on the couch. "When do you want us to go?"

He joined her on the couch and watched as she brought up the college's website. A part of him was proud of how quickly Zina learned the new technology. "I will take tomorrow off work. After shopping, we can have a date night."

She glanced at his face. "Date night?"

"An outing is long overdue. Dinner at a nice restaurant and a movie."

A slow smile transformed Zina's face. "Thank you, my husband."

Eziafa parked his car close to the mall entrance. He pulled out an envelope from his shirt pocket and handed it to Zina. "It should be enough to get the items on your list."

"You're not coming with me?"

"It is time for you to go places on your own."

Zina placed the money in her purse. She hesitated as her fingers curled around the door handle. "Where do I start?"

"When you get inside, you'll see directions to the information desk. They will give you a map."

Zina still looked uncertain.

"If you run into any problems, call me. After your shopping, wait here."

Three hours later, he found Zina standing outside the mall with several shopping bags.

"You found everything on your list?"

Zina gave him a proud look. "Yes. I even have change."

"Keep it. You'll need some pocket money. Now, get ready for an 'all-you-can-eat' dining experience."

"What does that mean?"

Zina's mouth opened when he told she could eat as much as she wanted without paying more. "My sister Ebele would have liked this restaurant," she said. "Ebele's stomach extends into her left leg."

Eziafa laughed as he started the car. As a teen, he was also a voracious eater. "When Ebele comes over for a visit, we'll give her an all-you-can-eat treat."

"Once Ebele sees this place, she will refuse to return home."

"In that case, it's best to send her pictures."

At the restaurant, red and gold lanterns floated near a painted sky-blue ceiling. Eziafa gave Zina a tour of the food stations. "I can write a manual on how to eat here."

Her eyes were wide as she took in all the food. "What would one do with such a manual?"

"It will help you maximize your money," he said.

"No wonder you like this place."

He ignored her statement. "When you visit this kind of restaurant, you have to take things slow. Make sure you wear loose fitting clothes. No tight trousers or skirts. Then, don't forget to pack some magazines for your reading pleasure. Some people watch Nollywood movies on their phones between their plates."

Zina laughed. "*Umu Naija* no go carry last."

"We do everything with excellence."

They stopped at the salad bar. "This is where your dining experience starts. Vegetables get the digestive system ready for other foods."

Eziafa piled Zina's plate with steamed broccoli, carrots, cauliflower, and green beans. He got his food and went back for large cups of iced tea.

Zina smiled at him. "Thank you."

He took his seat. "When I lived in Minnesota, the buffet restaurant I frequented didn't care if one spent the whole day there."

Zina's jaw dropped. "Whole day? It can't happen in Nigeria. The restaurant will not make any profit."

He forked a broccoli head into his mouth. "Those were good days."

Four dinner plates later, Zina groaned as she pushed aside a half-eaten plate of crab legs. "If I eat any more food, they will need a wheelbarrow to carry me out of here."

Eziafa laughed. "You didn't eat your money's worth." He pulled her plate close. "Buffet owners prefer customers like you."

Zina covered a belch. "Eating this much food is nothing but serious long throat."

Eziafa didn't see it as greed. He liked to get the most

value for his money. He made a show of loosening his drawstrings. "*Na you sabi. Onye ocha* no go chop my money."

"What's the point of eating your money's worth and then spending the rest of the day in the toilet?"

That had happened to him. "It's all about the savings."

When they finally left the restaurant, Zina insisted on going home. "I'm tired. Can we watch this movie on another day?"

Eziafa pulled out of the parking lot. Their movie was starting in less than an hour. "We're doing date night, not date dinner. How many days do we get to enjoy ourselves like this?"

Zina grimaced. "There's always next weekend."

His mood turned sour. "All I've heard since your arrival is how I never take you anywhere. I dedicated today to you, and all I get is complaints."

Zina turned her face away. "I already said I was grateful. Why must things be the way you want them?"

"The last time I checked, I was still the head of our household. You women say you're the necks. If you think this is how your friends get their husbands to carry out their wishes, you still have much learning to do."

They were still in the middle of the movie trailers when he turned to check on Zina. Her eyes were closed. Eziafa was sure she had willed herself to sleep.

Eziafa stretched his hand across Zina's back and rested her head on his shoulder. The woman would not kill him with her childish antics.

Chapter Twenty-Nine

ON THE FIRST day of school, Zina woke up before dawn. Eziafa snored beside her. To avoid waking him, she tried to stay calm as she lifted the duvet and slid out of bed. Brushing her teeth, she winked at her image in the mirror. *Zinachidi, you're going to school today.*

Zina wore the jeans and blouse she had ironed and laid out the night before. She styled her long, permed hair, applied the glitter lip gloss and smacked her plump lips. She liked the shine.

By the time Eziafa showered and dressed, breakfast was ready. "Good morning. Tea or coffee?"

Eziafa sat at the dining table. "Morning. Coffee please."

Zina hurried to the kitchen. Eziafa drank his coffee black. Her preference was milk, sugar and what Eziafa called a splash of coffee.

She popped out the multi-grain toast and buttered it. Eziafa thanked her as she placed a plate of scrambled eggs on the table. He picked up the fork. "Do you remember how to get back home?"

The previous evening, Eziafa went over the city bus schedule with her. "I do."

"Good."

The kettle whistled. Zina hurried off to make Eziafa's coffee.

Eziafa dropped her in front of the student building. Zina began to doubt her ability to navigate the day on her own. She stood on the steps and pulled out her to-do list for the day. A quick review settled her mind.

The main door opened to a large hall. She exhaled when a white sign with the words Student Registration caught her eye.

Zina joined the line. As they shuffled along, she hummed some Igbo church songs under her breath.

Zina's eyes were on the flaming red Afro in front of her when the girl turned around. "You're going to have to tell me what song you're humming," the girl said. "I'm not having much success with playing Name That Tune."

The girl's twinkling eyes made Zina feel at ease. "They're Nigerian choruses," she said.

"I'd guessed they were African from the melody."

The girl held out her hand. "Hey, I'm Nomzamo Gray."

She shook the offered hand. "My name is Zina Okereke."

"Some folks call me Nomzy, others, Nom. Your choice."

She gave Nomzamo a closer look. They were about the same height and had similar skin tones. Unlike her, Nomzamo was curvy. "I like Nomzamo. Are you African?"

Nomzamo shook her head. "The name is. I'm a Georgia peach."

"Why do you have an African name?" Zina asked.

"My momma named me after her Spelman College roommate from South Africa. Gorgeous woman. She's my godmother."

Zina was too shy to ask Nomzamo what she meant by being a Georgia peach. Maybe it was a pet name like Tomato Jos. "What does the name mean?"

"Momma said it means she who strives, or she who must endure trials." Nomzamo smiled. "Fits me. I'm a resilient five-star badass."

Zina smiled. "It's a nice name."

"Don't worry, I'm not going to ask you if you know my godmother."

Zina frowned. "How will I know her? She's from a different part of the continent."

"Exactly. I know Africa is not a country."

"People here don't know that?"

"Far too many people don't," Nomzamo said.

It turned out she and Nomzamo were in the same program. They completed their registration and hurried off to their first class.

When the female professor entered the room, Zina rose from her seat. She looked down when Nomzamo gave her a kick under the table. Nomzamo pointed to the chair.

The professor raised an eyebrow. "Do you have a question?" she asked.

Zina wanted to cover her face when she looked around and saw she was the only one standing. "No, ma'am."

Nomzamo teased her as they made their way out of the lecture room. "Sistah Girl, what were you doing?"

She gave Nomzamo an embarrassed look. "I thought students here also stand when a teacher walks into the classroom."

"Even kindergarteners stay in their seats," Nomzamo said. "You'd better not give these professors ridiculous ideas."

"It won't happen again."

Nomzamo glanced at her oversized chain watch. "We have another hour before our next class. I need to get to the bookstore. You want to come along?"

"Sure."

After Nomzamo ordered her books, they sat on one of the stone benches outside. The warm sun caressed Zina's exposed arms. She missed outside time.

Nomzamo gave a little wave to a tall, Black man. He returned Nomzamo's wave. She made a "call me" gesture with her hand.

"He's your friend?" Zina asked.

"I don't know the brother." Nomzamo nudged her with her shoulder. "I'm sure you noticed his cute butt."

Zina held up her left hand. "I'm married."

Nomzamo shrugged. "Your eyes still work, right?"

Zina laughed. "You're funny."

"Thank you. I was going to be a comedian slash beautician. I love making people laugh. I also love making people feel good about themselves."

Nomzamo didn't look like someone you could compel to do something she didn't want to. "So why the change to nursing?" Zina asked.

"I'm doing this for my baby brother, Trey. Two years ago, he was fooling around on a trampoline. A backflip broke his spine. The nurses who took care of him did a fantastic job. Without them, we wouldn't have been able to take him home."

Zina reached out and gave Nomzamo's arm a gentle touch. "I'm sorry to hear that."

Nomzamo gave her a wry smile. "Thanks. Sometimes, life provides us with the luxury of choice. Sometimes, it doesn't."

The words brought a heaviness to Zina's chest. "Your brother is still here with you."

Nomzamo took a deep breath. "He is. I'm glad I met you today, Zina with the contagious giggle."

Zina realized she may have found her first friend at the college. "Me too."

The rest of the day flew by. For the first time, Zina was happy to come home to an empty house. Tired, she stretched out on the bed and fell into a deep sleep.

Together every school day, she and Nomzamo became good friends. Nomzamo treated her as nineteen-year-old Zina and not as a married madam.

"I'm starving," Nomzamo said as they walked out of the lecture hall.

Zina rubbed her stomach. "I skipped breakfast."

At the cafeteria, they sat in a quiet corner of the room. Zina always treated herself to the Thursday lunch special. She had tried to make the barbecue chicken sandwich at home. It did not taste the same.

Nomzamo raised an eyebrow. "When are you inviting me to your place?" she asked.

Eziafa met Nomzamo during a surprise school pick-up.

He took an instant dislike to her. Zina deflected the question with a laugh. "Only if you promise to bring me a homemade pie for dessert."

"Deal. I'm an excellent baker."

"I'm talking about spicy Nigerian meat pie. Not apple pie."

"That's an interesting choice for dessert," Nomzamo said. "But, I'm willing to try something new."

Zina took a sip from her soda cup. The situation with Eziafa should have made her more careful with her words.

"You're missing home," Nomzamo said with a kind smile.

While Zina liked the ease and predictability of her new life, she missed her family and the sense of belonging. "Yes."

"It sounds like you need some cheering up. I'm going to see a movie this Saturday. Can you make it this time?"

Zina chewed on her lip. There was no point in telling Eziafa about the movie date. He would tell her to focus on her house chores, unwilling to accept that there was only so much cleaning and cooking one could do for a family of two.

"My husband had mentioned a weekend outing. Why don't I check with him and get back to you?"

"Sure," Nomzamo said.

They finished up their meal and headed to the lecture hall for their last class of the day.

During the bus ride back home, Zina came up with a plan. She waited until Eziafa finished his meal. "Today, our microbiology professor gave us a group assignment to submit by Monday. We need to finish it at the college library, and the others want us all to meet this Saturday."

Busy with counting money on the dining table, Eziafa gave her an absentminded look. "Okay. Make sure you don't stay out late."

"I can go?"

He gave her an impatient look. "Yes! Now I have to count this pile all over again."

As she washed the dishes, Zina imagined herself and Nomzamo arm in arm as they enjoyed the afternoon.

They met at the mall. She proudly paid for her ticket and food. With a tub of popcorn between them, Zina smiled when the theatre lights dimmed.

Nomzamo nudged her with an elbow. "Hey, I'm glad you made it this time."

"So am I."

After three successful visits to the mall, the lies came easily. Zina reasoned that her activities were harmless. It wasn't as if she was spending time with another man.

After the movie, Nomzamo dragged her on an impromptu shopping spree. They were standing at the checkout line when Zina glanced at her watch. Her eyebrows shot up. It was later than she'd thought. "I need to go home."

"I'm surprised you stayed this long," Nomzamo said. "Don't worry. I'll drop you at home."

She couldn't risk a meeting between Nomzamo and Eziafa. "I want to take the bus."

Nomzamo narrowed her eyes. "Are you in the CIA witness protection program?"

Zina grinned. "Anything is possible."

Nomzamo looked around. "Do we have a surveillance crew? Are they taking pictures? What's my code name? Tell me. Tell me."

"It's El Pollo Loco." The restaurant was one of Nomzamo's favourite places.

Nomzamo pouted. "I'm not a crazy chicken."

Zina winked. "It depends on the day."

After they said their goodbyes, Zina half-ran to the bus stop shelter. It was a good thing she had cooked dinner before she left home. With luck on her side, she would get back long before Eziafa did.

Chapter Thirty

EZIAFA SCOWLED AS he watched Zina hurry towards the bus shelter. See this foolish girl. He was sure Zina told him she had to be at school to meet up with her study group.

He waited until she was close by before he poked his head out of the window. "Mrs. Zinachidi Okereke."

Looking like she had heard the voice of a ghost, Zina froze.

He leaned over and pushed open the passenger door. "Get in."

At first, he thought she was going to refuse the command. She took slow steps towards the vehicle.

He didn't speak to her until their apartment door slammed shut behind them. "What were you doing at the mall?"

Zina's eyes darted around the room. "Um … I went with my friend."

"What friend? To do what?"

"Em, Nomzamo needed to buy a pair of shoes."

Eziafa narrowed his eyes. He had made it clear to Zina that he didn't want her spending time with another unsuitable friend. "Did you say Nomzamo?"

"This is the first time," Zina said as he stared at her.

Eziafa gave a sharp laugh. "You must think I'm a fool."

"I don't."

"Look at me when I'm talking to you! I'm sure you've been going with this Nomzamo woman to her man's house. And since she is generous, she found you a boyfriend."

Zina gave her head a vigorous shake. "I've never followed Nomzamo to a man's house. We've only gone to the mall."

"You see how you have trapped yourself? I thought you said this mall visit was the first one?"

Zina began her whining routine. "Is it a crime to spend time with my friend? What did Nomzamo ever do to you?"

Eziafa gritted his teeth. What would it take to knock some sense into her head? "This isn't about Nomzamo. If something horrific had happened at the mall, I would have thought you were safe at school."

"I didn't think of that."

"My exact point. You tend not to think things through. Adults should think before acting."

Zina grabbed a throw pillow off the couch and clutched it to her chest, "How can I act like an adult when you keep treating me like a child?"

"People who want adult status act like one."

She gave him a sullen look. "You don't want an adult wife. You want a child you can order around."

Eziafa sighed in exasperation. "See me see trouble o. Is it wrong for me to expect honesty from you? I'm not arguing.

If you can't be honest about where you're going, you are not ready to leave the house on your own."

Zina began to cry. "I want to go to school."

"I will decide on the best thing to do."

Zina was still crying when Eziafa picked up his car keys and left the house.

No woman was going to manipulate him with tears. She chose to disobey.

Once again, Eziafa found himself at Felix's doorstep. This time, it was Felix who asked that they have their conversation out on his porch steps. It was his daughter's birthday and her friends were visiting.

Felix closed the door behind them. "*Nna*, you're shaking. What is the matter?"

He hated that Zina had put him in this awkward position. His friend would think that he wasn't in control of his home. "This marriage business is giving me too much headache."

"Why? You people should still be in the super lovey-dovey stage."

"You were right. The women back home are no longer what they used to be. Zina is giving me some trouble."

"What happened?"

He recounted the mall incident. "Imagine. Zina was sneaking about right under my nose."

"That is it? You made it sound like she did something terrible."

"I don't want to wait until that happens," he said.

"What are you going to do?"

He didn't think Zina was capable of such blatant defiance. "I'm not sure. I didn't think that she would start misbehaving this early."

"Zina is still young. You have to be gentle with her."

"She wants to act like a teen. Unfortunately, that is no longer an option for her."

Felix started to say something. Instead, he clamped his lips together.

"If you were going to say I brought this upon myself, I already told myself that."

"*Nna*, take it easy. Sit down with her and talk things through."

"Why can't she just do as she's told?"

"Eziafa, if you want this marriage to work, you will have to make some changes."

"What kind of changes?"

"What is it that Zina wants the most?" Felix asked.

Eziafa pondered the question. "Independence."

"Then how can you give her some?"

Zina gave him a wary look when he asked her to sit down at the dining table. Eziafa pulled his chair up to the table and tried to look at her with kindness in his eyes. He remembered what Felix said about being gentle. He reached across the table for her hand. "I want you to tell me what's on your mind. What do you want me to change?"

Zina's hand was limp in his grasp. "I should tell you what's on my mind?"

Eziafa braced himself for her words. "Yes."

Zina pulled her hand away from his to scratch her

forehead. "You talk to me in this 'Papa and Pikin' tone. I don't like it."

Eziafa sat back in his chair. "I am not your father," he said. "And you're definitely not my child."

"You treat me like one. And you are always talking about money, about the price of an item. Now, I can't even enjoy an apple without converting the price to *naira*."

He had not realized how much his financial concerns impacted Zina. He gave her an apologetic look. "When one has lived with too little for far too long, one tends to get tight-fisted."

Zina's voice grew soft. "Mama used to say that when you keep your hand in a fist, nothing new can come in."

"Tell me something. What money have you been spending when you go out with your friend?"

"Once, I used my lunch money to watch a movie. I usually don't buy anything."

Eziafa believed her. He did not find any unfamiliar items when he searched their room. "Would you like to have your own bank card so you can buy something on an occasional basis?"

"Yes."

He dug a hand into his pocket and brought out the second bank debit card and slid it across the table to her. "Here you go."

Zina's mouth opened as she stared at him. "You're giving me a card?"

"There is a limit on how much money you can withdraw from the account. And I want to see receipts for all the purchases you make."

She jumped up and ran over to wrap her arms around his neck. "Thank you!"

"Before you start whining about how I treat you like a child, I need the receipts to balance our account. Please, don't make me regret this."

Her smile stretched from cheek to cheek. "You won't. I promise."

"Let's go and test your card to make sure it works."

She gave him a coy look. "How much did you say my daily limit is?"

Women. "It sounds like I've made a mistake. You have to give the card back."

Zina shook her head as she stepped away from him. "You must catch me first."

"My friend, *bia neba*."

Zina ran towards the bedroom. Eziafa chuckled as he raced after her. He was up for a game of small madam hides, and big *oga* seeks.

PART THREE

*When the drummers change their
beats, the dancers must also
change their steps*

Chapter Thirty-One

ZINA LIFTED THE sweaty lid of her jollof rice bowl and inhaled the spicy aroma. She'd been counting down to the lunch hour.

Elinma, a Nigerian nurse from the surgical floor, sat next to her. Zina was pleasantly surprised to discover that Elinma's village was down the road from Oji.

Elinma's deep-set eyes lit up as they peered into Zina's food. "My sister, I have to make a citizen's arrest of this rice."

Zina chuckled. "On what grounds?"

Elinma licked her lips. "For starters, inciting public envy and potential disorder."

"All this big grammar on top of your long throat?" Zina asked.

Elinma grinned. "My sister, I get clean spoon o," she said.

Zina moved the bowl so Elinma could reach it. "Come chop."

"Yaaas! You be better person."

The other nurses at the table chuckled at Elinma when she brought out a spoon from her lunch bag and began eating with Zina.

Chardonnay, a petite, bubbly nurse on Zina's floor, rolled her eyes. "You guys need to speak English," she said.

Zina smiled. "We were speaking pidgin English."

"Well, I don't understand it."

Elinma stuck out her tongue at Chardonnay. "*Na you sabi.*"

A nurse from Elinma's team shook her head. "Oooh, Chardonnay. I think Elinma just cursed you out."

Chardonnay narrowed her eyes. "Well that means I don't have to attend her Arbonne party."

Zina smiled to herself. Elinma was a hustler. She sold Tupperware, Arbonne, herbal supplements, insurance, and anything else she could find. When Zina asked why she did so much, Elinma said she had popped out four babies in six years, and children were expensive to maintain. And like Zina, she was also expected to pay black tax by sending money to her family members in Nigeria.

Zina turned to Elinma. "You know Chardonnay makes it rain. If I were you, I would apologize."

Elinma switched her accent. "Shorty, you know I was playing, right? Y'all better show up at my Arbonne party with lots of cash."

Chardonnay's booming laugh turned heads in their direction. "I got you."

"Billie Lou is heading our way," Elinma muttered under her breath.

Zina's spoonful of rice stopped halfway to her mouth. Which kind *wahala* be dis?

Billie Lou, a nurse on Zina's floor, was notorious for rude monologues started as soon as each nurse left the table. They were yet to figure how Billie Lou gathered the dirty titbits she shared.

Nomzamo swore Billie Lou had planted bugs on their

floor. She told the other nurses people like Billie Lou lived in her village. They were excellent eavesdroppers.

Chardonnay looked around the table. "Ladies, remember, no eye contact. I'll point my crucifix pendant at her and we'll clap as she disappears in a puff of smoke."

The previous month, someone plastered a Libertarian Party bumper sticker on Billie Lou's car. Billie Lou told anyone who would listen that Chardonnay was responsible. Chardonnay insisted that, until the incident happened, she didn't even know the type of car Billie Lou drove.

Billie Lou placed her lunch box on the table. Stringy auburn hair framed the heavyset woman's square face. "How y'all doing?" she asked.

The women kept their heads down.

Billie Lou brought out her food containers. "Girls, I tell you. There's nothing like day-old pork roast."

Zina was alone at the table when Billie Lou made it back from the microwave line. The others had fled. She would have joined them if she felt like carrying a half-eaten bowl of jollof rice across the room. Some people had already commented about the spicy smell of her curried goat meat.

Billie Lou gave her a blinding smile. "Honey, looks like it's you and me."

Zina stayed silent. *Chukwu biko* save your daughter from this woman.

After two bites, Billie Lou dabbed the corner of her lips with a checkered napkin. "Zee dahlin', since you're still kind of new here, it's up to me to tell you the truth about that girl, Chardonnay."

Billie Lou placed a hand on her chest. "At the last staff Christmas party, dear God in the mornin', Chardonnay was drunk as a three-eyed spider on a blue tick dog. Be careful around her. You don't want to get a reputation."

Zina coughed. She'd almost choked on a piece of goat meat. Drunk as a three-eyed what? She was still gathering her thoughts when Billie Lou moved right along. "So, tell me, are you a Republican or a Democrat?"

Taken aback by the question, Zina stared at Billie Lou. Years back, Nomzamo told her, in America, one did not talk about politics and religion in polite company. If she had done anything to make Billie Lou think they were friends, she needed to undo it.

Eziafa had not involved himself in the political process. To avoid any unnecessary *wahala*, neither did Zina. The bottom line was they were too busy with surviving, and from even the little she knew about politics, it seemed complicated. "I am an Independent."

"Saddened to hear that," Billie Lou said in her slow, southern drawl. "You Africans usually share our conservative family values. Imagine if we joined forces against them."

Who were these "them"? Zina took a long drink from her water bottle. She should have escaped when the others did.

"Hey, sistah girl."

Seven hallelujahs and three hosannas. Zina turned in her seat and beamed at Nomzamo. "Hey Trouble. Where were you?"

Nomzamo pulled a chair. "I had to make some personal calls."

Face contorted like she had just sucked on a lemon, Billie Lou packed up her things and left the table without saying another word.

Zina grinned. "Saved by The Nomzamo."

Nomzamo inclined her head. "It's good deed Friday."

They watched as Billie Lou navigated her way to another table. Its occupants packed up and left.

"I wish I could tell her not to sit with me," Zina said.

"What's stopping you?" Nomzamo asked.

"I'm not that kind of person."

"You just want to be liked by everyone."

"That's not a bad thing," she said.

"It's impossible."

"Next time, I'll get up and move."

"Your call." Nomzamo shuddered. "The woman gives me the heebie-jeebies. She must have some bad juju."

Zina grinned. One of her significant achievements was converting Nomzamo into an ardent Nollywood fan. Nomzamo's favourite movie was *Igwe 2Pac*. The main character's absurd attempt at an American accent had Nomzamo howling with laughter.

"You don't mess with people who have bad juju."

Nomzamo responded with a dismissive wave. "Girl, my mother's family has deep Louisiana roots. I've got powers, too."

"Please use them to make Billie Lou stay away from me. You should have heard the nonsense she was saying about Chardonnay."

Nomzamo's eyes lit up. "Tell me, tell me. Chardonnay's going to be hopping mad when she hears it."

Zina wasn't ready to start a feud on their floor. "It's not worth repeating."

Nomzamo pouted. "You're no fun. Miss Goody-Too-Tight-Weave."

She flicked her bangs. "You know you want my weave."

"Not that mop attached to your head," Nomzamo said.

Her weave was grungy. Thanks to Eziafa's strict budgeting, visits to the salon were on a schedule. She packed up her Tupperware containers. "I'm not going to dignify that with a response."

"Love ya," Nomzamo said with a toothy grin.

Zina feigned a sigh. She and Nomzamo stuck together through two years of community college and another two years of obtaining their Bachelor of Nursing degree. Nomzamo made life good. "I kind of love ya, too."

Zina stepped out of the elevators at the pediatric intensive care unit floor. As she pushed through the double doors, the clean, sterile smell and ever-present buzz of monitors and ventilators welcomed her.

It was Zina's sixth month at Mercy Cross, the biggest hospital in Houston. It was her first nursing job and she loved it. Since she could not change her career situation, she had come to accept it. The acceptance made life easier.

To her surprise, pediatric nursing turned out to be her calling. It was the children. The smiles on their faces when they finally felt better and could go home brought her much joy. She did not share the discovery with Eziafa. He would have laughed and said he knew he'd been right. Zina pursed her lips. Eziafa still needed to be right about everything.

She stopped by the automatic sanitizer dispenser before entering Genna's room. It was the girl's third admission for pneumococcal sepsis.

During her first stay, the teen tested Zina's patience. Genna was upset that she had missed a school trip to Europe. When Zina realized Genna's surliness masked legitimate fears that she might not leave the hospital alive, their relationship changed. The way Genna's chin quivered whenever she didn't get her way reminded Zina of her younger sister, Ebele.

Zina walked into a bright room. The nurse who covered her lunch must have opened the blinds. "Hey, Genna."

The frail brunette on the hospital bed turned away from the window. She gave Zina a weak smile. Over the past week, Genna's large brown eyes seemed to have taken over her face. The child needed to eat some solid food.

"Nurse Zee. You're still here."

"I have a few things to do before the end of my shift."

Genna stayed still while Zina took her temperature, which had spiked. Zina bit her lip.

Genna peered at her face. "What is it? Something's wrong."

The kids who spent too many days on their ICU floor were often anxious and they quickly became experts at reading facial expressions. "Remember, Billie Lou is going to be taking care of you while I'm off for a few days," she said.

Genna wrinkled her nose. "I don't like her."

Zina flicked the disposable thermometer cover into the trash can. "Why?"

"She has a permanent 'I need to take a dump' look on her face."

Teenagers. She gave Genna a disapproving look. "That's not a nice thing to say."

"Why can't Raven fill in for you?" Genna asked.

Raven earned Genna's devotion after she'd projectile vomited on him and he cleaned her up with a smile. Raven was great with children. And women. "He's not here today."

Genna fanned herself. "Raven is such a hottie."

"And you, my dear, are only fourteen."

"I'm almost fifteen, and people say I have an old soul."

"Your old soul is still in a minor's body," Zina said.

Zina noted how Genna's chest rose and fell rapidly under the thin hospital gown. She rolled the pump stand to the side as she wrapped the blood pressure cuff around Genna's bare upper arm. "It sounds like I need to have a chat with your mom."

"No! If you tell my mom about Raven, she'll have him fired."

Zina doubted the woman had such powers. "Then we'll have to make sure Raven stays away from you."

Genna scowled. "That's no fun."

"An unemployed Raven would not be having fun either."

"Are you going to call my mom?" Genna asked.

She laid a calming hand on Genna's arm. "Of course not. Raven is safe from you."

Genna giggled as Zina moved to the end of the bed and lifted the chart holder. She wrote down her observations and Genna's vital signs.

"I really have to deal with Billie Lou?" Genna asked.

"Yes, ma'am. And I want to hear you've been eating while I was gone."

Genna looked like a ten-year-old when she stuck out her tongue. Given all the challenges the girl faced, it was a wonder she managed to stay so upbeat.

Zina made sure Genna's wires were still attached to the sensors stuck to her chest, and smoothed her blanket. "Do you need me to pull the blinds?"

"No. I like looking outside."

Zina gave her a soft smile. All the poor girl could see from her window was the rooftop of the next brick building. There was a little sliver of blue sky. "I'll be back soon."

Genna lay against her pillows "Okay. Thanks."

"You're welcome."

Out in the corridor, Zina sent up a silent prayer. She needed Genna's blood culture results to come back clear. The girl had been through enough.

It was 7 pm by the time Zina completed her shift reports and discussed her concerns with the next nurse.

Nomzamo found her as she was packing up to leave. "Figured you would still be here. Am I going to see you at Chardonnay's birthday party?"

"Shoot! I completely forgot about that. And I told Chardonnay I was coming, too." Zina groaned. "I need to sleep."

"You work too many 12-hour shifts," Nomzamo said.

Zina agreed. Thoughts about their financial situation always brought on a bout of nausea.

"I don't have a choice," she said. "We need the money."

Nomzamo shrugged. "If you change your mind, we'll be at the karaoke bar on Westheimer Road."

Eziafa had relaxed his monitoring but she was sure he would not let her attend a night party without him. She would have to call Chardonnay and apologize. She wished she had the money to get Chardonnay a nice gift.

She gave Nomzamo a quick hug before plodding down the hall to the elevators. Their apartment was the last place she wanted to be.

Zina gritted her teeth. Oh, the joys of being Mrs. Okereke.

Chapter Thirty-Two

THE THROBBING IN Zina's head increased when she pulled into their parking lot and saw Eziafa's taxicab. The vehicle hadn't moved in ten days.

Eziafa told her his years at the meat processing factory had left him with chronic arthritis. The pain now made it difficult for him to drive.

Zina knew there was truth to Eziafa's words. Some of his fingers were deformed. Still, she struggled to find empathy for him when he spent hours flipping through his beloved building plans with the same fingers.

Glasses perched on the bridge of his nose, Eziafa was gazing at those house plans spread out in front of him when she walked in.

Once upon a time, Zina was invested in the building project. She lost interest when the building plans changed from a simple bungalow to a three-story mansion.

Zina dropped her purse on the couch. She would not be surprised by the addition of another floor. Oji's flat landscape was a perfect showcase for his McMansion.

Eziafa continued to ignore her. She wasn't surprised.

Before she left for her shift, they had exchanged some heated words.

She washed her hands at the kitchen sink. "I don't understand how a grown man can be this comfortable with staying home while his mates are working. Where's your sense of shame?"

Eziafa raised his voice. "Are you talking to me?"

Zina tore off a paper towel from the roll and dried her hands. "Since there's only one shameless man in this house, yes I am."

The veins in Eziafa's head popped. "Zina, me?"

She stood over him at the dining room table. "Why are you spending so much money on a house we're not going to live in?"

"The house is also for Nne and Evelyn. Where do you want me to put them?"

Her mother-in-law was a simple woman. For her sixtieth birthday, she had begged them not to throw a party for her. "I'm sure Nne did not ask you to build her a mansion. Even if she did, is my well-being not important too?"

"We all have to make sacrifices for the good of this family. It's your turn."

"I can't continue to do this all on my own. Your endless demands have me in a choke hold."

Eziafa pushed back his chair and stood. "Do you want my hands to become completely useless?"

"Go back to the doctor. Staying at home and doing nothing isn't going to help."

Eziafa waved her off. "I drive for a living, and the man prescribes a pain medication which impairs my driving ability. Is that one a sensible doctor?"

"Dr. Sharma is an excellent physician."

"The man is a first-class quack. Why can't you bring me something useful from work?"

Was he trying to get her fired? "I'm not a thief. Since you don't agree with Dr. Sharma, get a second opinion. You said we came to America to prosper. Laziness has never made anyone rich."

"Now, I'm lazy. How do you think I ended up like this? For five terrible years, I worked like a dog for you." Eziafa poked himself in the chest. "I, Eziafakaego Francis Okereke, brought you to this country. I fed you, paid for your school, and sent money to your parents. I bought everything you needed including your stinking sanitary pads. Is this how to show gratitude?"

Zina hissed. When she had offered to find a summer job, he'd said all she needed to do was focus on her classes. "Listen. There is nothing extraordinary about what you did. Some men feed hundreds of people on a regular basis. No one hears *kpim* from them."

"I'm sure none of these men you speak of are from your poverty-stricken family. It's not your fault. If you were still back in Oji, you would not be here saying nonsense to me."

Zina pictured the blue American passport locked away in Eziafa's fireproof box. On the day she got her citizenship, Eziafa had reminded her of how lucky she was that he had picked her from the line-up of village girls.

"I did not beg you to bring me here."

"God will punish you for your ingratitude."

She didn't think either of them was in God's good book. "God is fair. He will also punish you and men like you whose only ambition in life is to stay home and live off nursing salaries."

Eziafa shook his fists. "You dare curse me in my house?"

Zina stared him down. "What can you do to me?"

Eziafa's arms dropped to his side. "Be thankful that my father didn't raise a wife beater."

"Story, story." Her eyes swept over him. "You're not worth my time."

Eziafa called out her name as she walked away from him.

By the time Zina came out of the shower, she had convinced herself of the need to offer Eziafa an apology. Her frustration made her say too much.

Eziafa was on the phone. "Yes, Dede," he said. "You can go to the bank tomorrow morning to collect the money for the steel beams." He stayed quiet for a moment. "I know building materials are expensive. Still, please, try and stretch the money. Things are not easy here too."

The planned apology fled from Zina's lips. Dede Matthias would not stretch any money when Zinachidi, the Okereke Family cash cow, could work endless shifts.

Zina headed back to the bedroom. She had plaited her braids and swept them up into a French twist when Eziafa walked into the room.

"Where are you going?" Eziafa asked.

"A colleague is having her birthday party. I should be back by midnight."

"Who said you're leaving this house? Woman, see the clothes you're wearing."

She had changed into a blue lace blouse and a pair of black jeans. "What's wrong with them?"

"They're too tight. You are not a teen. Also, respectable married women don't attend night events without their husbands."

"In what century? You are free to come along."

Eziafa pointed in the direction of the bed. "Go and change into your nightgown."

His stony glare no longer intimidated her. Zina walked around him and ran out of the room.

Eziafa followed her. "Zina!"

She picked her handbag from the couch. "I'll see you later."

"I said, come back here!"

Out in the corridor, Zina smiled as she leaned against the closed door. The stunned look on Eziafa's face as she turned away from him was priceless.

Hearing footsteps from inside the apartment, Zina ran down the hallway. She was not going back inside.

Zina heaved a sigh of relief as she parked in front of Loonies and Tunes. She locked the car and hurried toward the bright entrance of the karaoke bar.

It was a crowded room. Chardonnay, Nomzamo and a couple of the other nurses were singing their hearts out on a rainbow-lit stage.

Zina turned when she heard someone call her name. "Hey, Zee!"

It was Raven Giesbrecht, Genna's nurse crush. She joined him at the back of the room. "Why are you not up there singing with rest of the girls?" she asked.

Raven's alabaster skin flushed. He held up a cobalt blue tote. "Someone had to watch our purses."

Zina laughed as she pulled a chair close to him. As the

only male nurse on their floor, Raven was one of the girls. "Nice. I see you traded in your man purse."

Raven winked. "This year's summer colours were irresistible."

She didn't keep up with fashion trends. "I'll take your word for it."

Raven pushed back his thick, black curls. "The girls finished our pitcher of Zombie. What would you like?"

Zina tasted wine on special occasions. But since she was already in trouble with Eziafa, she might as well have a good time. "Whatever you recommend."

"I'm having gin and juice," Raven said.

"That sounds like a good choice."

"You can taste mine to make sure it's what you want."

He wanted her to drink from his glass? When she hesitated, Raven winked. "I promise. I don't have lip fungus."

The words made her look at his plump lips.

"You like them?" Raven asked.

Flustered, Zina took more than a sip of the drink. She had not expected the sweet, floral flavour. "They're, I meant, the drink is nice."

Raven chuckled as he pushed back his chair. "I'll get you one."

As she drank from the tumbler, Zina stopped glancing toward the door. There was nothing to worry about. Eziafa wasn't coming for her. He probably told himself the proper thing to do with an errant child was to wait at home.

Against her best judgment, Zina said yes to a second drink. As the noise level in the room rose, she inched closer to Raven. Soon, their shoulders brushed. For the first time, she noticed the light brown specks in Raven's green eyes. On a second look, they seemed to have taken on a warm, hazel hue. It was fascinating. His eyes were making bold promises and she was unable to break their gaze.

Raven moved, and Zina caught a whiff of his cologne. Her throat choked up. Its light woodsy scent brought back memories of Ndu. A cousin of his visiting from Europe had given Ndu a half-empty bottle of the same or a similar cologne. She inhaled.

Raven leaned in until Zina felt the warmth of his breath on her skin. "Your gaze feels like home."

The whispered words snapped Zina out of the almost trance-like state. Mortified, she peeked through her slim fingers. "I'm sorry."

"Hey, I'm not complaining. You can stare at me all night long."

"Am I interrupting something?"

The sound of Nomzamo's voice made Zina jump back into her seat. Raven gave Nomzamo an easy smile. "Is it cake time?" he asked.

"No. I just noticed Zina was here. Chardonnay's favourite song is next."

Zina emptied her tumbler in one gulp. The alcohol went straight to her head. Nomzamo gave her a questioning look as they made their way to the stage. "I've never seen you drink before," she said.

Zina giggled. "Girl, there is a lot more to this beautiful face."

Nomzamo gave her a side-eye. "How many drinks have you had?"

"Two."

Nomzamo shook her head. "No more for you."

"I'm doing fantastic. Let's go rock this karaoke thing."

Standing on the stage, Zina froze when the lyrics for Rascal Flatts' "Life Is A Highway" came up on the screen.

Chardonnay gave her an encouraging smile. "Come on, Zee. You can do it."

After taking a deep breath, Zina joined the rest of the group in shouting out the lyrics. As the song said, life was short, the road long and rough, and all she wanted to do was stay in her lane without being flattened by Eziafa's inconsiderate dreams. She was working harder than him to make them come true.

Their rowdy group left the karaoke bar when it closed at 2 am. She arrived home and found Eziafa asleep on the couch. The television was on and his hand clutched the remote control.

She thought of waking him. His neck would hurt in the morning. Then, she remembered that she had been drinking. The smell of alcohol on her breath would spark a major fight.

Zina pulled the television's cord from the wall and headed for the bedroom. She would face the fallout from her actions in the morning.

Chapter Thirty-Three

A **SHRILL RING** woke Eziafa shortly before dawn. He staggered across the living room and picked up the telephone. "Hello."

Evelyn's solemn voice cleared his eyes. "Brother, good morning."

He yawned as he leaned against the wall. "My dear. How are you?"

"I'm fine. Please hold on. Nne wants to talk to you."

"Eziafakaego, are you there?" his mother asked.

He stretched from side to side to get the kinks out of his waist. "Nne, good morning."

"What is good about the morning?" she said.

Eziafa scratched his head. "What have I done again?"

"When I asked why I still have no grandchildren, you said it was because Zina was still in school. I folded my arms and waited. It has been almost one year since she started work, and you people have not called with good news. I ask again. Eziafakaego, where are my grandchildren?"

He could not tell her that having children was on hold

until he had completed the house. It was a money thing. "These things take time," he said.

"That is what people who don't know how to do their job say."

Did she just cast aspersions on his virility? "Nne, please, calm down."

"I will calm down when you do as I have asked."

Before he could respond, his mother ended the call.

Eziafa spun around and saw Zina's car keys on the dining table. So, she is back. His mother's angry voice echoed in his ears as he marched to the bedroom.

Zina was still asleep. He sat at the edge of the bed and stared at her. Through parted pink lips, he saw the glint of Zina's silver braces. She no longer had to cover her smile. Her boyish figure was gone. While he was not paying enough attention, Zina had bloomed into a stunning woman.

Eziafa knew the long hours at the hospital were hard on her. On some days, she fell asleep in the middle of her meal.

He had tried to find a different job. There weren't many employment options for middle-aged men with limited work experience. He'd even contemplated starting a business. The lack of capital made that near-impossible.

Zina's disdain for the building project was valid. He should have stuck with their original building plans. Yes, he had made some miscalculations, but Zina still needed to respect him as the head of their family.

Eziafa took a deep breath. The look of defiance in Zina's eyes as she stomped out of the house for her party had scared him. He would get back to work so he could get more money for them to finish the house before getting Zina pregnant. A baby would keep Zina distracted from these friends of hers and get his mother off his back.

He stared at his knobby knuckles. His situation called for a clear head and a new strategy.

Eziafa cooked a full breakfast; scrambled eggs, sausage, bacon and hash browns. He even made some French toast.

Zina took hesitant steps into the kitchen. "Good morning."

He flashed a big smile. "Morning, my dear."

She glanced at the set table. "What is going on?"

He was taking back control. While he was in Oji, Dede Matthias told him women don't respect weak men. Zina needed to understand he was strong enough to do a woman's job, too.

"I made us breakfast."

Zina's eyes darted between his face and the table. "You cooked all of this food?"

Eziafa smiled. "I was taking care of myself before you came to America."

"You're not angry with me?"

"It's a new day. Sit down. Let me serve you."

She gave him a wary look. "I can serve myself."

"This woman, I said sit down. Must you fight everything?"

Zina complied. Her food sat uneaten. "You're not hungry?"

"My stomach feels a little queasy," she said.

"Drink your tea. It might help."

Eziafa finished his meal and placed his dishes in the kitchen sink. "Are you going anywhere today?"

Zina shook her head. "I'm off for the next four days. There's plenty of house chores to do."

He adjusted his trousers. "I'm leaving for work."

Zina gaped at him. "Work?"

"Yes. I should be back around ten pm."

Zina scrambled to her feet. "Do you have a packed lunch?"

He pointed to his lunch box. "I already took care of it."

Zina looked dazed as she walked him to the apartment door. "Have a good day," she said.

"You, too."

Out in the parking lot, Eziafa groaned as he unlocked the car door. It was going to be a long day. Since he was no longer motivated to work, his need to prove to Zina that he wasn't a lazy man had to be his driving force.

That evening, he basked in Zina's admiration. She didn't hesitate when he asked her for a back massage.

"Today was good," Eziafa said as Zina kneaded out the knots.

"*Jisie ike*. And I'm sure tomorrow will be better."

Eziafa closed his eyes. Yes, tomorrow had to be better.

By the fourth day, Eziafa was leaving home only to park his cab in places safe enough for him to take long naps. He felt like a fraud as Zina continued to cheer him on. Since his heart was no longer in taxi driving, he had to find another job, even if it was a lower-paying one.

A random conversation with another cab driver landed

Eziafa a job at a local tortilla factory. The automated processes meant reduced hands-on time.

The phone interview with his new boss was a formality. The nepotistic machinations of "man-know-man" also worked in America. Its fancy name was networking.

On the day before he started work, Eziafa wandered down the shoe aisle at their local Walmart. The only explanation for his backward movement was he must have done something to offend his *chi*.

The work boots stayed in his car. There was no need to tell Zina about the new job. With the way he felt, the weight of her pity might break him.

Chapter Thirty-Four

EZIAFA THREW TWO apples in the open lunch box. "Before I forget, as of next week, I'm going to be very busy. I got a contract with a new company."

Zina turned off the kitchen tap and placed her water bottle on the counter. "What will you be doing for them?"

"I'll be moving personnel between their different offices," he said.

"It won't affect your regular work?" Zina asked.

Eziafa shook his head.

"This is good news," she said.

"It does mean that my work hours will change. I'll have to work based on their shifts. Soon, we'll put this village house business behind us, and our primary focus will be on starting our family."

The passage of time had dulled Zina's yearning for a baby. "Look at the hours I work. Where will I find time to take care of a child?"

"We will manage," Eziafa said.

Zina knew the primary caregiving would still fall on her. She picked up her water bottle. "I have to go."

"Have a good day."

"You too."

During the drive to work, Zina thought about Eziafa's baby comments. She would get some paid time off, and either of their mothers would jump on an airplane if needed.

There was no point worrying. First, she had to get pregnant, and then, they would have nine months to figure things out.

Nomzamo's face was the first thing Zina saw when the elevator opened on their floor. Nomzamo waited for her to step out. "Here comes the twerking queen," she said.

Zina laughed. "I don't think that uncoordinated mess counts as twerking."

Nomzamo lowered her voice. "You were putting on a show for Raven. And he was just loving it."

"I was not."

"Girl be quiet. I know what I saw."

Nomzamo's words knocked the blinders off her eyes. Genna was right. Raven was a hottie. He had a Ryan Gosling look. "What do you think about him?"

"Raven?"

Zina nodded.

"I've always found him interesting."

"Interesting good or bad?"

Nomzamo cocked her head. "A bit of both. Like the rest of us, he's flawed. Why are you asking?"

"Just curious."

"I found out that Raven crochets the baby blankets we give out."

"Are you serious?" Zina asked.

Nomzamo nodded. "Chardonnay told me. They once had a thing."

She couldn't picture them together. "Oh."

Nomzamo grinned. "Raven also dated Jackie in neurology and one of the residents. The man gets around. Just thought you should know."

The words felt like a dash of cold water. "It's none of my business."

"If you say so."

She needed to end the conversation. "Where are you headed?"

"Upstairs. I'll be back soon."

"Okay."

Zina was still thinking about Nomzamo's words when she ran into Raven.

A big smile brightened his face. "Hello, Superstar. Have you recovered from your singing debut?"

Zina shrugged. "It was just karaoke."

"You were hot on that stage. I couldn't take my eyes off you."

She did a double take. "Are you hitting on me?"

"Am I succeeding?"

"You're truly a woman *wrappa*."

Raven frowned. "A woman rapper?"

"A *wrappa*. It's the long piece of cloth African women tie around their bodies."

"Why would you call me that?"

Zina cleared her throat. "It's the Nigerian term for a man who would do anything to get a woman's attention or approval. It also works for a chronic womanizer."

Raven leered. "Girl, I do wanna reach out and wrap ya."

Zina giggled. "You're so original."

"Isn't the whole point of communication making yourself understood? Come closer. You know you want the chunky touch."

Her body went warm. Raven's intentions were loud

and clear. She stepped away from him. "Weren't you headed somewhere?"

"Yeah. I forget what I was going to do. I see you have
your lunch bag. I'll walk you to the break room."

"Okay."

"So, what do you think about my proposal?"

Raven's eyes were making her married body tingle in
places it shouldn't for another man. "You have issues."

"Don't we all? I practice my sweet nothings on you
married girls since it costs me nothing. And when the right
girl comes along, bam, I'll be ready."

Zina opened the door to their break room. The aroma of fresh coffee lifted her spirits. She sent up a quick
prayer for the person who had turned on the coffee maker.
"Wow. A cheapskate woman *wrappa*. You're a prize catch."

Raven followed her, closed the door and leaned against
it. "That's what my kindergarten teacher said when I gave
her a half-eaten Snickers bar on Valentine's Day."

Zina opened the fridge and placed her lunch bag inside. Raven's presence seemed to have sucked up all the air
in the room.

When she had the courage to face him, Raven's expression was serious. "Your husband's pretty lucky to have you."

Zina snorted. "He doesn't think so."

"Hmm. What are you doing for lunch today?"

"I'm eating here. Why?"

He made some comical gestures with his hands. "I'd
love to hear more about this woman body wrapping thing."

Zina leaned against the fridge door. "You'll have to
pay for the info."

Raven winked. "I'll pay in cash or kind. Whatever you
want."

What did he mean by in kind? "I only take traveller's cheques."

"Done. See you at lunch?"

Zina bit her lip. Colleagues eat lunch together. Raven was her colleague. So, there was nothing wrong with eating lunch with Raven. "Sure."

Raven waited as she made herself a cup of coffee. He opened the door for her. "After you, sweet thing."

"There's nothing sweet about me," she said.

"Liar, liar, G-string on fire."

Zina giggled. "I'm a fan of full coverage underwear."

Raven kept a straight face. "You may be due for an upgrade. I offer customized lingerie assessments."

"This married woman does not need your service."

"That is just too bad."

Zina took a deep breath as she walked out of the room. It was too early in the day for heart palpitations.

The lunch date with Raven turned into several more. He was relentless in his pursuit. Zina knew that, despite what Nomzamo had told her, she wasn't exactly putting up much of a defense.

Like her, Raven was a farmer's child. He grew up in a rural Mennonite community outside Millersburg, Ohio. While she couldn't stop talking about her family, Raven said little about his. His stories were often about his pot-bellied pig, Myrtle. Her little cousins back in Oji wouldn't believe her if she were to tell them some people kept pigs as pets.

Raven hummed under his breath as they took a walk

around the hospital grounds. Zina glanced at him. "I enjoy spending time with you," she said.

"Time with you makes me happy too."

Even though people could see them, she didn't pull away when Raven reached for her hand. She told herself his touch was harmless. More importantly, it comforted her.

Alone in the small lunchroom, Zina rested her head on the table. Minutes earlier, the hospital lobby's ATM had declined her card. Upset, Zina had called the bank's customer service line. They told her their account was overdrawn for the second time that month. Their credit cards were maxed out and she had left home without packing a lunch. She wanted to call Eziafa to give him several pieces of her mind. But it would not get her any lunch.

Zina looked up at the sound of footsteps. It was Raven.

"There you are."

She was silent as Raven pulled up a chair and sat across from her.

"What's wrong?"

She couldn't understand how Eziafa worked two jobs and brought in less money. "The man in my house is frustrating me."

Raven gave her an apologetic smile. "And then another man shows up to bug you."

"You're on my side."

He smiled. "I'm glad you think so."

She broke the prolonged eye contact. "Are you going home this summer?"

Raven's forced smile reminded her of a hurt little boy. "My home is here. No more uncomfortable family gatherings for me. My paternal grandfather, Grosspapa, and my dad can't get over the fact I'm not coming back to the family farm."

"They're not proud you're a nurse?"

Raven snorted. "My dad told me men who lack the brains to become doctors are the ones who end up as nurses. And Grosspapa, God bless his failing heart, never misses an opportunity to tell me I'm doing a woman's job."

"I'm sorry to hear that."

He shrugged. "It is what it is."

"For what it's worth, you are a phenomenal nurse. And I wish I could be in Ohio to give your family members a piece of my mind."

"You're serious?"

She'd said the words without giving them much thought. "Of course."

Raven gave her a teasing smile. "Then it's a good thing you have CPR training. After you march into the farmhouse in your Dora Milaje outfit, you'll need to use it."

She was surprised Raven knew the character. "You watched *Black Panther*?"

"Didn't we all?"

"We should ask Billie Lou if she did."

Raven grinned. "We both know the answer to that. Ms. Billie Lou is in a class of her own."

Zina winced when she tried to laugh. Her shoulder muscles were all bunched up. She rubbed a hand along her neck. "Aargh, I could use a good massage."

He flexed his fingers. "I can give you one."

She was sure Raven would do a great job. "Don't tell me you worked as a masseuse, too?"

"Yup. All through my college and university years. I was a pizza-delivering, dog-walking, burger-flipping, tele-marketing, part-time masseuse."

It was hard to tell if Raven was joking. "Why did you have to do all those jobs?"

"When you run away from home as a teen, you wander down a lot of interesting paths." He flexed his fingers. "My magic kit is at home. Petroleum jelly will have to do the trick."

"It's okay. I'll book an appointment when I'm off next week."

"Zee, come on, you're hurting right now."

"You're not going to dislocate anything?"

"It's only a neck massage."

She could always ask him to stop. "Here?"

He looked around. "How about I go grab a tube and meet you down in the linen room?"

Behind the closed door, Raven's warm fingers worked their way up to Zina's shoulder blades. She closed her eyes.

"You're so tight," Raven said.

Zina, you're playing with fire. "I ... I am?"

His body brushed against her back. "Uh-huh. You know stress isn't good for you."

As the heat from her body meeting the jelly radiated all over, she relaxed against him. Raven's warm breath fanned the top of her earlobe. "Am I being gentle?"

A moan escaped from her lips when Raven touched the sensitive spot below her ears. She flew off the linen cart. "We shouldn't be doing this."

"Doing what?" Raven asked.

Zina stepped back. She was a quarter way to having sex with him. "I'm sorry. I shouldn't have said yes to this."

"Zee, I'm …"

Afraid that he would say something that would make her damn the consequences, Zina opened the door and ran down the hall.

Chapter Thirty-Five

FROM THE WAY Genna's eyes had followed her since she arrived in the room, Zina could tell there was something on the girl's mind.

"Nurse Zee why are you and Raven being weird toward each other?" she asked.

Zina stopped writing in Genna's chart. She wasn't surprised the nosy teen had noticed the change in her behaviour. If she happened to be in the room when Raven stopped by to say hello to Genna, Zina would immediately step outside for a while. She gave Genna a casual look. "What do you mean by weird?"

"Yesterday, Raven kept looking at you and making the sucky face puppies make."

Zina held in her laughter. The description was apt.

Genna touched her arm. "Girlfriend to girlfriend. Tell me, what did Raven do?"

The touch of Raven's fingers made her forget her marriage vows. "You will make a great actress," she said.

Genna grinned. "Hollywood isn't ready for me yet. I'll

grace them with my presence after a year of backpacking through Europe."

It would be wonderful to see Genna leave the hospital. "Can I come along?"

"You haven't answered my question."

Chei. Genna was one persistent girl. Zina resumed her writing. "Raven didn't do anything. Stop worrying your pretty head."

"I'm sure you can tell Raven likes you."

"Of course, he does. He's my friend."

Genna rolled her eyes. "I mean *like* like."

Zina helped her patient back on the bed. She frowned. The girl felt lighter than the previous week. "That's too bad since I only have eyes for Mr. Bruno Mars."

"Sorry, my Bruno's not into grandmas."

Genna loved the artist. She had several posters of him pinned up near her bed.

"Excuse you?"

"I know you have a nice face and all ..." Genna said.

"Me, a grandma?"

"You have to be like ... thirty?"

Zina narrowed her eyes. Thirty must seem like grandma age when you're fourteen. "For payback, this grandma is going to make sure you eat your supper."

Genna held her hands in front of her face. "No."

She pulled the dinner tray close. "Mm, yummy bland peas and mashed potatoes."

"I'm sorry. Bruno would leave me for you in a heartbeat. Who wouldn't? You're gorgeous."

Zina scooped some peas. "Too late. Open your mouth."

As always, Nomzamo hummed as she chewed. Zina smiled. It was a good thing she didn't have to coax Nomzamo into eating the lunch she'd packed for her.

Nomzamo gave her a side-eye. "Even though this meal smells and tastes like a bribe, I'm going to eat it and offer you a piece of my mind for dessert."

"What do you mean by that?" Zina said.

"When was the last time we hung out?"

They saw each other at work. It wasn't the same. "I'm sorry."

Nomzamo shrugged. "That trifling Raven has your mind all wrapped up. I'm beginning to feel like the side chick."

She rolled her eyes. "You're extra."

Nomzamo picked up her fried chicken drumstick and took a bite. "So, what do you guys talk about?"

Zina lifted a banana from her lunch box. "We're two farm kids reminiscing about our childhood."

"Hmm. I also have some farming experience."

"From where?"

"You should see my patio-grown tomatoes. Those babies are huge."

"Sounds like I'm overdue for a visit," Zina said.

"You're always welcome at our place. With proper notice, of course. Don't call me when you're already standing at my door."

Zina smiled. "Yes ma'am."

"While I can't stand your man, I'm glad you and Raven are behaving. I'm no saint. You know I've got lots of issues. But cheating is one thing that rubs me the wrong way."

The animosity between Eziafa and Nomzamo was

mutual. Despite Zina's best efforts, they had not recovered from their first and only meeting. Nomzamo felt Zina shouldn't take Eziafa's crap. Eziafa blamed Nomzamo for teaching Zina to disrespect him. They had one thing in common: Neither of them recognized that she was her own person.

She wasn't the complete *mumu* Nomzamo made her out to be. She fought back in ways her friend didn't understand. "Cheating? I haven't even kissed the guy."

Nomzamo narrowed her eyes. "You want to, don't you? I'm sure in your mind you've kissed Raven a thousand and one times."

Girl, double that number. Zina peeled her banana and took a big bite.

Nomzamo made an air check mark with her finger.

Zina rolled her eyes.

"Speaking of He-Who-Must-Not-Be-Challenged, what is the man up to these days?"

It was Nomzamo's new name for Eziafa. Zina swallowed her food. "I'm furious with him."

"What did he do?"

The night before, Eziafa had called a budget-trimming meeting. She'd stopped herself from laughing in his face when he told her the agenda. There was nothing left to trim.

Yet he'd managed to surprise her. By the end of their meeting, he'd placed them on a cash-only system and collected her bank and credit cards. Each Sunday, after filling her car with gas, he would give her an allowance of $20 for her weekly spending. If keeping her car hadn't been a job requirement, she was sure Eziafa would insist she take the bus.

She gave Nomzamo a rundown of their latest argument.

"Wow. The guy is a master jerk."

"Don't call him that."

"Why are you defending him?"

Nomzamo could not understand the burden of duty she and Eziafa carried. "He is still my husband."

"Well, I'm not interested in hearing you sing a pitiful cover of 'Stand by Your Man'."

"Can you not just listen to me without insulting him?"

Nomzamo made a serious face. "I guess I can try."

"Thank you."

Nomzamo gave her a pious look. "Non-judgmental listening mode activated."

Zina sighed. "I always wanted to go to school because I knew it was my path to independence. Look at me now. I'm working hard, but have nothing to show for it. It hurts that I can't offer financial help to my family at home. My mother has stopped asking for money."

Nomzamo cleaned her hands with a moist towelette. "It's time for you to open a private bank account."

"With which money?"

"Go down to HR, ask them to split your paycheck into two deposits. That's how I save."

"Hey, ladies."

Zina turned around at Elinma's husky voice. "My sister, how now?"

"I dey o." Elinma pulled up a chair and dropped her lunch box on the table. She gave Nomzamo a bright smile. "The American Nomzamo. It's been a while."

Nomzamo returned Elinma's smile. "You no longer visit our floor," she said.

"Girl, some days, I'm not sure if I'm coming or going." Elinma turned to Zina. "My sister, you look worried. What's going on?"

"I'm having some problems with saving money. Nomzamo said HR could split my paycheck."

Elinma nodded. "I had to do the same thing with my husband. The man was spending my money on his conquests."

Zina gaped at her. Elinma's candor was rare. Most Nigerian women kept their distressing marriage stories to themselves. "I'm sorry to hear that."

Elinma shrugged. "My sister, there's no longer any shame in my game. It's why I have all these side businesses. Although he still lives at home, the man chooses to act like a freeloading roommate."

Zina gave Elinma a sympathetic look. At least Eziafa spent her money on real estate.

"I still don't understand why you continue to put up with him," Nomzamo said to Elinma.

Elinma flashed her big smile. "Everything in its due course. Now that you're both feeling sorry for me, you must order some Arbonne. We just launched a bunch of new products. The energy fizz drinks are great."

"Girl, you're a shark," Nomzamo said.

Elinma winked. "I'm a bidness woman. What can I get you?"

"Hmm. I could use some of that exfoliating facial scrub," Nomzamo said.

"God bless you." Elinma turned to Zina. "My *omalicha*, what should I get you? Perfume, powder, lipstick, shoes, frying pan, a baby goat?"

Zina pictured Elinma standing in traffic with an

open coat displaying items for sale. "You no go kill me with laughter."

"Never. Prison Orange is not my colour." Elinma placed a comforting hand on Zina's shoulder. "My sister, we will laugh through these hard days and overcome."

Elinma left.

Nomzamo gave Zina a pointed look. "See why you need to hang with me? I bet Raven wouldn't have been able to get you that crucial information."

"You're not going to let this Raven thing go, are you?"

Nomzamo stuck her nose in the air. "Nope. I'm not good at sharing my people."

The conversation with HR was quick and productive. To avoid raising Eziafa's suspicions, Zina asked for a ninety-ten percent split of her earnings. It was a start.

At the end of her shift, Zina drove to a nearby bank and opened a checking account and applied for a bank credit card. Nomzamo had told her she could use her address for any correspondence. Zina walked out of the bank with a huge smile. See how the lack of knowledge had kept her in bondage?

On her way home, she thought about Titilope. It'd been a while since they'd spoken and it was her fault for not returning Titilope's voicemail messages. Zina bit on her lower lip. Nomzamo was right. She had allowed thoughts of Raven to preoccupy her.

She pulled over and dialled Titilope's number. The call forwarded to a new one. When prompted, Zina left a call-back message. She hoped Titilope wasn't mad at her, too.

Nomzamo's call came in right after she'd hung up. "I need a status update."

"Account, credit card, check and check," Zina said.

"You go, girl. What did you do with all the papers you got at the bank?"

"They're in my purse."

Nomzamo clucked her tongue. "That's not how to do it. What if when you get home, you trip over your big feet, your purse flies into Eziafa's lap, the bank papers drop out and say, Hey Papi?"

Nomzamo's imagination was a thing of beauty. "You're just jealous you have bird-size feet."

"Whatever. Get a plastic bag from that messy trunk of yours, throw them papers in it, and stuff the bag inside your glove compartment."

"Eziafa was right. You are a bad influence."

Nomzamo snorted. "About time I lived up to my reputation."

Chapter Thirty-Six

ZINA LEFT THE nurses' station and dragged herself down the empty hallway. With four hours left on her shift, she hoped a chocolate bar would give her a much-needed boost.

Focused on punching the right vending machine button, she didn't hear Raven walk up behind her. He jingled the coins in his pocket. "Hey. Let me buy that for you," he said.

Zina fought the urge to fall into his arms and demand mouth-to-mouth CPR. She blamed the delirium on low blood sugar. "Aren't you the big spender?"

"For making that astute observation, you've also earned yourself an over-priced bottle of one hundred per cent mountain spring water."

Raven inserted some coins, retrieved the items and handed them to her.

"Thanks. I'll see you later."

"Zee, wait. I am trying to buy your friendship."

Don't look him in the eye. "We're cool," she said.

"No, we're not. I crossed the line with the neck massage. I'm sorry."

"Apology accepted."

Raven looked relieved. "I know I have a reputation around here. I earned it. But I truly care about you. I want things to go back to the way they were. Before you say yea or nay, I'll admit I find you attractive. If it were possible, I'd want more than a friendship. But you are married, so I'll respect any decision you make."

"It wasn't as if you dragged me kicking and screaming into the linen room. I ran because I like you too. Since this can't go anywhere, I thought it was best to give you some space."

"Forget space. I want to spend time with you."

"So much for respecting my decision."

"Okay. I lied. I don't care that you're married."

Zina took a backward step. She was having a hard time remembering that too. "I'm sure you've noticed how the bubbly new nurse melts when you walk into the room."

He moved closer. "To keep my player badge, I need more woman *wrappa* training. I'm hoping that, as my friend, you'll take pity on me. I'll do anything you want."

Zina gulped as Raven's eyes sucked her in. What she wanted was for him to kiss away the acrid taste of regret in her mouth.

Mama's clear voice rang in her head. *Zinachidi, be careful. What you don't want to eat, you don't smell.*

Every rule had exceptions. "I can give you a few tips."

Raven leaned forward and kissed her forehead.

The music from the satellite radio stopped as a call came through the car's Bluetooth. The screen on the dash flashed an unknown name and number. Zina frowned. Who could it be? Curious, she took the call. It was Titilope.

"*Na wah*. So, you still remember me? I tried your house and cell number several times. They were both out of service. What happened?"

"I got a new number," Titilope said. "Things have been busy."

After a glance at her rear-view mirror, Zina turned on the left turn signal and switched lanes. "Busy good or bad?"

"All good. We're now living in New Orleans. I got a job here."

"Wow."

"After Tomide moved back to Nigeria, I decided it was time for a change. Between selling our house, finding a new home, a school, time got away."

"Tomide went back to Nigeria?"

"He sure did."

From the little she'd heard about him, Tomide didn't sound like someone who would have gone back home to start over. "What happened?"

"Remember I'd told you Tomide couldn't find another job in his field?"

"Yes."

"He got tired of searching. A relative of his who is minister of something-or-other gave him a PA job."

"Serious enjoyment for him."

"The absurd thing is that Tomide, the personal assistant, also has an assistant."

From the little Zina knew, working the Abuja political

scene wasn't for the faint of heart. "He must have the right packaging."

"Tomide can be quite charming when he wants to be. I don't doubt, that before the end of the year, he will announce the arrival of the third Mrs. Ojo."

Zina snorted. "Good luck to her."

"Who knows, Tomide may be a better husband the third time around. A part of me is glad he's far away from us even though Tomide has been on his best behaviour since the divorce. However, during his visits to see T.J., his presence makes me feel on edge."

If something came and spirited Eziafa away for some weeks, Zina would throw a dance party. "Does T.J. miss his father?"

"It depends on the day. I do see some trips back home in our future. Talking of husbands, how are things between you and Eziafa?"

Eziafa had turned into Mr. Contrary. If he could, he would blame grass blades for not growing in the same direction. "Both of us are still alive."

"Good. No one should take being alive for granted."

"You sound tired."

"Nothing a good night's rest won't fix," Titilope said. "How was your day?"

"Long. One of my patients left us this morning. I was happy he was finally well enough to go home."

"Are you headed home?"

Zina slowed down at a four-way stop sign. "Yes. I'm ready to put my feet up."

"How do you watch children go through so much pain without losing your mind?" Titilope asked.

Zina turned onto her street. "It's hard when we lose a patient. We grieve. We remember them. We keep fighting for the ones who still need our help."

"Thank God for you guys. You must work with some amazing people."

Raven's face popped into her mind. "I do. Speaking of colleagues, I need to run a dilemma by you."

"I'm listening."

"During your marriage, were you ever attracted to another man?"

"No. Most days, I was too busy loathing the one I lived with." Titilope's speech became hesitant. "Are ... are you seeing someone?"

"Me? No o. It's about this ... this married woman at work. She's struggling with romantic feelings for her fitness coach. The closeness during gym time is making her, em, uncomfortable."

"I hope you told her to cancel the coach's services."

"No. I don't think my colleague is ready for that kind of advice. The problem is she's married to a certified toad. From what she's told me about this fitness coach, he's nice to her."

"Who says this coach is not another toad in disguise?"

Zina's laugh sounded forced, even to her. "You make it sound as if we're in the middle of an amphibian infestation."

"That's my negative baggage showing."

Potential toad or not, she couldn't stop thinking about Raven. "I understand."

"Zina, be honest with me, what's his name?"

Now it was her turn for hesitance. "What are you talking about?"

"When people say this or that happened to a friend or acquaintance, it's usually about them. Is there something you want to tell me?"

Zina knew her secret would be safe with Titilope. "There is someone. We spend time together. Nothing's happened between us."

"I have a feeling that could change."

"I do have self-control," Zina said.

"What were you hoping to hear from me?"

It was foolish to expect Titilope's approval. "I don't know."

"I have an opinion. I've also vowed to stop dishing out unsolicited advice."

Zina was glad she didn't have to suffer through a lecture. "We can talk about this some other time," she said.

"Okay."

"Now, that you're living closer to me, we should plan a reunion."

"You're the lady with the busy work schedule. Tell me when you can see me. I'll work around it."

By the end of the year, she would be able to pay for a mini-vacation from the money she was squirrelling away. The main problem was how to take one without Eziafa's knowledge. "Let me see what I can do."

"Spoken like a boss lady."

Zina laughed as she pulled into her parking lot. "I'm home."

"I'll let you go. Take care. Limit your contact with toads."

Zina smiled. "I thought you said no unsolicited advice?"

Titilope laughed. "Forget this Americana accent. At my core, I'm still a Nigerian."

Chapter Thirty-Seven

NOMZAMO SLAMMED HER fist on the wobbly Formica table. "I'm done with this job!"

Zina was glad they were alone in the lunchroom. Every day that week, one or two colleagues had threatened to walk off the job. Due to a Methicillin-resistant Staphylococcus aureus (MRSA) infection outbreak on their floor, they were all running on empty as they worked their regular shifts and covered for sick colleagues.

"Take a deep breath," Zina said.

"Girl, this MRSA is kicking our butts."

"We have a zero-fatality rate. We're winning."

Nomzamo scoffed. "You're coming with me?"

"Are we going to another hospital?"

"No. We're taking courses through an online esthetician school and opening a full-service salon."

Zina gaped at her friend. "You want us to work as estheticians?"

"It's another way of caring for people."

"That's a huge pay cut. Eziafa would lose his mind."

"You know what I want to say about that man."

"Remember, Karma walks amongst us."

Nomzamo rolled her eyes. "On this matter, she'll give me a high five."

"And the fact that you're allergic to aerosol hairsprays?" Zina asked.

"There are masks on the market. I could make it work. You just don't want me to leave you behind."

"That, too."

Nomzamo groaned as she rubbed her face, hard. "Zina, I think I'm burning out."

"We've just started our careers. Maybe you need a week off?"

"You know they're not going to approve a vacation request while we're dealing with these evil bacteria."

"Girl, I'm worried about you," Zina said, frowning.

"Next week, let's go to Vegas. I'll pay for the trip. We are off work for three days."

Zina was yet to travel out of Texas. "Done."

Nomzamo gave her a weak smile. "Hearing you say you'll come with me, I feel better already."

"Hey ladies."

Nomzamo's expression soured at the sound of Raven's voice. She stood. "I guess we'll talk later."

Zina glanced over her shoulder. Raven was heading their way. "You don't have to leave," she said to Nomzamo.

"I know you want to talk to him."

Raven had travelled to Ohio for his brother's university graduation. "I do."

Nomzamo grimaced. "Since Raven is now your number one priority, I should get used to figuring out things on my own."

"That's not true."

"I don't encourage self-delusion," Nomzamo said over her shoulder as she walked away.

"Did I interrupt something?" Raven asked when he reached Zina's side.

"We were having a serious conversation."

"I'm sorry."

Zina shrugged. "You couldn't have known."

Raven sat. "Nomzy and I used to be cool. I don't know what I did to her."

"Nomzamo thinks something is going on between us. She disapproves."

Raven winked. "Since she already thinks it, why don't we make it happen?"

"This isn't the time for one of your jokes."

Raven gave her a pained expression. "I was trying to lighten your mood."

Zina watched Nomzamo's retreating back. She should have said: "Yes, I want to talk to Raven. But it can wait."

"I guess you didn't miss me as much as I've missed you," Raven said with a pout.

Annoyed with herself, irritated by the accusatory tone of Raven's voice, Zina stood. "I guess I didn't. I'll see you later."

By the end of her shift, Zina was sore everywhere. At home, she soaked herself in an Epsom salt bath and tried not to think about the conversations with Nomzamo and Raven. She couldn't seem to please either of them.

She consoled herself with thoughts of her parents. They, at least, wholeheartedly approved of her. During her

last telephone call to Oji, Mama told her how proud they
were of her, and how appreciative they were for the money
she'd been able to send over the past three months. It was
a good thing Eziafa did not call her parents. They would
have thanked him too and ruined her precious secret.

Relaxed from her bath, Zina plopped onto the couch
and reached for the laptop.

Curious to see Eziafa's mansion, she had asked her
sister Ebele to email her some pictures.

Zina opened the email. She did a double take. Ebele
must have sent her a Photoshop image. The monstrosity
on her screen looked like three bungalows piled atop each
other at odd angles. She re-read the email. Ebele didn't
drop any hints to suggest the picture was a joke.

As if the shape wasn't bad enough, Dede Matthias
had used gold bathroom tiles for the outside walls. Un-
believable.

When Eziafa finally returned, Zina shoved a printout
of the photo in his face. "How in the world could you
have authorized this mess?"

"What are you talking about?"

"Behold your pride and joy."

Eziafa took the paper from her. As he stared at it,
sweat beads popped out on his forehead. "Impossible." He
dropped the paper and pulled out his cell phone. "It has to
be another person's house. Dede Matthias would not do
this to me."

Zina hovered. "I can't wait to hear his explanation."

Eziafa glared at her. "Step away."

"No. Put it on speaker."

"Zina, I said leave me alone."

"I must hear what your uncle has to say. Put it on

speaker." Zina pressed the button when he ignored her request.

Dede Matthias sounded annoyed when he finally answered. "Eziafa, we were already in bed."

Eziafa's babbling was pathetic. "I'm sorry, I had to know something. The house walls. We said gold paint. I just wanted to confirm that's what you used."

"Actually, the painter and me, we decided to use gold tiles."

Eziafa gasped. "What?"

"If I had listened to your request, by this time next year, you would need to repaint the building. This way, rainwater will keep the walls clean."

Zina felt hysterical laughter bubble up her throat. What rain?

Eziafa looked as if he was going to explode. "Dede, how could you have done this to me? You didn't use tiles for your house."

Dede Matthias's voice grew cold. "Is this the thank-you I deserve for saving you money?" he asked.

"Uncle, is it a crime to trust your blood? You have turned me into the village laughingstock."

Zina was sure her in-law heard her cackling sounds. "You didn't ask him to send you pictures of the house?" she whispered.

"I don't like how you are talking to me," Dede Matthias said.

Eziafa disconnected the call without saying goodbye.

Zina clapped her hands. "Congratulations on the bathroom house. Your friends can bring cartons of tile cleaners to the housewarming party."

Eziafa had trouble controlling his breathing as he

tried to stare her down. "Brilliant idea. Since the house belongs to the both of us, tell your friends to bring scrubbing brushes."

She snorted. "That eyesore is not my house. I would rather sleep on a mat under the stars than put a foot inside that thing."

Eziafa glared at her. "What would you say is chasing you from your husband's house?"

Zina refused to let her burning tears flow. "You wait and see."

Chapter Thirty-Eight

DURING THEIR BREAK, she and Raven sat on an outdoor bench. He had begged her to come with him. Raven took one look at the house pictures on her phone and turned beet red. "You've got to be kidding me. Did this dude tile inside the house too?"

Zina wanted to smack herself when her eyes filled with tears. She'd done too much crying since she saw the pictures.

Raven gave her a quick hug. "I'm sorry."

Zina sniffed. "It's not your fault."

"How about I take you out for lunch?"

"I'm not hungry."

Raven smiled at her. "Please. A little treat to cheer you up." Raven drew circles on the back of her hand. "There's a Japanese place that's not too far from here. We'll be back in no time."

Zina exhaled. Why wasn't she married to someone like Raven? "You spoil me."

Raven wiped her tears away with his fingers. "Don't be so easy to please. I'm just getting started."

The waitress ushered them into a private room. Given the number of people waiting at the front desk, Raven couldn't have reserved it that morning. "You were pretty sure I was going to come for lunch today, weren't you?"

Raven gave her his little-boy grin. "I have absolute confidence in the potency of my charms."

No one could accuse Raven of modesty. "Be grateful I like free food."

"I was counting on that, too."

They sat at a cooking table and watched as the Teppan-yaki chef arranged his ingredients. He poured some cooking oil on the steel grill. "Are you guys celebrating something special?"

Raven's eyes held hers. "We're celebrating life."

The chef tipped his hat. "To life."

She wrinkled her nose when Raven tried to feed her sushi from their appetizer plates. "I'm allergic to raw fish."

Raven dipped the sushi roll in the green wasabi paste. "You're missing out."

"You enjoy."

Raven nudged her when the chef used his knife to shape the fried rice into a heart. "To life and love," the chef said with a bow.

A nervous giggle escaped as she moved away from Raven. "We're not in a relationship."

The chef frowned. "No?"

Zina held up her right hand. "I'm married."

The chef gave her a puzzled look. "Marriage is not relationship?"

Zina dropped her voice. "To another man."

The chef's thin lips were set in a straight line as he scattered the heart-shaped rice.

Raven's hand hovered over his mouth. She could tell he was trying not to laugh out loud. When the chef left, Raven lost it. "Oh my God, my ribs hurt."

Zina scowled as she glanced in the direction of the service entrance. "I'm sure the chef is busy telling the kitchen staff about the scarlet woman in the dining room."

Raven wiped wet eyes with the back of his hand. "Don't worry about it. I'm sure the guy has seen and heard worse."

"How is that statement comforting?"

Raven pointed at her bowl. "I'm sorry. Eat up."

Zina's hand shook as she picked up her fork. What on earth had moved her to blurt out such private information?

Her mood had lightened by dessert. The server persuaded them to have some mochi. She and Raven shared a bowl of the balls of ice cream in delicate shells.

"Do you think there's only one person in the world meant for you?"

People who lose spouses find other mates. "No."

"I think it would have been perfect if we came into the world with the names of our future partners tagged to our toes."

Zina wasn't sure how that would work. "Really?"

"Think about it. Parents get to keep the name tags until the child becomes an adult. When they're ready, the adult then sends a text, a boomerang, smoke signal, something to their soul mate saying: Are you ready to meet?"

"It's impractical," Zina said. "What if the designated mate didn't make it past childhood? Does it mean their partner loses out on experiencing true love?"

Raven grinned. "I didn't think of that. Two sound heads are certainly better than one."

"If only you knew how confused this head is."

Raven gently pulled her hand to look at her watch. He frowned. "Duty calls."

It didn't feel like they'd been there for an hour. Zina withdrew her hand from his. "Thanks for lunch."

"Anytime. Even though you're married, you're still my girl."

Zina peeked at Raven during their drive back to the hospital. She would have loved it if she were born with his name on her tag.

Billie Lou was the first person they saw. Zina braced herself for Billie Lou's nosy questions.

"Where are you young'uns coming from?" Billie Lou asked.

They answered at the same time.

"Lunch," Raven said.

"A walk," Zina said.

Billie Lou coughed out a loud "ahem". "Do you need time to get your stories straight?"

Raven gave her a dazzling smile. "We meant to say we took a walk around the block after sitting outside for lunch."

Billie Lou's eyes swept over them. "It's 85 degrees outside. You both look fresh."

"We took slow steps," Raven said with a wink.

What is this man saying? Zina thought. She wanted to stomp on Raven's foot.

Billie Lou looked at their hands. "Hmm. You must have eaten your lunch boxes too." She walked away before they could give a response.

Zina bit her lip. There was already chatter about the time they spent together. They had just given the busy-body more ammunition.

"Next time, we need to do better," Raven said under his breath.

She stared at Billie Lou's back. "Who says there will be a next time? We're on her radar now."

"You want me to stay away from you?" Raven asked.

"It's the best thing for us," Zina said. Even to her ears, she sounded unconvinced.

Raven gave her hand a quick squeeze. "Zee, I have tried. I can't. It will take the hordes of hell to keep me away from you."

Chapter Thirty-Nine

STANDING ON NOMZAMO'S screened-in porch, Zina leaned against the folding table, and dug her fingers into the potting soil. They were transplanting Nomzamo's new batch of tomato seedlings into small pots. Nomzamo had offered her gloves, but Zina craved the familiar feel of dirt.

Out of the corner of her eye, Zina saw Nomzamo put down her pot.

"Zina?

She turned her head. "Yes?"

Nomzamo had a thoughtful look. "Have you ever stood in front of a person, looked into their eyes, and asked yourself where in the world did their soul go?"

Zina shook her head. "No."

Nomzamo shrugged. "Me neither."

Zina smiled as she dusted off her hands. She no longer wondered about what led to Nomzamo's random, often odd questions. They just popped in and out of the woman's head.

"Thanks for letting me help," she said.

Nomzamo snorted. "It's your punishment for showing up unannounced."

Zina didn't feel that she'd had any choice. Since the lunchroom incident, Nomzamo had been keeping to herself. "I didn't think you would invite me over."

"You're right."

"Why are you so mad at me?" Zina asked in a soft tone.

"Honestly, it's not all about you and Raven's shenanigans."

"What's going on?"

"I'm stressed to the max. There are mass layoffs at Momma's job. We don't know what's going to happen."

Ms. Gray had a great job at a Fortune 500 company. "Are they offering severance pay?"

Nomzamo nodded. "It won't be easy for her to find another job. Not at her level. All this stuff has me worried about Trey's future. Momma and I won't be around forever. Who's going take care of him?"

Zina knew how much Nomzamo struggled with guilt over her brother. Their mother had told Nomzamo not to let Trey play on the trampoline. Trey was grounded for something no one remembered. Tired of his whining, Nomzamo had let him go outside. On the anniversary of Trey's accident, Nomzamo moved around like a zombie.

"You know, one of the doctors in hematology has paraplegia. She's amazing."

"I've heard about her," Nomzamo said.

"She's not the only professional in Houston with a spinal cord injury. Trey's an honour roll student. I'm sure he has plans for himself."

A smile tugged at a corner of Nomzamo's mouth. "That boy always has grand plans."

"And you have to forgive yourself. This guilt is eating you alive."

"Girl, it's hard. I keep wanting to go back to that day, so I can change my part in it."

"You're torturing yourself."

"That's what momma said."

"We both know your momma is a wise woman."

Nomzamo pulled up two plastic chairs. "The other day, when I was talking about the online esthetician school, I was serious about doing something else."

Zina sat back in her chair. "What do you have in mind?"

"I think I'm going to become a nurse practitioner."

As a registered nurse, Nomzamo would need to earn her master's degree in nursing and apply to the Texas Board of Nursing to get an advanced practice nursing license. Once that was sorted out, Nomzamo would be able to join a practice under the supervision of a physician.

"As a nurse practitioner, I can work regular hours. I'll be able to make time when Trey needs me."

"It's a great plan."

Nomzamo gave her a doubtful look.

"It is. Will you go back to school full-time?"

"I can't afford to. There are lots of online options." Nomzamo batted her eyelashes. "Are you going to do this with me?"

The thought that in the future there would be a time she wouldn't see Nomzamo on a regular basis already made Zina sad. "But I'm not interested in working as a nurse practitioner," she said.

"I have an option number two. A Master's in Nursing program with a specialization in nursing administration. It's the ideal combination of nursing expertise and business. We can take one course per semester."

The idea of getting a graduate degree was tempting. With her 4.0 grade point average, she would probably get an entrance scholarship. "Let me think about it."

"Okay." Nomzamo stood. "Let's get washed up. Before you leave, you have to taste my homemade pasta sauce."

"Deal. Are we cool?" Zina asked. "I hate it when we fight."

Nomzamo gave her a grudging smile. "For now, we are."

Chapter Forty

"**C**ODE **BLUE, PEDIATRIC** Intensive Care Unit, Room 102. Code Blue, Pediatric Intensive Care Unit, Room 102."

Zina bolted for the elevators. That was Genna's room. The code team was there when she arrived. Through the frosted glass, she could see one of the doctors performing CPR.

She grabbed the nearest arm. "What happened?"

The medical student gave a nonchalant shrug. "The patient was unresponsive."

Zina refused to accept what those words meant. "Her name is Genna!"

Wide-eyed, the student backed away from her. "Sorry."

Zina glanced at the door. Genna, *biko*, don't do this.

A voice from the room yelled: "Clear!"

Zina leaned against a nearby wall and prayed under her breath. "Papa God, I know I haven't spoken to you in a while. But this prayer is not about me. Please, if You let Genna live, I promise I will go to mass tomorrow. I won't flirt with Raven again. Even if Eziafa were to poke me in the eye, I won't fight with him. Let her live. *Chukwu, biko.* You don't need Genna now."

Zina's eyes flew open when she heard clapping sounds. The medical student gave her a thumbs up sign. She bent over and began to laugh through her tears. *Thank You. Thank You.*

Raven found her in Genna's room. Her parents had gone to get some coffee. "Hey Zee."

"Hey."

"Chardonnay filled me in. How's our girl doing?"

Zina rubbed her eyes. "She's stable. I'm waiting for her to wake up."

Raven walked back and closed the door. "You look like you need someone to hold you up."

As he hugged her, Zina clung to him. "I was terrified."

"Genna's a fighter. She'll be alright."

They turned their heads at gurgling sounds. Genna's eyes were open. Intubated, she couldn't talk.

Zina hurried to the girl's side and squeezed her cold hand. "Sweetie, you're going to be fine."

Genna returned Zina's squeeze.

Raven joined them. "Hey, kiddo."

Genna held her other hand out to him. Raven squeezed it.

Zina placed a hand on Genna's cheek. "Try and get some more rest. We'll listen to your babe Bruno Mars when you wake up."

Genna's eyes smiled before she closed them.

"Zee?"

Zina lifted her wet face from the table at the sound of Raven's voice. He walked across the empty cafeteria and sat next to her. The sight of his red-rimmed eyes brought fresh tears. "She's gone, Raven. Genna's gone."

The charge nurse told her Genna passed away less than two hours after Zina went home. Another cardiac arrest. They couldn't resuscitate.

Raven sat next to her. "Zee, I'm so sorry."

"If I had been here, things would not have turned out this way."

"Zee, you know you can't own this outcome. You did your best."

Her best would have been making sure Genna got sent home. A sob caught in Zina's throat as she thought of Genna's parents. Her hysterical father had to be sedated.

Raven drew her close. "Let me take you for a quick drive to get some fresh air. You'll feel better."

"I can't leave. I must go back upstairs. I need to ... I need to ..." Zina couldn't remember what she needed to do.

Raven's thumb stroked the back of her hand. "You're not in any state to help anyone. Nomzy said the nurse on call is taking over your shift."

"Okay."

Zina came downstairs and found Raven's car idling by their staff entrance. She opened the door and settled back into the leather seat.

"We don't have to go for a drive," Raven said. "I can just take you home."

Eziafa was waiting there. "Drive first."

"Have you been to the Williams Waterwall?"

Zina shook her head.

"If we park on a nearby street, we'll be able to see the wall," Raven said. "You might find it relaxing."

Zina didn't care where Raven took her. She nodded.

When Raven switched on the car radio, she leaned back and closed her eyes. A short while later, she felt the car stop. "We're here."

Zina opened her eyes and saw a horseshoe-shaped structure. Lights mounted on the wall caused a dramatic rainbow effect as the water cascaded down the structure. "It's beautiful."

"I knew you would like it."

A laughing voice from the radio filled the car. "Hello, Houston. It's your girl, Tamara Brown. Welcome to another Friday night edition of Midnight Smooches. We're kicking off today's segment with a request from one of our listeners.

"Ayesha, this is an oldie but goodie from your boy, Sean G. It's Wyclef Jean featuring Mary J. Blige in '911'. Enjoy."

She glanced at Raven as his arm curved around her shoulders. His eyes were closed. She leaned against him, conscious of the heat rising from his body. Or was it from hers?

Zina stiffened for a split second when Raven planted a hesitant kiss on the side of her head. She didn't push him away.

He leaned over her and she felt her seat recline backward. Raven's lips became bolder, more demanding. Their fingers tangled as they both tried to lift her scrub blouse. She dropped her hands and allowed him to take it off. The rest of her clothes followed.

Raven moved away, and Zina shivered from the sudden cold. His eyes sought hers. She felt herself drowning in the molten gaze. "Is this what you want?" Raven asked.

She couldn't remember the last time—if ever—a man in her life had asked her that question, on any subject. She stared at his face. Every conversation, the lunch dates, all they'd shared had led to that moment. "Yes."

Raven rifled through the glove box, and she heard the tearing of foil.

She hadn't thought about the need for protection. For a brief second, it felt as if her wedding ring tightened around her finger like a little noose. She pushed the image of Eziafa's face to the back of her mind.

Zina wanted to forget about death. About duty. She did not want to think about the unfulfilled backpacking travel dreams of a laughing teen. Or feel anger over a bathroom-tiled house.

Hot tears made their way down her face as Raven's lips met hers. She could taste the saltiness as she held on to him.

The gear stick dug in Zina's thigh as they manoeuvred their limbs in the back seat. As the heat built, so did her moans. When Raven's hard body settled on hers, the ball of heat twirling in Zina's core exploded. And for a far too short time, she did forget about it all.

Chapter Forty-One

ZINA WAS SURE Eziafa would sniff Raven's overpowering scent off her body the moment she walked into their apartment. Instead, busily rifling through a pile of documents, he paid her little attention.

Stuck at home for three days, Zina turned into a wreck. Guilt and disappointment were a toxic mix. She couldn't understand why Raven hadn't contacted her. He had her number. A simple text to say hello would have been enough.

Her apprehension grew as she drove to the hospital on the fourth day. What if it had been meaningless sex to him? She ran names in her head. There were many willing women. Did he drive them to the same location or take them to his place?

Mama's stern voice had joined the others in her head. It was growing louder. *Zinachidi, confess this abomination now and live.*

Zina silenced her mother's voice with a determined shake of her head. Land spirits like their ancestor, Oji, were unable to travel over water. For as long as she stayed in America, she was free from retribution.

Raven and Chardonnay were standing and talking in the hallway when Zina arrived at work. Raven saw her first. "Hey, Zee."

How was Raven able to look so relaxed while her breathing came in shallow spurts? "Hey."

Chardonnay hurried to her side. The tight hug gave Zina some fortification. "Honey, I'm so sorry about Genna."

Zina stared at Raven's face over Chardonnay's shoulder. Did you think of me?

When Chardonnay stepped away from her, Zina glanced in the direction of Room 102. She wasn't ready to face the memories in Genna's room.

"Your new patient is in 96. I switched rooms with you."

She gave Chardonnay a grateful look. "Thanks."

Chardonnay turned to Raven. "It was nice of you to drive Zina home the other night."

"My pleasure," Raven said.

Zina's toes clenched inside her shoes as she flashed back to the hour spent in Raven's car.

"I need to stock the drug cart before I leave," Chardonnay said. "Catch you guys later."

"I've got to go, too," Raven said as Chardonnay walked away. He brushed against Zina and slid something into her pocket.

Zina waited until she was alone before she fished the item out. It was a little Mars bar with a yellow note taped to it. The words 'Missed you. Meet me on level one at lunch' were printed in block letters.

In the parking lot Zina stepped back when Raven tried to kiss her. "We shouldn't."

"I thought things were different now."

"Raven, what we did was wrong."

"Nothing about our time together felt wrong. Zee, you do know you don't have to spend the rest of your life married to a man who makes you desperately unhappy?"

"You can't understand the ties between Eziafa and me."

"Make me."

Zina peered at his face. Was it possible? Could she make Raven understand?

"Felix and Nkolika invited us over for dinner on Saturday," Eziafa said from his spot on the couch. She'd noticed the place where he spent so much of his time had begun to sag.

Zina pursed her lips as she looked up from her romance novel. Eziafa's words had yanked her out of a steamy scene. The interracial couple in the book could have been her and Raven. "That won't work for me. I have a double shift on Saturday."

Eziafa frowned. "Didn't you have this weekend off?"

Zina used a finger as a bookmarker. Eziafa knew her regular shifts. She had to keep a copy of her work schedule posted on the fridge. "I did. One of the other ladies had a family emergency. I offered to take her shift since I'll get paid time and a half."

Eziafa's frown faded. "I'll attend on our behalf."

Zina went back to reading her book. She was no longer interested in playing the dutiful wife.

The drive to Humble from Houston took them about thirty minutes. She and Raven were spending the afternoon at the city's summer festival.

The crowd was larger than Zina had expected. In the concert area, Raven held her hand as they walked through people dancing to what Raven called swamp-pop music. Until that day she hadn't known the genre existed. Raven said it was a fusion of rock 'n' roll, rhythm and blues, country, and Cajun music. Zina found herself bobbing her head along to the beat.

Hungry, they made their way down the row of food vendors. One of them sold fried ice cream. "Who came up with this idea?"

"A visionary. You have to try some," Raven insisted as they watched the vendor drizzle honey on the fried ice cream ball.

Zina bit into it and concentrated on the flavours. It was a mixture of hot, cold, crunchy and sweet. And more sweetness. She handed her cup to Raven. "Too much sugar for me."

"You're missing out," Raven said before demolishing the ball.

After a stop at the fried turkey legs stand, Raven insisted she watch her first crawfish race.

The Crawfish Race Commissioner yelled: "*Ils sont partis!*" And the race began. The numbered crawfish inched their way up the racecourse as owners and the crowd cheered them on.

"That was exciting," Zina said when the race was over.

"I told you it was going be fun. What next?"

Zina mulled over the question. "I saw a vintage clothing and jewellery stand on our way here. I want to get myself a Southern Belle lace parasol."

"If that's what my lady wants," Raven said with a little bow.

Zina was trying on a rhinestone link bracelet when

Raven mumbled some words under his breath. She looked up. "What's the matter?"

"It's Billie Lou."

Zina gritted her teeth when she saw Billie Lou's barracuda grin. The woman was like an evil wind.

Billie Lou beamed. "Zee, Raven. Isn't this a lovely surprise? When I spied you guys, I thought these poor old eyes were playing tricks on me."

"Those poor old eyes sure don't miss much," Raven said in a wry tone.

"They haven't failed me yet." Billie Lou turned to Zina. "That's a lovely Juliana bracelet you're holding. I wouldn't have thought it would be your taste."

The vendor had told her the name of the gemstones. "I happen to like garnets," she said.

Billie Lou craned her neck and scanned the area. "I presume your husband's around somewhere?"

Zina dropped the bracelet back on the table. "I came on my own. He's a little bit under the weather."

"That's too bad. I've been looking forward to a meeting." Billie Lou lifted an eyebrow. "You ran into Raven?"

Raven spoke before she did. "This is a yearly thing for me. A friend of mine runs the beer tent."

"You sure have interesting friends," Billie Lou said.

Raven acted as if he hadn't heard the snide tone. "I should introduce you. This year, festival-goers can create personalized bottle labels for their craft beer selection."

Zina gave Raven a puzzled look. Why would he want to keep Billie Lou around them?

Billie Lou's lips twisted as if she'd sucked on a sour lemon. "No thank you. I'm an apple cider kind of girl."

Raven gave Billie Lou a wink. "Aha. That explains your tarty sweetness."

"Oh, stop it," Billie Lou said with a wave of her hand. She glanced at her watch. "I must hurry along. See you at work."

Zina was silent as Raven wished Billie Lou a good day.

"I can't stand that woman," Zina said after Billie Lou left.

"She's okay."

"*Okay?* You must be feeling generous."

"Relax. What's the worst Billie Lou can do?"

Zina stared at Billie Lou's retreating figure. How could she ever explain to Raven that one should never underestimate the destructive power of the village gossip?

Chapter Forty-Two

THE LONG YAWN made Eziafa's eyes water. He shouldn't have agreed to fill in for a coworker who needed the day off. The back-to-back work shifts made it hard for him to keep his eyes open. Hoping that fresh air would help, Eziafa opened the driver's side window. It didn't.

Desperate, he turned on the car radio and began counting backward from 50 in a loud voice. Twenty more minutes of driving and he would be safe at home.

Loud honks from several cars woke Eziafa. He realized he had fallen asleep. The car was now in the other lane, and bright headlights from an oncoming vehicle shone on his face. Blinded by the glare, Eziafa swung the car to the right and almost sideswiped the truck behind him. He was fighting to gain control when he struck the guardrail on the side of the road. A headlight shattered on impact and Eziafa banged his head on the steering wheel.

Badly shaken, Eziafa managed to park the car. He screamed in frustration. Who had he offended? The person's *otumokpo* was potent. A curse was the only way to explain his continuous bad luck.

Calming his thoughts took a long time. Finally, he turned on his caution lights. The last thing he needed was someone running into him as he figured out what to do.

Eziafa weighed his options. An officer could pull him over because of a broken headlight. With the way things were going in the country, the encounter could cost him more than a fine.

He would have called AAA for help if he hadn't cancelled his membership. He remembered Zina's frustrated expression when she insisted they needed the service. If he called Zina for help, she would laugh in his face.

Felix was the only option. He would call him and ask for a ride home. In the morning, he would figure out what to do with the car. Felix took his call and told him to wait. Thirty minutes later, Felix showed up with some good news. Their friend Dinesh knew someone who owned a towing truck. The friend had agreed to help Eziafa tow the car to a repair shop. They waited inside Felix's car.

"Eziafa, what is going on with you?" Felix asked. "You could have killed yourself, or somebody else."

"I know."

"I'm worried about you. You've not been yourself. *Ogini?*"

He stared at Felix's tired face. Whenever he thought about the house in Oji, the pictures Zina had presented to him returned to torment him. "The house in Oji is sucking my blood."

Felix leaned back and closed his eyes. "This man. We agreed you would build something manageable."

Eziafa squirmed in his seat. "I got carried away. I started dreaming of a house I could retire to."

"Is that still your plan?"

Eziafa was in love with the romantic idea of a homeland which no longer existed. "No."

"At one time, Nkolika and I wanted to move back to Nigeria. Not anymore. By the time we're ready to retire, our children will be adults. They won't follow us home. And we would be deceiving ourselves by thinking it would be easy to adapt, in our old age, to the many challenges we'd encounter. We abandoned our building project. I hear the structure is now a reputable lizard refuge."

"I couldn't let my mother live inside another uncompleted building," he said.

"You were in a difficult position."

He was glad Felix understood his dilemma.

"Where were you coming from?"

Eziafa had feared the question would come up. "I should have told you about this earlier. I took a job at the tortilla factory in East Houston. I've been working all the shifts I can."

Felix shook his head. "No wonder you have lost so much weight. People have been asking me if you're sick. Is the house almost done?"

An angry Dede Matthias summoned Nne and declared that he would no longer oversee the housing project. It took a month of family meetings before Dede Matthias returned to the building site. The delay had cost Eziafa more money, time and sleep. "They just installed the flooring."

Felix gave him an encouraging smile. "You're close to the finish line."

From where he stood, everything was still blurry. "If I had known it was this difficult to be a man, I would have come as a woman."

"Women don't have it easy either. I swear it's this adult life which brings suffering."

Eziafa snorted. "Valiant Defender of the Womankind."

Felix inclined his head. "Na me be dat."

"I guess you have to be when you have a houseful of them."

"Even if I were a father of sons, it would not be different."

Eziafa clenched his jaw. "As you said, the finish line is in sight." He would crawl there if he had to.

"Brother, we went for the walkthrough as you requested," Evelyn said. "The house is ready."

He heaved a sigh of relief. "Nne, did she like it?"

"She couldn't stop crying."

Silent tears rolled down Eziafa's face. It was over.

"Brother, thank you for all you have done for us. It could not have been easy for you to build this house while you were also paying my school fees and sending maintenance money. *Chukwu gozie gi.*"

"Evelyn, I must thank you too. Anyone can provide money. The real work belongs to the person who provides direct care. *Jisie ike.*"

"Brother, we thank God. Now I can tell you my big news."

Eziafa sat up. "Is it good?"

"Yes. I found a job at Makurdi. I leave home next month."

"Congratulations, my dear."

"Thank you."

"But why Makurdi?"

Evelyn giggled. "There's someone there."

Eziafa tapped his toes on the carpet. "Someone?"

"My boyfriend."

Eziafa frowned. "You're moving in with him?"

"No o. I'm going to rent my own flat."

Evelyn's response was a little too quick. Eziafa reminded himself that Evelyn was now in her thirties. She was old enough to make some decisions.

"I know you wouldn't want Nne alone in the house. So, we came up with a solution. Aunty Buchi said her grandchild, Phillipa, could move in with her."

Aunty Buchi was their maternal aunt. They should have consulted him before speaking to her. "How old is this child?" Eziafa asked.

"Twelve. Phillipa is old enough to take care of herself."

The child was school age. No doubt, his mother would be expected to pay for her education. Eziafa's head ached as he pictured a new column on his spreadsheet. "Let me know the final decision."

"I will."

He settled back on the couch. "So, who is this man spiriting you away from us?"

"His name is Eyinnaya Ozumba. Before you ask the question, yes, he is an Oji man."

It would be easier for Nne to research this man's family. "Good. When are we hearing from his people?"

"When we're ready, you'll hear from them."

"What do you mean by this we? Are you marrying yourself? This Eyinnaya needs to know that marrying a beautiful university graduate is not for the faint of heart. It's time I made back some of the money Zina's family took from me."

"Brother, since you brought up the topic, we want to postpone our traditional wedding. Eyinnaya is ready to pay the bride price so we can get married in church. After we have settled down, and saved some money, we will do the *igba nkwu*."

Evelyn's request was not unusual. He knew of people who did the ceremony long after all their children were born.

"Dede Matthias and our other kinsmen would have to be in agreement with this arrangement."

"I'm sure they will be glad that a man has finally come to ask for my hand in marriage," Evelyn said in a dry tone. "Once Dede Matthias says yes, the others will swallow any disagreement."

Evelyn's advanced age would certainly be considered. "What if Dede Matthias says no?"

"You will have to help me beg him. Brother, I love Eyinnaya. We have been seeing each other for almost eight years. He is a good man."

Love-tainted eyes often make inferior men look good. "Why did he wait so long?"

"Eyinnaya wanted to make something of himself."

Since the young man wanted to marry a wife without doing things the proper way, it sounded like he had not succeeded. "Have you told Nne about your plans?"

"Not yet. I wanted to get your support."

"What does this Eyinnaya do?"

"For now, he teaches at a private primary school. We are looking for another job."

Eziafa frowned. Teachers were paid peanuts. All this "we" business did not sit well with him. "Who is doing most of the looking? You or him?"

"Brother, does it matter? We're building a life together."

He didn't want his sister tied to a man who waited for her to make things happen. "Tell Eyinnaya I want to speak with him tomorrow. After our conversation, I will let you know my thoughts."

"Eyinnaya will call you," she said.

"Greet Nne for me when she comes back from her women's meeting."

"I will. My greetings to our wife."

Zina was still at work. "She will hear."

He was still on the couch when Zina returned. She didn't look pleased to see him. "Have you left that chair today?" she asked.

Eziafa bit back an angry retort. Because he took a couple of days off from work, she had been spoiling for a fight. "Welcome, dear. How was your day?"

She sat on the armchair and loosened her shoelaces. "What do you want?"

"Nothing. Evelyn called. Nne has the house keys."

Zina raised her hands. "Hallelujah!"

"My dear wife, without all your hard work, this day would have been impossible. I'm grateful."

Zina gave him a rare smile. "I'm sure Nne's happy."

"Evelyn told me she was. I have been thinking. A pregnancy announcement would make her Nne's joy complete."

Zina's smile disappeared. "Pregnancy?"

His excitement grew. "Yes. Once we pay off our credit card debt, we will put the extra money into a baby account. A month before the baby is supposed to arrive, one of the mothers will come to help. In fact, we ..." Eziafa stopped at the distressed look on Zina's face. "What is the matter?"

"This baby thing seems a little sudden."

"My wife, we have been married for almost seven years. Some of your mates in Oji already have two or three children."

"You've created a baby column in your almighty spreadsheet?" Zina asked.

He refused to acknowledge the irreverent tone in her voice. "Please, make an appointment with the gynecologist. We no longer need the IUD."

"You want them to take out the IUD?"

He couldn't understand Zina's reluctance. "Do you need me to come with you?"

Her eyes flashed. "I'm not a child. I can take care of it myself."

"You seem confused."

"This isn't the kind of demand you spring on someone who worked a long day."

Demand? He remembered how unhappy Zina was when he had insisted on the birth control. Now, she seemed unhappy at the thought of removing it. "I thought you would be happy at the news."

Zina pulled herself from the chair. "I'm going to take a shower."

He gave her a hopeful look. "Can I join you?"

"You don't need to get infected with hospital germs."

In recent weeks, Zina had become even more aloof. He tried his best to be patient with her. Still, for how long does a man remain patient with a wife whose body stays cold when he makes love to her?

"That was not in an issue in the past," he said.

"Like everyone, you're getting older. The last thing you need is an infection."

Eziafa was silent as Zina stood from couch and walked

away. His gaze followed her retreating back. Something had happened to his wife.

Eziafa made sure he drove Zina to her doctor's appointment. The IUD was taken out. That night, she didn't move away when he reached for her. Eziafa thanked her by taking his time to do everything he knew she liked. Zina didn't say no when he rolled over to her side of their bed for the second time.

Weeks passed, there was still no baby for them to celebrate. Desperate, Eziafa bought the daily supplements his pharmacist friend Nuru recommended. Zina refused to accept the supplements he bought for her. Every day, Eziafa pondered on what else to do.

From where Eziafa laid on the bed, he watched as Zina changed out of her day clothes. Her stomach was still as flat as ever.

"Don't you think this baby thing is taking too long?" Eziafa asked.

Zina pulled the nightgown over her head. "Staying on birth control for a long time can affect fertility. If you had let me remove the IUD when I wanted to, we wouldn't be having this conversation."

"We could not afford a baby then."

Zina snorted. "Frankly, with all the credit card debt, we still can't afford one now."

He refused to get drawn into a fight. "I think we should book a doctor's appointment."

Zina sat on her side of the bed. "The recommendation

is to see a specialist after six months of trying. If you don't believe me, feel free to make an appointment."

He pondered on her words. Zina was a medical professional. "Since you said it's normal, we can wait for a little while."

Felix listened as Eziafa moaned about their infertility problem. "Older men get several women pregnant. What is wrong with me?"

"What kind of underwear do you wear?" Felix asked.

He blinked. "Underwear? What has that got to do with this problem?"

"I've heard tight underpants can do serious damage to a man's testicles."

"Felix, which half-baked *dibia* gave you this information?"

"I didn't consult an herbalist. My friend, this is biology. Original science. Not hocus pocus. They say it's like when the vehicle's carburetor overheats, and the engine begins to misbehave. It's good for that area to maintain a normal temperature."

Eziafa mulled over the information. It made sense. "How come they don't teach such valuable information in biology class? It is osmosis and photosynthesis they were shoving down our throats. How has that lesson helped my life?"

"Leave that matter. Go and buy those boxer shorts young men wear. It allows for better airflow."

The heaviness on Eziafa's chest lifted. "Thank you,

my brother." Eziafa looked at the large wall clock. He had to get to the mall before it closed. "I have to be on my way."

"You can't leave without tasting my honey beans," Felix said.

Eziafa wrinkled his nose. "Beans?"

Felix grinned. "I promise you this pot of beans has no rival. Before she left for work, Nkolika was making mouth about my cooking. She'll eat those words today. Do you want to drink *gari* with it or should I fry plantains?"

He shook his head. "I'm not hungry."

"You know Nkolika's number one house rule. No one comes here and leaves without a full stomach. Please, don't get me into trouble with her."

A feeling of envy overwhelmed him. "Women like your wife are scarce."

"I won't lie. The woman makes life sweet. We complement each other. She has flaws. Like I do. *Onaghi ezu cha*. Marriage is never perfect. For it to last, one must work hard and take the bitter with the sweet."

Most days, he wasn't sure of how to approach Zina. His presence had become an irritant to her. "Felix, what is happening to us? Our women seem to have gone mad."

"How?"

"Look around us. Our marriages are going through difficult times. This living abroad thing is ruining things."

"From what I hear, marriages at home are struggling, too," Felix said.

Eziafa shook his head. "No be like dis. What do these women want from us? From one side of their mouths, they're saying you're the man, take care of us and pay all the bills. From the other side, they're saying, *biko* free me from your demands, give me equality, I want to be Mrs. Independent. They should choose one struggle."

"My late cousin, God rest his soul, used to say: 'When drummers change their beats, we the dancers, must change our steps.' *Nna*, the marriage drums of these times are speaking a different language. If we want our marriages to survive, we must learn these new dance steps."

"*Must*? Tell me, where is the space for choice?"

"Eziafa, we are talking about survival."

"At what price? The language these drums speak is not ours. Why must we dance to it? I accept that we live in different times. But ... but must these women poke us in the eyes because some of them now pay the lion's share of the bills?"

"I've never supported disrespect in any relationship," Felix said.

"You know these women want to be the head and neck. They won't be content until we men are under their feet."

"All I know is that, for our marriages to work, we must learn from each other and make compromises. Whether we are living abroad, or at home."

Eziafa pursed his lips. As far as he saw it, everyone expected men to bear the burden of the compromises. "Is it worth it? This acceptance of new ways?"

"There is nothing new about making life easy for the people one loves. *Biko*, learn to bend a little."

Eziafa gritted his teeth. The men around him seemed to have turned into jellyfish. Thank God he had a spine. And if he bent it any further, he would break. Eziafa stood. "*Nna*, let me be on my way. Time is going. I have some shopping to do."

Chapter Forty-Three

ZINA WALKED ONTO their hospital floor and met most of the team huddled around the central desk. "Hey, guys."

They were all quiet.

Raven stepped forward. "Zee, I'm afraid we have some bad news."

The others watched as Raven took away her purse, dropped it on the desk and held her hand. "Elinma died last night."

The words slammed into Zina's chest. She gasped. "Elinma did what?"

Raven squeezed her hand. "I'm sorry. The email went out this morning."

Elinma's cheerful face flashed before Zina's eyes. "But I saw her earlier this week. What happened?"

Chardonnay spoke up. "One of the surgical nurses said it was her husband. E finally kicked him out of the house. The children said things got heated when their dad brought them back from a visit. Right in front of them, he shot E and then turned the gun on himself. They brought them here." Chardonnay's voice broke. "E was DOA. The lowlife's on life support."

That they'd separated was news to Zina. Those poor, poor children.

Raven reached for her hand. "I know Elinma was your girl. Do you need to go home?" he asked.

Zina shook her head. The living still needed help. "I can do this."

As she repeated the words to herself, Zina began to cry. This time she didn't care who was watching as Raven pulled her into his arms.

After her shift, Zina went to the parking garage and sat in the car. Was this how she would see her beloved sister no more? Perhaps if she had not joined Elinma in laughing away her problems, she would have been able to help her. Zina bit hard on the inside of her lips. Foolish woman, have you helped yourself?

Zina rolled the car windows up so she could scream her dirge for Elinma:

Obu onye k'anyi na acho?
It is Elinma we are looking for.
Elinma left for the land of plenty and didn't come back home.
Elinma is not at the market, neither is she at the stream.
Listen. Elinma's age mates are singing. Elinma's voice is missing.
When Elinma's children cry, who will hold them to their bosom?
Obu onye k'anyi na acho?
It is Elinma we are looking for.

Tears ran down Zina's cheeks as she called Nomzamo's cell. She had to let her know before she heard it on the news. "Hi. Where are you?"

"At home. Trey and I are getting ready to bake cookies."

"Oh."

"Is everything okay? You don't sound good."

"It has been a long day. Can I stop by for a quick visit?"

"Sure. We can always use an extra dough-mixing hand."

"I'll see you soon."

Zina didn't remember much of the drive. Nomzamo welcomed her with a tight hug and a frown. "Your eyes are bloodshot. Are your work kids okay?"

Zina was gathering her thoughts when Trey wheeled himself over to say hello. She gave him a high five. "You're getting bigger."

"That's because he eats like a horse," Nomzamo said.

Trey pouted. "I do not. I have better manners."

"Your sissy meant to say you eat a lot," Zina said.

Trey grinned. "Yeah, that I do. Sissy, are we still making the cookies?"

"Of course. Zina came to help us."

Trey spun his wheelchair around. "Sweet."

Zina dragged her feet as she followed into the kitchen. She helped Trey line up the baking supplies and utensils on the lower counter installed for him.

After washing his hands, Trey wheeled his chair underneath the counter. "I'm ready."

Nomzamo gave him a thumbs-up. "Let's do this."

Zina held the recipe card and read out the steps while

Trey measured the ingredients. Nomzamo did the mixing, used a spoon to drop the dough on the baking sheets, and slid them into the heated oven. "Some yummy cookies are coming up soon."

Trey placed the dirty bowls in the sink. "It always takes too long."

Nomzamo wagged a finger. "No pacing in front of the stove. You make me dizzy with all that back and forth."

"I want the cookies to be all done," Trey said.

"I promised Momma you would have done your chores before she gets back."

Trey pouted. "I hate doing chores."

Nomzamo began washing up. "No one loves them. Go and sort your laundry."

When Trey left the room, Nomzamo turned to Zina. "You've been super quiet."

Zina took a deep breath. "There's something I need to tell you. I didn't want Trey to hear it."

Nomzamo raised her voice. "Trey, Zina and I are going to step outside for a minute."

They sat on the porch swing.

Zina couldn't bring herself to say the words. "Something happened to Elinma."

Nomzamo's hand flew to her mouth. "How bad?"

She whispered the words. "It was fatal."

Nomzamo pounded a fist into her thigh. "Damn it!"

"It feels as if I'm dreaming."

Tears filled Nomzamo's eyes. "I haven't paid her for my last Arbonne order."

Zina swallowed hard. Neither had she.

"What happened?"

"Her husband shot her."

Nomzamo gasped. "Why?"

"Apparently, they were separated."

"That shouldn't be a death sentence," Nomzamo said, sadly. "Elinma was so full of life."

Zina's fingers clenched as she imagined a stiff body lying in an icy morgue. She wanted to tell Nomzamo that Elinma was in a better place. The words stuck in her throat. She didn't know it for a fact. She was no longer sure of anything. She remembered Elinma's children. She gagged. What would happen to them?

They turned when the front door opened. Trey stopped in the doorway when he saw Nomzamo's face. "Sissy, why are you crying?"

Nomzamo tried to wipe the tears rolling down her cheeks. "I'm not."

Trey frowned. "You told me it's wrong to tell lies."

Nomzamo's voice shook. "You're right. I am crying."

Trey wheeled himself over. "Did something happen to Momma?"

Nomzamo laid a hand on his shoulder. "No. Momma's fine."

Trey gave Nomzamo a disbelieving look. He knew how much his sister tried to protect him.

"It's okay," Zina said. "Your mom's fine. Your sissy is upset about work stuff."

"Did something happen to one of the kids?" Trey asked.

Zina shook her head. "No."

Trey's worried expression cleared.

Nomzamo shot her a grateful look. "Come. We should check on those cookies."

As the door closed behind Nomzamo and Trey, fresh tears rolled down Zina's cheeks.

Chapter Forty-Four

ELINMA'S DEATH DID not stop time. Nothing could. Every morning, Zina got up and went through the motions of living even though it felt llike trying to crawl out of a dark hole. No matter how hard she tried, the sand kept falling on her face.

There were days when Zina could swear she saw Elinma's faint silhouette in the distance as she turned a corner. Other times, goosebumps covered her skin when Elinma's tinkling laughter filtered through the fog around her.

Raven and Nomzamo tried to reach her. She pushed them away. Zina could not explain even to herself why this death had hit her so hard.

It was Eziafa who helped on the day he came home and found her crying as if her body was made up of broken bones.

Solemn-faced, Eziafa sat beside her and waited until she had nothing left to give. *"Nwunye m, gini ka m ga eme?"*

Zina stared at him. She couldn't remember the last time Eziafa's sincerity lowered the wall between them.

"I'm tired," she said.

"Please, tell me what you want."

Zina just wanted to talk. Eziafa listened as she talked about Elinma, about how she struggled to move out of the grip of her grief.

Eziafa's expression didn't change when she told about the sightings of Elinma. Zina wasn't surprised. Where they came from, it was a given that life was more than the physical realm.

"I don't know if it's all in my mind, or if I truly see Elinma's spirit."

"When I was a little boy, one of our neighbours, Mr. Ifeanyi, died." Eziafa's eyes clouded over. "That day, I was coming back from school when I saw him at the end of the street. Mr. Ifeanyi lifted his hand and smiled at me. It was how he always greeted me. I didn't believe my mother when she told me he'd died that morning. For many months, I was afraid to close my eyes in the dark."

Zina had heard similar stories. "But why do their spirits roam?"

Eziafa shrugged. "There are some things about this life we will never fully understand. We can only pray Elinma's spirit finds rest."

She took a deep breath. "*Daalu.*"

Eziafa pulled himself up from the couch. "For what? A man takes care of his own."

At the end of their shift, she and Nomzamo stood in the parking lot. Nomzamo reached out and squeezed her hand. "You look so much better."

The fog was lifting. "I do feel a little better."

"I don't want to dampen your mood. But I thought you would want to know we're taking up a collection for Elinma's children."

Elinma's children were leaving for their paternal uncle's home in Colorado. Their father was still on life support. Even if he made it, he wouldn't be coming home.

"I'm glad you told me. How much should I bring?"

"People are giving what they can," Nomzamo said.

"You'll get my contribution tomorrow."

Nomzamo cocked her head. "I need to know something."

"What?"

"We all knew Elinma's husband was a deadbeat. Did she tell you he abused her?"

Zina frowned as she recalled conversations with Elinma, the few visits to Elinma's house, interactions with Elinma's jovial husband. From what she saw, they both seemed to have accepted their separate lives. "No. I guess we all keep secrets."

"I miss her presence," Nomzamo whispered.

"Me too."

That night, as they sat up in bed, Zina gave Eziafa the update on Elinma's children. "They're leaving next week."

"The relative is taking all four of them?" Eziafa asked.

Zina had worried they would have to be separated. "Yes."

"To take in that many children in this economy, the relative must have plenty money."

"No. I heard he's a school custodian."

"Hmm. Some people have good hearts. Elinma's life insurance money will help."

The hospital provided them with free coverage to the equivalent of two years' salary. "That money won't go far," she said. "Those children still have a lot of growing to do. The hospital staff are contributing to a tuition fund. I have to bring in mine tomorrow."

"I wish we could help. Anyway, we'll keep the children in our thoughts and prayers."

Nonsense and ingredients. "Eziafa, when was the last time you prayed or gave significant thought to anything but the monstrosity you built in the village?"

Eziafa frowned. "Zina, this house matter is done and over. *Biko*, let it rest."

"How? I can't help my friend's children because of the debt it saddled us with. It was a grave mistake and you know it."

"I admit that I am not perfect. Neither are you. And it is not a crime to want a visible testament to my success in America."

Zina scoffed. "Your success?"

Eziafa waved his hand. "My success, your success, it's the same."

"You have forgotten that, when you only look in one direction, your neck becomes stiff."

He laughed. "See this small girl, quoting proverb for me."

"Eziafa, while you were not paying attention, I grew up. And one does not need to be old to recognize the truth."

"Since you want to carry someone else's problem on your head, go and start a GoFundMe campaign."

"I should ask strangers for money?"

"It's what everyone does these days. I'm sure you have Elinma's pictures on your phone. Find a nice one. Put it there. *Inugo?* Make sure the campaign story says you're raising money for four African orphans whose father killed their mother."

Eziafa tugged on his ear. "Do not forget to share it on social media. Since you women are always on the internet, I'm sure you could make the campaign link go viral. Who knows, you may even raise up to a million dollars."

"I didn't know you were this heartless. You should be ashamed of yourself."

Eziafa scowled. "Who do you think you're talking to?"

Dazed, Zina felt like for the first time she was seeing the real version of her husband. She remembered Nomzamo's question about whether she had ever stood in front of a person, looked into their eyes, and asked herself where in the world their soul went. If Nomzamo were to repeat the question now, she would be able to give her an emphatic yes.

Eziafa's lips were still moving when Zina stretched out on the bed and turned her back.

On her way out of the house the next morning, Zina stood in the hallway and stared at Eziafa. He was shouting at the television as he watched a soccer match.

Her mother had told her love would come after marriage. She didn't even like Eziafa. He looked up and caught her staring at him. "*Ogini?*"

"I just wanted to remind you that I won't be back until tomorrow afternoon."

Eziafa turned his attention back to the television. "Okay."

Zina squared her shoulders as she opened the door and walked out.

After some second thoughts, Zina left her overnight bag in the car. Raven had sounded uncertain when she asked if she could come over to his place. It was her first visit.

He welcomed her with a big hug. "I wasn't sure you would show up."

"I almost didn't."

"I'm glad you're here."

She turned away from him. The large sectional sofa gave the living room a cozy look. A half-finished baby blanket laid on it. A warm feeling went through her. "You do knit those blankets."

Raven gave her a sheepish grin. "My mom taught me. It was our secret."

Zina inhaled. He was her secret. "You have a nice home."

"Thanks." He reached for her hand. "I'll show you around."

The kitchen with painted white cabinets and black appliances made her smile. With all the palm oil splatters, she would not be able to maintain a white kitchen.

"Do you want to see the bedroom?" Raven asked.

Zina smiled. "If you want to show it to me."

"It's nothing special."

"You let me be the judge of that."

She followed Raven as he walked down a bright hallway. The white room had an indigo accent wall behind the king-sized bed.

Zina read aloud a quote from someone named Zig Ziglar printed on the cream plaque Raven hung above the bed: "Failure is an event, not a person."

Raven stood beside her. "I've repeated those words to myself on many days."

She noticed a panel on the wall. "What is that?"

"It's the alarm for my wake-up calls. Every morning it plays a song and tells me to go slay some dragons."

She didn't understand why everyone was consumed with dragon-slaying. She felt a little danger kept the senses sharp. "Really?"

Raven smiled. "Actually, it sings to me. That's why I come to work with a big smile and some pep in my steps."

Zina shook her head. "Why can't you set a simple alarm like everyone else?"

Raven wound an arm around her waist. "I'm not like everyone else."

That uniqueness was part of why she was so smitten with him. She knew that, if they were to have sex again, she had to make it clear to Raven that it was what she wanted. "I hope you're not against serving breakfast in bed?"

Raven blinked. "Breakfast?"

Zina nodded. "Unless you don't want me to spend the night."

Raven's eye colour shifted to a deep jade. "What kind of friend would that make me?"

Chapter Forty-Five

ZINA SNEEZED INTO the crook of her arm. The sharp scent of the muscle cream had drifted up her nostrils.

Her fingers continued to knead imaginary knots from Eziafa's shoulders and back. Life with a controlling and hypochondriac husband was hell. Thank God for Raven.

Eziafa moaned his pleasure. "God bless you."

Zina bit hard on her lip. When Eziafa was home from work, all he did was sit on the couch and stare into space. His headaches had become indicators of brain tumors; phantom facial twitches sure signs of stroke. All the test results were negative.

She stared at Eziafa's head. The sight of the bald, puckered spot at the top made her want to empty a bottle of Rogaine on his head.

Zina squeezed her eyes shut as a wave of shame ran through her. Eziafa was responsible for many things, but he did not create himself.

Her eyes flew open when Eziafa flipped onto his

back and fell on her. He gave her what he must think looked like an appealing sensual wink. "How far? It's been too long."

Irritated, Zina moved away. The man deserved an A for persistence. "We don't have time for this. I still have to go grocery shopping before I leave for work."

"The groceries will wait. I'm your number one priority."

Be deceiving yourself. "Eziafa, *biko*, I don't have time for nonsense."

"Sex with your husband is now nonsense?"

"Will it fill your stomach?"

"There are different kinds of hunger."

"Please, just leave me alone."

He gave her a sullen look. "Is it a crime for a man to love his wife?"

Zina snickered. Story for the gods.

"Time is going by. At forty-five, I'm overdue for children. Zina, *biko*. Do you want me changing baby diapers in my fifties?"

"Tell me, all the sex you've been having, where is its result?" she asked.

Eziafa took a deep breath as he rolled away from her. Relieved, Zina scooted out of bed and changed her clothes. Eziafa was still facing the wall when she walked out of the room.

Zina was in the middle of making a cereal choice when Raven called her cell phone. "Hello, Mr. Giesbrecht."

"Hey, babe. Are you still coming over to my place?"

Thanks to Mr. Eziafa, she had less time to get things done. "I don't think I can make it today."

"I want to see you. Please."

Zina glanced at her wristwatch. "It would have to be a quick visit."

"I'll take whatever I can get. See you soon."

Zina sped through the rest of her shopping.

When she got to his place, Raven wouldn't let her leave. They ended up on his couch, talking as "All I Want Is You" by Banky W & Chidinma played from the iPod dock. Raven loved her collection of Nigerian music.

When he began nuzzling her neck, she pushed him away.

"What's the matter?" Raven asked.

"Is sex all you think of when you see me?"

"You know my love language is physical touch."

"It's time to learn another language."

Raven moved away from her. "I thought you enjoyed being with me."

The sex was great. His company greater. But she was finding it harder to silence her mother's warning voice. "I don't have time. I'm sure Eziafa's wondering ..." Zina stopped mid-sentence.

She'd agreed not to mention Eziafa's name while they were together. She gave Raven a look under her eyelashes. He didn't comment on her slip of the tongue.

"You look stressed. Call in sick and spend the night with me. I promise to be on my best behaviour."

She shook her head. "The kids at work need me."

Raven pouted. "I need you, too."

"You're a big boy. Your needs can wait."

Raven stood from the couch. "Will you stay if I dance for you?"

She shook her head. "Careful now. You might break something if you try and move those stiff hips."

After doing the white man's overbite dance, Raven spun around. "Let the dance-off begin."

Her shoulders shook with laughter. "You're an *onye ocha* feeling funky."

Raven frowned. "What does that mean?"

Zina didn't want to tell him she had called him a white person. It was a fact. But Raven was a bit sensitive about his alabaster skin tone. He couldn't tan. "I said you're a boss."

He pouted. "Yeah, yeah, laugh at me. Once Rosetta Stone starts offering Igbo language lessons, you won't be able to get anything past me."

"Good luck with that. My shift starts in half an hour."

"Leave your frozen food items here and pick them up afterward."

It made sense since her place was farther away. She would call Eziafa and tell him there was an emergency and she had to head straight to the hospital.

The ladies were huddled around the central desk. Zina slowed her steps. She couldn't handle any more bad news.

Her eyes met with Chardonnay's. Chardonnay grinned before she gave a low whistle. "Attention ladies. Miss Florence Nightingale is in the building."

Zina's jaw dropped when she saw the huge floral arrangement placed on the desk. There had to be at least forty long-stemmed, white roses in the vase. "Wow. Whose birthday is it?"

Nomzamo gave her a questioning look. "Apparently yours."

"You know it's not my birthday," Zina said.

"Well, the card has your name on it," Nomzamo said.

Zina stared at the arrangement. "Who would send me such gorgeous flowers?"

"This should answer that question," Chardonnay said as pulled out the sealed florist envelope from the arrangement and handed it to Zina.

The card was signed "Myrtle's Dad." It was the four-month anniversary of the evening at the waterfall. Zina gave a silly laugh as she avoided Nomzamo's eyes. "Oh. It's from a former patient."

Billie Lou's smile didn't make it to her eyes. "Good for you."

Zina disliked the phrase. She could never tell when it was a compliment or the North American version of "go hug a transformer." Zina slid the card back in the envelope. "It does feel good to be appreciated."

Billie Lou's steely gaze stayed on her. "Bless your little heart, dear. For a moment, I thought the flowers were from Raven."

Zina lifted her chin. "And why would they be from Raven?"

Billie Lou didn't blink. "With the way you two have been carrying on, despite that wedding band on your finger, it seemed like a logical conclusion."

"Well, you're wrong," she said.

"Silly old me. What was I thinking?"

You're silly all right. "The real problem is that you don't think."

Blood drained from Billie Lou's face. "Pardon me?"

Zina's hand went to her mouth. "Oops. Did I say that out loud? I wasn't thinking, either."

"There is no need for insults," Billie Lou snapped.

"Insults? That was a factual observation."

Billie Lou blinked. "Excuse me?"

Zina lifted her chin. Since she'd said more than she intended to, she might as well go all the way. "I wasn't speaking a foreign language. Feel free to wash down those words with a tall glass of apple cider, Miss Tarty Sweetness."

Billie's face turned red. "This ... this is bullying. I'm going to H.R."

"Two can play that game. See you there."

Holding her head high, Zina picked up the floral arrangement and marched away from the desk. Where would she put the damn thing?

Chapter Forty-Six

ZINA'S MIND WANDERED as their nurse manager outlined some important monthly stats. She made a pretense of taking notes. All she had on her pad were meaningless doodles. It didn't help that Nomzamo sent her a death ray whenever their eyes met.

When things were quiet on the floor, she pulled Nomzamo into an empty patient room. "I've been neglecting us. I'm sorry."

"I'm not mad at you."

"The looks you gave me this morning painted a different picture," she said.

"Zina, I'm furious at you. This nonsense with Raven isn't helping your reputation. After you walked off with your flower pyramid, Billie Lou went on and on about how she ran into you and Raven at some festival and how you'd tried to avoid her and ended up crashing into a food truck."

"We didn't crash into any food truck," Zina said.

"You were at the festival with Raven."

"Yes. But Raven and I don't have a thing," she said.

"I'm keeping my nose up to avoid smelling the bullshit you're peddling."

"Nomzamo, I—"

"You forget we've been friends for way too long for me to believe your lies. You are having an affair with Raven."

"You don't understand."

Nomzamo folded her arms. "Make me."

Where would she begin? "For almost seven years, I have lived under Eziafa's giant thumb. Most days, it seemed all that thumb wanted to do was grind me into the dust until there was nothing left of me."

"We're on the same page about your husband's control issues," Nomzamo said. "I'm also somewhat old-fashioned enough to think the one-man-at-a-time policy is not a bad way to live. If you no longer want your marriage, pack your things and leave."

Her parents would be devastated. "I can't."

"So, you want to keep both men?"

What she wanted was love. "Raven loves me. Eziafa doesn't."

"You told me you didn't marry for love."

Nomzamo, with her privileged life, couldn't understand. "I'm not a gold-digger!"

"That's not what I said."

"It's what you implied. It was never about Eziafa's money. My parents gave me no choice."

"Zina, I know it was like the man got a mail order bride with a warranty, but it still isn't right."

"While I still have the opportunity, I want to wake up in the morning and feel excited about my day. Nomzamo,

I'm twenty-five years old. This isn't the time in my life when I want to hear about bowel problems and aching bones."

Nomzamo shrugged. "We all age."

Raven was twenty-six, a year older than her. "I don't want a man who needs my young body to push his wheelchair around."

"Say what?"

Zina's hand flew to her mouth. "I'm sorry."

Nomzamo turned away from her. Zina could tell from the way she wrapped arms around her body that she was fighting to control her emotions.

"I'm sorry. You know I love Trey."

"Saying sorry doesn't fix everything," Nomzamo said.

"What can I say to make this better?"

Nomzamo's eyes were shiny when she turned around. "Because Raven has your trifling mind all twisted, I'm going to pretend I didn't hear those words."

"This is not Raven's fault."

"Girl, part of it is. Raven is making you gamble with your life. Have you forgotten what happened to Elinma, to those other ladies you told me about?"

Zina knew of six other Nigerian women, all nurses, who were killed by their husbands. The men were much older, like Eziafa.

She clenched her teeth. "Contrary to what you all think, I'm no longer the naïve African girl."

"Zina, I have serious doubts. You're publicly messing with a man who's convinced that he owns you."

"Eziafa isn't violent."

Nomzamo gave her a frustrated look. "I think you're being irresponsible."

"I have a right to change."

"Yes, you do. You also have to understand that change has its attendant circumstances. Positive or negative, you'll have to deal with them."

"Please, be happy for me."

Nomzamo sighed. "Just remember that it's open season."

After work, Zina headed to Raven's place. She took the flowers with her. Before she left home, she'd told Eziafa she was working an overnight shift.

They ate dinner in front of the television. "The girls were talking about me."

Raven grinned. "That was the plan."

A foolish one. "In case there's a next time, please note that it wasn't one of your best plans."

Raven gave her a sullen look. "I couldn't have the flowers delivered to your house."

"You should have kept them here for me."

"I wanted the other girls to see them. I thought you girls like to make each other a little jealous."

Billie Lou was jealous all right. "Maybe your boatload of ex-girlfriends got a kick out of that. I don't."

"Boatload? I try to do something nice and I don't even get a thank you."

"I would have appreciated discretion."

Raven dropped his fork. "Fine. Next year, I won't make the mistake of sending you flowers."

"Since I'm new at this, what's the average lifespan of an affair? Six months, one year, two tops?"

Raven's eyes darkened. "Pardon my overconfidence."

A broad smile masked Zina's hurt feelings. "You said this is all fun, games and sex, remember?"

"You agreed to those terms."

Zina clenched her jaw. She had. But what she now wanted from Raven was an assurance of exclusivity. An unreasonable demand when she still lived with her husband.

Raven ran a hand through his hair. "Zee, I'm confused. What exactly do you want?"

It was hard for her to find words to express her dreams. She pulled her legs up and wrapped her arms around them. "Nomzamo and I had a painful chat about you."

Raven grimaced. "I guess she told you about our conversation."

"What conversation?"

"Well, last week, I was foolish enough to do some whitesplaining about why folks get mad about Black Lives Matter." Raven gave her a rueful smile. "Nomzy told me that because one of my body parts has been inside a black woman does not make me an expert on race relations."

Zina flinched. An angry Nomzamo pulled no punches. Nomzamo hadn't said anything to her. The new unwritten rule in their unit was no discussing political issues during their shifts. It had caused a lot of bad blood.

"You know Nomzamo likes you."

"I think she liked me more when I stayed in my race lane."

"Nomzamo isn't that kind of person."

"It didn't sound that way to me. I want to tell Nomzy to mind her own damn business. But I'm sure she wouldn't hesitate to cut me with a scalpel."

"Nomzamo looks out for me."

"I'm never going to hurt you. I promise."

"I'm going to hold you to it."

Raven cleared his throat. "I do want to know what you think. Are such topics a no-go between us?"

Zina took a deep breath. Unsure of how Raven felt about the issues, she had deliberately said nothing. It was cowardice and she knew it.

She picked her words. "I think you should be part of the ongoing conversations. But you can't dominate it. You have to listen and learn. As an African immigrant, I'm learning too."

"You'll let me know when I'm crossing boundaries?"

"Deal."

Raven looked excited as he dug a hand into his pocket. "I have something else for you."

Zina's mouth opened when Raven brought out a wrapped box and handed it over. Her fingers shook as she tore away the wrapping paper.

She opened the box and found a platinum link chain with a key pendant. A wave of disappointment overwhelmed her. "What is this?"

"The key to my heart. Do you like it?"

She'd thought he was giving her a ring. "It's ... pretty."

Raven's face fell. "I think the real answer is no."

Zina blinked back her tears. It wasn't Raven's fault she now wanted more. "I thought you were giving me the key to your apartment."

"Oh. Sorry. I can make one for you."

Nomzamo's words came to her mind. Yes, there were times when sorry didn't help.

"Let me put it on for you." The pendant key nestled in her cleavage. It was the right length.

Raven kissed her on the forehead. "You're one of the people I need most in my life."

You just don't need me enough to make things permanent. "Okay."

"Zee, what's going on today? Your mind isn't here."

"You're right. I need to go somewhere else to find it."

"Please stay. I was going to offer you a sappy movie and a foot rub."

On another day, Raven's offerings would have made for a perfect evening. "I'll take a rain check."

"Okay. Are you still coming on the training trip?"

The wise thing would be to tell her supervisor she couldn't travel to New Orleans because of a family emergency. She would then take time off from work, check herself into a hotel, and figure out her life. "Yes. It would be a great opportunity to see my friend, Titilope."

"I'm glad." Raven stroked her cheek. "*Ick heff di leev.*"

Zina's body sagged as she blew out air. Raven's first language was Low German. "I love you, too."

Chapter Forty-Seven

DRESSED IN A pair of red boxer shorts with a Cupid motif, Eziafa paced the bedroom. He was eager to test Felix's theory. He had not bothered Zina because he knew she was grieving over her friend. But it was time to focus on their family.

When he heard the front door open, Eziafa ran to the bed and dove under the duvet.

Zina tiptoed into the room. As she undressed, he yawned as if her movements woke him. He turned around with another louder yawn. "Zina, is that you?"

She gave him a cursory glance. "Were you expecting somebody else?"

Eziafa, no arguments. "Is it not good to check?"

Zina turned away.

He waited in bed while she took her shower. She came out, donned her pajamas and curled up on the other side of the bed.

He knew Zina's turned back was her 'do not disturb' sign. He rolled over and placed an arm and leg on her body. Zina moved to the edge of the bed.

Today na today. Eziafa cleared his throat and began to sing. "Oh, my darling. Oh, my sugar. When I think of you, my heart dey make *jigigi* like a railway."

"Eziafa, do you know what time it is?"

"Can a man not serenade his wife?"

Zina groaned. "*Chi m*, what have I done to deserve this punishment?"

"I'm just expressing my love." Zina squirmed as he tried to wrap his arms around her waist. "*Achalugo nwanyi*, relax."

She pushed him away. "Eziafa, leave me alone. I need my sleep."

He tried to keep his playful tone. "This woman. We can't be fighting every time. Haven't you missed me?"

"It's almost midnight," she said. "Can we talk about this tomorrow?"

"That's what you keep saying, tomorrow, tomorrow. No. We're talking about this now."

She eyed him. "Okay o. I'm listening."

"You seem to have forgotten that I am your husband."

"Because I no longer jump whenever you cough?"

"Zina, I want a child."

Zina shrugged. "We all have our wants."

Begging Zina for sex made him feel inadequate. He tightened his grip on her waist. "What have I ever done to you?"

"Please leave me alone."

"You're the one making this harder than it has to be. It won't take long. I promise. Just give me fifteen minutes."

"No!"

As Zina tried to pull away, her sharp elbow jabbed his

stomach. Eziafa relaxed his hold. "Okay, I'll manage with ten minutes."

"What part of no don't you understand?"

Zina didn't seem to realize how important this was to him. As Eziafa tightened his grip, Zina jerked her body. They fell off the bed. Eziafa's head hit the edge of their oak bedside table. Hard. He groaned.

"See what you've done to yourself," Zina said.

Eziafa fought to control his emotions. During their struggle, his red boxers had slid to his knees. Cold air from a floor vent blew on his exposed buttocks. Neither of them moved.

Felix's words came to his mind. The changing and bending thing had worked for his friend. "Zina, I'm sorry. I'm really sorry."

All he heard was her heavy breathing.

"I know you're angry with me. Please, how can I make things better between us?"

Zina's muffled response sent a chill through him. "There is no us."

Still in a daze, Eziafa dressed and left their apartment. He got behind the wheel of his taxi and headed for Felix's house. Somehow, he made it there without hurting himself or someone else. Relieved to see Felix's car, he parked and took slow steps up the porch stairs.

Dressed in his pajamas, Felix came to the door. He looked alarmed as he ushered Eziafa in. "What's going on?"

"It's Zina."

"What happened to her? Is she okay?"

"Yes."

"Thank God," Felix said as he turned on the living room lights. "Please, sit."

Before he could speak, Eziafa heard Nkolika's voice. "Sweetheart, *onye?*"

"It's Eziafa."

"Greet him o."

He gave Felix a pleading look. "Please, tell Nkolika to join us. I need her help, too."

Minutes later, Felix came back with his wife. Their faces were sombre as they sat across from him.

Eziafa shook his head. "It is with a heavy heart that I tell you that Zina is cheating on me."

Felix sat up. "Did you catch her in the act?"

Eziafa tapped on his heart. "I know it in here."

Felix gave him a reassuring smile. "I think this is a case of when one's goat goes missing, the aroma of a neighbour's soup becomes suspicious."

Eziafa clenched his jaw. He wasn't paranoid. "My intuition has never failed me," he said.

"There is always a first time," Felix said.

Nkolika's expression remained unchanged. Eziafa concluded she knew something. "*Nwanyi oma*, please, what have you heard?"

Nkolika pursed her lips. "I don't repeat gossip."

"My dear, you know something?" Felix asked.

"Yes," Nkolika said.

Felix gaped at his wife. "How could you have kept this information from me?"

"Grown men who go home and marry children should expect to get dirty while playing with them in the sandpit."

"You keep saying Eziafa went home to marry a child. Zina was eighteen."

Nkolika glared at her husband. "Our Amara will be eighteen this year. Are you telling me that if one man comes from Timbuktu and says he wants to marry Amara, you would hand her over?"

"Our daughters born here are different. They are delicate, unable to deal with the hardship our people experience at home. Zina grew up in the village. From the day she was born, she was raised to be a wife and mother."

"The girls born at home need protecting too," Nkolika said. "Eziafa should have married Jovita. She was a grown woman."

"My dear wife, it is not your place to tell Eziafa who he should have married. And the last time I saw Zina, she wasn't a child. The main issue here is that a wife is cheating on her husband. Did you hear that? If you now think adultery is acceptable, please, give me notice so I can prepare myself."

Nkolika rose from her seat. "Because your friend's wife may be cheating on him, I'm now an adulteress?"

They seemed to have forgotten his presence. "Enough, I beg. I didn't come here to cause trouble," Eziafa pleaded.

Nkolika took her seat and faced him. "Only a wicked person pours pepper into another's open wound. I'm sorry for my harsh words."

Eziafa nodded. "It takes strength to admit a fault. Thank you."

Nkolika crossed her legs. "If you think it will help, I will talk to Zina."

"*Imeela*. You both have a long day tomorrow. I should go."

They all rose.

Felix hugged his wife. "*Daalu*. I'm sorry for my words."

Nkolika turned to him. "*Kachifo*."

"*Ka omesia*."

Nkolika excused herself and returned to their bedroom. Felix insisted on walking Eziafa to his car. They sat on the hood.

"This must be hard for you," Felix said.

"If what I suspect is true, Zina has killed me."

"*Nna*, why are you talking like this?"

A gush of air escaped from Eziafa's mouth. "I'm dead."

"Take it easy. Assumptions are often wrong. Is Zina not an Oji woman? She knows what happens to adulterous women. She won't risk her life. Please, don't kill yourself with worry. Remember what happened to Obikwelu."

Obikwelu, the friend who kept them entertained with his pointless jokes, died the previous summer. Obikwelu collapsed in Family Court. Chigo, the imported wife his parents found for him, told the court Obikwelu was an abuser. She said he assaulted her and the children with a cowhide whip imported from Nigeria. Obikwelu told his friends Chigo's parents bought the *koboko* at her request. He swore he had never laid a hand on his wife.

Their circle knew Obikwelu was not a violent man. Yes, the man often spoke without thinking. He was fiercely committed to his ideas, especially the foolish ones. Above all, there were no doubts in their minds that Obikwelu loved his children.

By the time the dust settled, Chigo had what she wanted. Obikwelu lost his home, his children, and his pride.

Obikwelu was still alive when the ambulance carried him away from the courthouse. He died a week later.

Their association taxed members to ship Obikwelu's body back to his people.

In a matter of weeks, Chigo sold their house and disappeared from Houston. Back in Nigeria, Obikwelu's family was still calling for Chigo's head.

The clouds moved and the moonlight left a silvery sheen on Felix's face. Eziafa stared at it, desperate to believe his friend's words. "What if Zina has a boyfriend?"

"Then you have to tell our people at home what's going on."

"I just want to pack up and leave for Nigeria. We will settle ourselves there."

"I doubt Zina would go back with you. My brother, this is a bitter pill to swallow. You must remember that a little life is better than a little death. If Zina wants to go with this other man, let her go. It is not too late for you to start over."

Eziafa exhaled. "I have lived in America for twenty years. Where do I start from?"

Felix gave him a sad look. "Go home. Try and get some sleep. I'll call in the morning." Eziafa clenched his teeth as he started the car. It was easy for Felix to say to let Zina go when his wife and children slept peacefully inside their house.

Chapter Forty-Eight

INSTEAD OF GOING home after his shift at the tortilla factory, Eziafa drove around the city. The car's movement calmed him.

Desperate for some direction, Eziafa went over the many conversations with his father. Papa always encouraged him to come prepared with questions about life. Nothing useful came to Eziafa's mind. What to do when his wife decides to sleep with another man was not an issue they had discussed. Eziafa stared at the dark sky. It may not be too late. Dead or alive, parents are supposed to watch over their children.

"Papa, what should I do?" he whispered.

The prolonged silence amplified Eziafa's racing thoughts. He would take a booming reaction from the sky, a flash of letters across his windshield, anything. Nothing came.

"Ask Zina," the voice in Eziafa's head commanded.

His ears perked up. The voice sounded like his father's.

"Papa?"

"Go home and ask her."

He was afraid of Zina's response. "What if she says yes?"
There was silence.

His groan filled the car. "Papa, *biko*, talk to me."

Eziafa began to wonder if he'd imagined the voice. He
shook his head. No. He knew his father's voice. He decided
that the old man was silent because he wanted to see what
Eziafa would do. It was a test.

By the time Eziafa arrived at their apartment complex,
the morning sun had brightened the sky. He frowned at
the sight of Zina's car. She should have been at work. Stiff,
he hobbled towards the front lobby doors.

There was a suitcase standing by their bedroom door.
For a moment, Eziafa panicked. Zina was leaving him!
Then he remembered she had a week-long work training in
New Orleans.

His heart rate settled as he walked into the room and
heard Zina singing in the shower. Sitting on the edge of
the bed, he removed his socks.

Zina's bag was on the bed. Eziafa gave it a thoughtful
look before glancing in the direction of the bathroom. He
could still hear Zina's voice. He pulled the bag close, unzipped it, and began his search.

Inside one of the side pockets, he found a pink compact case. He turned it around in his hand. Back in the day,
his mother had owned similar-looking brown powder cases.
To think of it, he'd never seen Zina use that kind of powder.

Curious, Eziafa opened the case. He saw several rows
of pink pills. Surprised, he closed the case, only to open it
again. He took one of the pills and peered at it. What were
they? He hoped she didn't have a medical condition she
was hiding from him.

Eziafa heard the shower stop. He quickly placed the

compact case back in the bag and pushed it away from him. He slipped the pill into his pocket.

When Zina walked into the room, her eyes widened when she saw him. "You're back."

"Yes." Eziafa waited for Zina to ask him why he was coming home at dawn. She didn't.

Zina went over to the dresser. "I left the contact information for my hotel on the dining table. I'll also have my cell phone with me."

Eziafa, ask her. "No!"

Zina gave him a puzzled look. "Sorry?"

"Nothing."

Zina kept looking at him as she dried herself and applied lotion.

"Do you need me to drop you off at work?" he asked.

"No, thank you. I have a couple of errands to run before we leave for the airport. The car will be safe at the hospital."

Eziafa gulped. *Zina, are you sleeping with another man?*

She shook out her braids and rearranged them into a bun. "I made you some food for the week. You'll find the labeled bowls in the freezer."

"Thank you."

Zina gave him another inquiring look before shrugging. There was a lightness to her steps as she walked away from him.

Eziafa took the pink pill out of his pocket and examined it for markings. It had none.

Eziafa brought out a prescription bottle from his

nightstand drawer. He dropped the pink pill inside. He would ask Nuru.

He was relieved to see his friend at the pharmacy. "My brother, good morning."

The pharmacist beamed. "It has been a while."

They shook hands. "Where have you been?" Eziafa asked.

"My brother and I opened a small African food store near his house. Since it's new, I have to keep an eye on it."

To think that Nuru started life in America as a grocery packer. Eziafa was beginning to accept that he was cursed. "Congratulations. More blessings."

"Thank you, my brother. What brings you in today?"

Eziafa placed the prescription bottle on the counter. "Last night, I found a strange pill in my medication."

Nuru looked puzzled. "What did it look like?"

He handed over Zina's pink pill. The pharmacist frowned as he turned it over in his hand. "This was in your medication bottle?"

He nodded. "It was a good thing I looked before tossing it in my mouth."

"Please wait."

Nuru returned with a worried look. "This is a birth control pill. I can't figure out how it got mixed up with your medication."

Eziafa braced himself against the counter. "A birth control pill?"

Nuru nodded. "A relief pharmacist was covering for me around the time you got this prescription. But he should have noticed the difference in colour."

Eziafa stared at him. A birth control pill?

Nuru placed a hand on his chest. "As the manager, I

accept full responsibility. Next time you come, please don't pay for your order."

Eziafa forced a smile. "I'm not upset. We all make mistakes. What could have happened to me? Bigger breasts to match my pot belly?"

Nuru gave an uneasy laugh. "My brother, thanks for understanding."

Eziafa held his smile until he was outside the pharmacy. Inside his car, Eziafa rested his head against the steering wheel.

Zina knew how much he wanted children and she was taking birth control pills? He remembered their conversation about the effect of the IUD. All along, she'd been playing him for a fool.

Rain clouds gathered as Eziafa drove to the hospital. Zina must tell him what his offence was. Parked by the curb outside the main entrance, he was planning his confrontation when a woman's laughter rang out. The cheerful tone of the laugh caught Eziafa's attention before it registered as Zina's.

There she was. His dear wife holding hands with another man in broad daylight. The man walked with the confidence of someone who thought it was his right.

Eziafa stared at the young man's face. In his mind, he'd built up the image of an imposing muscular man. Someone fit to challenge him. This pudgy, ghostlike creature was his adversary?

As they made their way toward Eziafa, he anticipated Zina's reaction. There was no way she could continue her walk of shame past his car.

Zina did. The treacherous woman did.

The shock brought a sharp pain to Eziafa's chest. He gasped.

Before Zina and the man disappeared into the parking structure across the road, they stopped and shared a brief kiss. Mouth to mouth. In broad daylight.

A numb feeling radiated from Eziafa's face to the back of his neck. He gripped the steering wheel.

So, when Zina closed her eyes during their lovemaking, and a smile flitted at the corner of her mouth, she was thinking about this thief and not him?

Eziafakaego, stop punishing yourself.

The voice made him sit up. "Papa, is that you?"

He heard silence.

Eziafa closed his eyes. Since their wedding day, he had been dreaming of the two children he and Zina were going to have. They were going to be The Okerekes, a party of four, the perfect American family. The name he'd picked for his daughter was Obiageli. A beauty blessed with his mother's smile. Nnanna, his son, would have come into the world with his grandfather's quiet wisdom and strength.

The tightness in Eziafa's chest moved to his shoulder. Panting, he fumbled in the glove compartment for a bottle of baby aspirin. After swallowing a pill, he leaned back against his seat. The physical pain eased.

Be grateful she didn't give you another man's child to raise.

Eziafa's entire body jerked at the thought.

It began to rain during the drive home. The downpour turned the road ahead into a little stream. He held on the steering wheel as if it were a lifeline. Even the heavens were weeping for him.

Chapter Forty-Nine

ZINA STOOD IN front of the closet mirror and smoothed her dress with a shaky hand. She should not feel this nervous about meeting with Titilope.

Raven helped with her chain clasp. "I'm beginning to wonder if you're meeting up with a dude."

"I am. What are you going to do about it?"

Raven stepped away from her and cracked his knuckles. "I hope you're ready to be on the evening news. I'll be introducing these beauties to his face."

"You're all mouth and no trousers." Zina had heard the phrase from a British girl at work.

Raven winked. "Good thing I don't need to wear trousers when I'm around you."

"You no well."

Raven leered at her. "I be sharp *onye ocha* man."

Zina giggled. Raven now knew what the term meant. She pulled on her knee-length boots.

He walked her to the hotel room door. "Say hello to your friend, Titilope."

When Raven said the name, it rhymed with canta-loupe. She couldn't help teasing him. "I haven't told *Tea-Tea-Law-Pay* about you."

"You should." Raven reached out and stroked her cheek. "This is no longer a temporary thing."

"It's not?"

Raven shook his head. "There's a cost to living a life less than what you need. Zina, I need you."

Zina was afraid to give herself to the joy that burst inside her. "Have you told your friends about me?"

"I told Tim."

Tim was Raven's only friend from back home. Her response was a wide smile.

"He can't wait to meet you."

Zina stood on her tiptoes and kissed him. "We'll finish this conversation when I get back."

Raven winked. "Among other things."

Standing outside the hotel, Zina took a deep breath. It was a beautiful fall day. She was meeting Titilope at a place called Limpopo, an African restaurant only a block away.

Zina arrived early at the restaurant and checked in her coat. As she sat in the lobby, the fluttery sensations in her stomach grew by the minute.

The outer doors slid open. Zina pulled herself up after a woman in a blue dress coat walked in. "Titilope?"

The woman spun around. "Zina?"

They hurried toward each other and hugged.

Titilope held on to her hands. "Is this really you?"

"It's your little Zee Zee from Texas."

Titilope laughed at the exaggerated drawl. "You've become a Southern lady."

Zina stepped back and took another look at Titilope. Time had blended in her facial scarring. Zina wondered if the years had lightened her emotional scars as well. "You look beautiful."

Titilope gave a self-conscious laugh. "The lighting in here can't be that dim."

"You want me to repeat it. At the least, pay for my dinner before you start fishing for more compliments."

Titilope smiled. "You look great, too."

While they waited for their meal, Titilope shared T.J.'s recent school picture with her.

"Eeyah. He has grown."

"My sister, the teenage years are here."

Zina remembered the envelope in her purse. While searching for old documents, she found the pictures Eziafa took at the airport so long ago. She handed them over. "Better late than never."

Titilope's jaw dropped. "Wow. I forgot we took pictures."

"I laughed when I came across them."

Titilope held up a picture. "You still have your baby face."

"All I see is a skinny girl in a not-new pair of stonewash jeans." Johnny-Just-Come Zina was clueless about the challenges which laid ahead.

"There's nothing wrong with second-hand clothing. Look again. I see someone who was excited about her future."

If only that fresh-off-the plane Zina knew what lay ahead of her. "You on the other hand, have always been a trendy woman. You were well-dressed then, you're an even better dresser now.

Titilope laughed. "Me? Trendy? I've never been accused of such a thing."

"I find that hard to believe. You're the epitome of class."

"Oh, stop it."

"I'm serious."

Titilope chuckled. "I can see you've become an accomplished liar."

Zina flinched.

Clearly, Titilope realized the teasing remark hit a nerve. "I'm sorry. I didn't mean to offend you."

"The words do have some truth to them. I ..." Zina stopped when the waiter arrived with their plates of *mogudu* and couscous.

When he left, Zina pushed aside her plate. "There is something I have to tell you."

"What is it?"

"I'm leaving Eziafa."

Titilope didn't look surprised. "Why now?"

Knowing Raven loved and needed her made the difference. "There is someone else."

"Oh."

"His name's Raven."

Titilope raised an eyebrow. "The imaginary fitness coach?"

If Zina were white, her face would have turned beet red. "Yes."

"A good friend of mine once told me any hand stretched out to a drowning person becomes a lifeline. Is that the case with Raven?"

"No. I'm not using Raven as an escape. I haven't told him I'm leaving Eziafa."

"I'm confused."

"Even if there was no Raven, I can no longer live with Eziafa. We're not good for each other. I'm not proud of the person I've become in this marriage."

"What did Eziafa say when you told him?"

"He doesn't know."

"Hmm. Prepare for a messy fight."

"Thank God we don't have children. There's nothing else for us to fight over. He can keep everything. I only want my freedom."

"I don't think it's going to be that easy," Titilope said. "A despot king demands the loyalty of his subjects."

"Eziafa can find himself another queen. I want nothing from him."

"That, there, is the reason why Eziafa will fight you."

Zina frowned. "I don't understand."

"Our men are experts at dealing with our uneasy silences, at managing our outbursts. But, indifference? Hmm. That emotion drives them right over the edge."

Zina was confused. "Are you saying I shouldn't leave Eziafa?"

"What I'm saying is please be careful."

Her heart rate settled. "You worry too much."

"I know my experiences have coloured the way I look at things. Months after we left Tomide's house and moved into our apartment, I flinched at the slightest sound." Titilope gave her a wry smile. "There were days I was afraid to open my closet doors because my mind insisted Tomide was hiding inside. I couldn't believe he had let me go."

"At the end of the day, nothing happened to you," Zina said.

Titilope took a deep breath. "You're right."

To calm herself, Zina took a sip of cold water. She was

determined to make a new life for herself. With or without Raven. "My main problem right now is how to break the news to my mother."

Titilope twisted her lips. "If your mother is anything like mine, she's not going to handle it well."

Zina sighed. "How many Nigerian mothers would handle it well? Sometimes, I wish I could disappear for a while. By the time I get back, everyone would have missed me too much to care about my divorce."

"There's nothing you can do about their reaction. Since this is what you want, you'll have to ride the wave of your family's disapproval."

The distance from home would help. "Thanks for the encouragement."

"You're welcome. Let's eat."

Grateful for the change in subject, Zina picked up her fork. "What do you think of you and T.J. coming to Houston for Christmas? I'll have my apartment by then."

Titilope grimaced. "We're going to Nigeria."

"Is this a new development?"

"Yes. T.J. wants to see his father. I'm certainly not sending him on his own."

"Maybe you can visit during your spring break?"

Titilope gave her an apologetic look. "I promised Holly that T.J. and I would spend the week with them in Delaware. The boys miss each other. I also want to see Holly. They're expecting a little girl."

Zina still couldn't wrap her head around how Titilope had maintained a close relationship with Tomide's first wife. Titilope was in the bridal party at Holly's second wedding.

"The boys must be excited about getting a little sister," she said.

Titilope smiled. "T.J. wants us to move to Delaware so he can be around her all the time."

"Have you thought about remarrying?" Zina asked.

"No. I'm just finally open to dating."

"Any prospects?"

"I went on my first date last week. It was okay. We had lots to talk about. There might be a second date. For now, my focus is on T.J."

"Since you can't do Christmas or spring break, you must visit next summer. Unless you don't want to see my face?"

Titilope smiled. "Nonsense. Summer works. Once I know my work schedule, we'll plan the visit."

At the end of the evening, the women stood in front of the restaurant. The temperature had dropped since Zina's arrival. She rubbed her hands together.

"Are you sure you don't want me to drop you off at the hotel?" Titilope asked. "It's on my way."

"Raven is coming to walk me back. He'll be here soon."

Titilope glanced at her watch. "I should get going."

She gave Titilope a hopeful look. "Raven would like to meet you." She didn't give voice to her other thought, which was that she wanted, desperately, Titilope's opinion of Raven.

"Another time. I must pick up T.J. from his friend's place. I told the mom I wouldn't be late."

Zina held her arms wide open. Titilope stepped in and gave her a tight hug. "I look forward to seeing you next summer," Titilope said.

Zina fought back unexpected tears. "Me too."

Chapter Fifty

THE METALLIC RING interrupted Eziafa's racing thoughts. He walked across the room and picked up the telephone. "Hello."

"Hi. May I speak with Zina?"

The cheery voice irritated him. "Zina is not here."

"Oh. When will she be back?"

Good question. "I'm Zina's husband. Who is calling?"

The woman hesitated. "My name's Nomzamo. I work with your wife."

Eziafa pursed his lips. The Instigator. "Is there a problem?"

"We're trying to reach Zina. The nurse who was supposed to work the shift called in sick. Zina is the back-up."

"Zina is yet to return from her training trip."

"You mean the New Orleans trip?"

Eziafa frowned. That's where Zina told him she was going. "Yes."

He didn't miss Nomzamo's sharp intake of breath. "Oh. My apologies. I forgot about that. Thanks for your time."

Nomzamo disconnected the call before he could ask questions.

Eziafa stared at the phone. He didn't need a psychic to tell him Zina had lied about the extra training days. She was with him.

He was pacing the room when the doorbell rang. He looked through the peephole and saw Felix's anxious face. *Ezigbo enyim.*

Eziafa rested his forehead on the door for a moment before opening it. "*Nna*, how now?"

Felix stepped in. "What's going on? Why have you not returned any of my phone calls?"

"My house is on fire."

"What! In the village?"

Eziafa bared his teeth. "I kept telling you Zina was cheating on me. I saw them with these two eyes."

Felix's eyes bugged out. "You saw your wife, Zinach-idi Okereke, with her lover?"

"Yes! They were laughing and holding hands in broad daylight."

Felix's hands went to his head. "*Ewo!*"

"My brother, I'm finished."

Felix looked around. "Where is Zina?"

"She is at his house. Zina told me she was travelling for work. But, for the past ten days, she has been with him."

"Who is this man?"

Eziafa pictured the thief in scrubs. "I don't know his name. I think he's one of Zina's co-workers."

Felix ran a hand over his face. "I hope you remember that you must not have sex with Zina until a cleansing ceremony is done?"

He did. Oji men who had sex with adulterous wives before a cleansing ceremony ran mad.

Eziafa shook his head. "You still believe in those superstitions?"

"These eyes have seen things. I would rather you not incur the wrath of any real or imaginary demon."

"How do I tell my mother that I was unable to manage the wife she found for me?"

Felix laid a hand on his shoulder. "You are not responsible for Zina's actions."

Eziafa's mind raced as he thought about the logistics of a cleansing ceremony. It must take place in the village stream. "Zina will not go back to Oji."

"If Zina will not travel home for the ceremony, let her go. This marriage thing is not a do or die matter. Sooner or later, Zina will face the consequences of her actions."

"I should let Zina go?"

"Yes."

He could not live with the impact of another loss. "No."

"What other choice do you have?"

Eziafa clenched his fingers. Why did Zina have to change? He hadn't. "I should have married Jovita."

"Remember, Jovita was not what you wanted."

They could have moved away from Houston and started a new life where no one knew of Jovita's history.

"Jovita would not have cheated on me."

"Eziafa, looking back will do you no good."

"There is nothing to look forward to."

"Please, come home with me. You shouldn't be alone. Together, we'll brainstorm on how to break the news to our people."

Bad news can always wait. "It is best I stay here," Eziafa said.

Felix gave him an uncertain look. "Are you sure?"

"Yes."

"It doesn't look as if you've slept or showered in days."

Eziafa's eyes ached. All week, his dreams—when he could sleep—were about Zina. They started off where they had ended the previous night. In every one of them, Zina was having sex with the man from the hospital.

"After you leave, I'll shower and eat. I may even go for a walk. The fresh air should clear my head."

"Promise?"

"You have my word. I'm tired. Tomorrow, we'll sit and decide on a plan."

"Do you want me to come here?"

"No. I'll come to you."

Felix looked relieved. "I'll expect you later in the day."

At the door, Eziafa gave Felix a tight hug. "Thanks for checking on me, for being a real brother. Human beings like you are rare."

Felix gave a dismissive wave. "No be today *yansh* get centre parting. You would have done the same for me."

Eziafa took a shower, dressed and went on a long walk around the neighbourhood. It was a beautiful day. When he returned, he moved his car to the parking lot across the street.

Hungry, Eziafa made himself some toast and scrambled eggs. He washed it down with scalding hot black coffee. He washed the dishes, dried and put them away, straightened up the living room, drew all the curtains, and moved the armchair so he could sit and face the door. Something told him Zina would be home soon.

Chapter Fifty-One

RAVEN'S ALARM WOKE Zina up. The upbeat tempo of a song she didn't recognize failed to lift her dark mood. It was homegoing day.

Zina shivered when her toes touched Raven's foot. What are the odds of one woman having a husband *and* a lover with cold hands and feet?

Before they left New Orleans, Raven begged her to spend the weekend with him. It wasn't hard to say yes. All week, they'd crept in and out of each other's hotel rooms while Nomzamo and the rest of their team watched with disapproval they no longer tried to conceal.

Since she and Nomzamo were yet to have a conversation about what Nomzamo said to Raven, the growing distance between them suited her just fine. Zina bit on her lip. That lie was wearing thin. She missed her friend's company.

The call to Eziafa was easy. He sounded preoccupied and didn't interrogate her. She should have tagged on more fake training days. After ten nights of falling asleep in Raven's arms, the thought of going back to Eziafa made her want to get on the first Greyhound bus out of town.

Raven stirred. "Hey, gorgeous."

"Morning."

Her skin tingled as Raven's warm lips left kisses along the nape of her neck.

When he looked at her, Zina saw that the light brown specks in Raven's green eyes had taken on a warm hazel hue. It was fascinating how Raven's eye colour changed with his mood.

She suppressed a yawn. "I'm starving."

"Me, too."

It was Raven's turn to make breakfast. "I'll pass out on you if I don't eat soon."

Raven scooted off the bed. "I'm about to amaze you."

She was in the mood for a big breakfast. "If you don't have sausages, I'll take bacon."

"Bacon? I was talking about premium microwaved oatmeal."

Raven was trying to eat healthy. She didn't have to. "Oatmeal is not amazing."

"Wait until you eat this oatmeal and organic fruit mix."

Zina rolled her eyes. "I'm super impressed."

Raven grinned. "I knew you would be. Breakfast in five minutes."

Zina threw the rumpled clothes into her open suitcase and slammed it shut.

In the living room, Raven patted the spot beside him on the couch. "I need to say something before you leave."

She sat, and Raven reached for her hand. "Zee, this

week confirmed that I don't want to spend any more time away from you."

The words came out in a rush. "I know I'm not the pick of the bunch. I'm tardy. And I ... I don't do well with sharing my feelings."

Zina's mouth went dry.

"I love you, Zee. When you're not with me, it feels like a part of me is missing."

"Raven—"

"Please wait. I need to finish this while I can. I know family and traditional stuff are important to you. I'll visit Nigeria to ask for your father's permission."

She gaped at him. He genuinely wanted to marry her.

"I've been watching some YouTube videos of Igbo marriages. Even though the thought of buying you leaves a nasty taste in my mouth, I'm down with paying the bride price. You tell me what I need to do."

"You're not buying me," Zina said. "The bride price is a symbolic gesture."

He raised an eyebrow. "Really?"

"Yes."

Raven looked relieved. "Okay. I must be honest about something. My parents will not welcome you right away."

"Why?"

"I'm ashamed to say this. My family has a hard time accepting people who don't look like them."

Zina's heart sank. "They won't like me because I'm black?"

"No man in my family has ever brought a black woman home. I do, did, have one cousin who ran off with a black guy. For her, it was instant shunning."

Raven was watching Zina's face carefully and didn't wait for her question.

"My cousin was disowned by her parents. From that moment, she ceased to be a member of our community. We couldn't even talk about her. It was like she had never existed."

"Just because she married a black man?"

"Yes."

Zina shook her head. "How did you turn out to be so accepting?"

"Even as a little boy, somehow, I knew all the nasty, racist and sexist things my grandfather said were not right. One day, I told him so."

"That's why you left home."

"A big part of it. I had to save myself. My grandfather's words were messing with the person I wanted to be."

Tears welled up in her eyes. "I love you."

Raven tightened the grip on her hand. "So, what do you say? Are you willing to cast your lot with this neurodivergent, ex-Mennonite farm boy?"

As her silence lengthened, Raven's face paled. "This wasn't the response I hoped for."

Even though she'd enacted the moment in her mind on numerous occasions, Zina started to cry.

The tips of Raven's ears turned a bright red. "Are you crying because you have to say no?"

The objections to their relationship would not be one-sided. There would be no visit to Oji to meet her parents. Rather than welcome her divorced daughter's boyfriend, Mama would choose to heap burning coal on Zina's head. Despite her disapproval, Mama would share in the shame when the other women gossiped about her wayward daughter.

"Zee, please, look at me."

She lifted her head. "I can't accept your proposal while I'm still wearing his ring."

Raven frowned. "You can take it off."

She stroked Raven's cheek. "I have to tell Eziafa I'm leaving him. When I come back, please, ask me again."

He squirmed in his seat. "Do you mean that?"

She smiled through her tears. "Yes."

Raven smacked his forehead. "Shoot. I forgot about your ring. I've been holding onto it for a while." He dug a hand into his pocket and brought out a box. "I hope you like it."

The garnet ring reminded Zina of the ring she'd tried on during their visit to the summer festival. "Raven. It's beautiful."

"If you're serious about us, you have to take the ring from me before you leave."

"Let's make a compromise. I'll wear it on my chain, and you can put it on my finger when I get back."

"Deal."

Raven unclasped her chain, slid the ring on it, and put it back on her. He buried his face in her neck. Zina clung to him. He was worth the sacrifice.

"I have something else for you," Raven said as he brought out a shiny new key from his other pocket. "This is your home now."

Zina took the key from him. "I need to get my own place."

"What matters most is that now my love for you can be as bold and loud as you need it."

Zina bit her lip. Raven was making it hard for her to leave.

"Do you want me to drive? I can wait for you down the street."

Zina squared her shoulders. Raven's presence would be like shaking salt granules on Eziafa's open wound. "I'll be fine."

He stroked the side of her face. "Promise me you're not going to change your mind when you see him?"

"I promise."

Zina glanced at the clock. "I should be back by 5 pm." If she had to, she would call Eziafa and ask him to come home.

"I'll book a dinner reservation at the new Thai restaurant downtown. We need a celebration."

As she stared at Raven's face, her fingers curled around the metal in her hand. She had the keys to the heart and home of this flawed being whose magic had transformed her life. What more could any girl want?

"I love you with all my strength, Raven Giesbrecht."

His face glowed. "I love you more Zee soon to be Giesbrecht. Hurry back."

Chapter Fifty-Two

AT THE NEXT stop sign, Zina pressed a knob on the CD player, and tunes from Nneka's "Book of Job" filled the car.

She took a deep breath as she clutched her engagement ring. Away from Raven's anchoring presence, she was a cowardly mess. The cautionary words from Nomzamo and Titilope played like a continuous loop in her mind. She began to doubt the wisdom of confronting Eziafa on her own.

Woman, pull yourself together. Zina turned into the parking lot of a strip mall. She needed to think of the right phrases to say to Eziafa. The words forming in her head sounded harsh. Despite everything Eziafa had said and done, she did not hate him.

She pulled out a notepad from her purse. Things might go better if she had a prepared speech. Something short and straight to the point. She stared into the rearview mirror as she recited the few lines she wrote. No matter how much she softened her voice, the words sounded brusque.

Zina crumpled the piece of paper. After several attempts, she had a short script she could use.

She made a list of the essential things she needed to get from the house. She couldn't count on Eziafa letting her back in.

It occurred to her that her cell phone was still switched off. Zina turned it on. She had several missed calls from Nomzamo.

Titilope also sent her a text message. She wanted an update. In her response to Titilope's text, Zina stated that the conversation with Eziafa was yet to happen, and she would call her back as soon as it was done.

Zina could not remember Nomzamo's work schedule. They had not spoken since leaving New Orleans.

Nomzamo didn't pick up. Zina's second call went to voicemail. She decided to leave a message.

"Hey, it's me. Guess what? Raven asked me to marry him. I said yes. You may not care, but you're the first person, the only person, I wanted to tell. I'm on my way to let Eziafa know I'm leaving him. I don't know if you can tell from my voice, but I am scared silly because Eziafa is not going to take it well. Call me. *Please.*"

On second thought, she decided to check in with Chardonnay. It could be something about one of her patients. That call also went to voicemail. She left Chardonnay a call-back message.

Her next call was to Oji. She needed to have one good conversation with her parents before Eziafa called them. It was true that if they hadn't forced her to marry Eziafa, she would not be in her current predicament. She also reminded herself that, if they hadn't, she'd never have met Raven.

Mama picked the call. Both her parents were late sleepers and early risers. "Zinachidi, *nwa m, kedu*?"

Zina forced some cheer into her voice. "*Odinma*. How are you?"

"I am fine. How is your husband?"

"Eziafa is fine."

"We thank God. Your other mother was here in the morning. She came to invite us to your housewarming mass. Zinachidi, I was proud when she sang your praises. Your husband told her he could not have built the house without your help. Thank you for making us proud."

"I'm glad you're happy."

"Is Eziafa there? I want to congratulate him."

Zina grimaced. "He's not here. I'm calling you from my car."

"It is important we speak to Eziafa too. You have both done all we could have expected from responsible children, and more."

Zina heard a muffled voice in the background. "Is that Papa?"

"Yes." She heard Mama's smile in her voice. "He said I should stop wasting your phone credits."

Worried about the international phone rates, her father timed their conversations. "Didn't you tell him I now have an unlimited phone plan?" Zina asked.

"I did. You know him."

"Please give him the phone."

"Your father is getting ready for bed. He sends his greetings."

She had wanted to hear his voice. "Before you go to sleep, please tell Papa I'm sorry."

"Sorry for what?" her mother asked.

"For changing."

Mama's voice became alarmed. "Zinachidi, what are you talking about? Are you okay?"

Zina fell back against her seat. "Mama, I'm fine. In fact, something great happened to me today."

"Then why were you scaring me with those words?"

She could picture her mother's worried look. "Mama, I'm sorry. I wasn't thinking."

"Call me when you get home so I can greet your husband."

"It will be too late to call Nigeria by the time Eziafa gets home. I will call tomorrow."

"We will be waiting."

Zina's eyes filled with tears. It would be the first time saying the words to her mother. She hoped they captured all the regret she felt. "I love you."

Mama giggled. "I am in love too. *Omalicha m*, you are now *Onye Bekee*."

"*Kachifo*."

After having a good cry, she wiped her eyes and dialled Raven's number to tell him she would be back by seven at the latest.

Raven picked up on the first ring. "How did the conversation go?"

"It hasn't happened yet. I'll call you when it's over."

"Should I cancel the dinner reservation? We can go tomorrow."

Nothing was going to ruin their special night. "Push it back to eight. I'll see you soon."

"Please call if you need me."

Raven made loving him easy. "I'll be okay."

Zina let out a huge breath when she saw that Eziafa's car was missing from the parking lot.

If Eziafa came back during her packing, she would tell him about the divorce, as planned. If not, she would ask for a meeting on neutral ground.

Before Zina left her vehicle, she slid Eziafa's rings off her finger and placed them in her jeans pocket. She would leave them on the dresser.

At the apartment door, Zina paused for a moment before inserting her key in the lock. She refused to let fear paralyze her. After Eziafa calmed down, he would accept that she was doing them both a favour. Everyone deserves to be with someone who wanted them. No doubt, people would talk, but she was not the first woman who came to America and left her husband. She was willing to bet her life that she would not be the last.

Chapter Fifty-Three

EZIAFA SAT UP when he heard a key turn in the front door lock. His wanderer was back. The door opened, and Zina walked in. She gave a startled cry when she switched on the living room light and saw him. "You scared me. Why are you sitting in the dark?"

Silent, he continued to stare at her.

Zina dropped her bag on the couch and pushed the long braids away from her glowing face. "Are you okay?"

Eziafa snorted and pursed his lips at the concern in her voice. Like she cared whether or not he was okay "Where have you been?"

Zina stopped two feet away from his chair. As she took deep breaths, the sheer fabric of her pink blouse strained against her chest.

Eziafa's pulse quickened. Zina came back to taunt him with her tainted body. His fingers clenched as he became aroused. He mumbled a prayer and clamped his thighs together.

"We need to talk," she said.

He continued to stare at Zina's heaving chest. An unfamiliar, aromatic scent drifted towards his nose as Zina stepped forward. The maleness of it made Eziafa wrinkle his nose. Zina had dared to walk into his house with that thing's scent all over her.

Zina squared her shoulders. "There is no easier way to say this. Eziafa, I want a divorce."

"You want to leave me?"

"I know I have been a disappointment to you and—"

Eziafa jumped to his feet. "Save the 'it's me, not you' speech. The answer is no."

Zina's voice grew gentler. "You have done a lot for my family and me. We're grateful. When I spoke to my mother today, all she did was sing your praises."

"Did you tell your mother you were going to ask me for a divorce?"

Zina shook her head. "This is between the two of us. Eziafa, for too many years, I've not been happy. I can't continue to live this way. I can't."

Eziafa could hear hot blood rushing through his veins. It was the sound of war. "Sit. Let us talk this out."

Zina shook her head. "There's nothing else to say."

"Admit it. You want to leave me because there is another man."

Zina averted her eyes.

"Answer me!"

Zina brought out something from her pocket. When she held out her hand, Eziafa saw her engagement and wedding rings. "I'm sorry."

As he stared at the rings, white-hot rage coursed through his body. "I should take back the rings I gave you?"

"I no longer need them," Zina said. "I promise to re-fund the bride price you paid. Even the cost of the gifts to my family."

He laughed. "Foolish woman. You don't have enough money to pay for my blood, sweat, and tears."

"Eziafa, I don't love you. I never did."

"I don't care. You married me. You will honour and respect your vows."

"Those vows no longer mean anything to me."

Eziafa saw red as he lunged at Zina and grabbed her arm. The rings fell to the floor. At the growing fear in Zina's eyes he felt nothing but glee. Yes! Let Zina fear him. One does not disrespect what one fears.

"Tell me. What is this thief giving you?"

"I don't know what you're talking about."

"Enough of the lies! I saw the two of you in front of the hospital."

"It's not what you think," Zina said.

Eziafa creased his nose. "I can smell him all over you."

"Please, let go of me." Zina whimpered as his nails dug into the fleshy part of her arm. "You're hurting me."

He wanted Zina to feel some of his pain. "Tell me what he's giving you!"

Saliva drops sprayed his face as Zina spat her words. "Fine! His love. His respect."

"A man who has no regard for things that don't belong to him loves and respects you?"

Zina sneered. "I am not a thing. And, yes, he does. How can I not love and respect someone who sees me as a complete human?"

The words froze Eziafa's heat into a cold fury. "Only a shallow woman confuses furtive, meaningless sex with love. Why do you think I worked like a dog to send you to school, to feed you, to put clothes on your back? You think I did all those things because I hate you?"

"Eziafa, you did those things for yourself. I was only your rainy-day investment. As soon as you could get away with it, didn't you sit on your buttocks all day while I slaved for you?"

"I was sick!"

"You were lazy."

"Fine. You say you were only an investment? Investments should yield dividends. Zina, where are the children I deserve to get from you?"

"A child should be born to two people in a loving relationship. You should let me go because you will never get a child from me."

Zina's words were like a spear imbedded in his back. "I found your birth control pills." Eziafa gave a bitter laugh. "And I thought there was something wrong with me."

"For that, I'm sorry. It's not too late. There are other women out there who will be willing to have your children."

He drawled the words. "I should find myself another woman?"

"Not everything about you is bad."

"You expect me to be grateful because my magnanimous whore of a wife has given me permission to replace her?"

"I'm not a whore!"

Eziafa tapped a finger on his forehead. "Hmm. What other name do you give a married woman who goes around sleeping with other men? Ha, yes. Public toilet. Tell me, Porta-Potty, who else have you been servicing?"

Zina lifted her chin. "Your insults will not make me change my mind."

"Back in Oji, you know we strip whores naked and push them out for the world to see. There is nothing wrong with doing the same here."

He grabbed her blouse with both hands and yanked. The fabric ripped apart.

Zina screamed. "No!"

"I am sure that is not what you say when your *onye ocha* boyfriend paws you. Say, Eziafa darling, yes, oh please, yes."

Zina gave her head a vigorous shake.

He held on tight. "Still, no? That is sad because you're not going to escape from me."

"Please, don't do this. Oh, Raven."

The sound of the name made Eziafa bare his teeth. It made sense. Zina committed an abomination with a cursed bird. "Why did you allow the despicable thing to prey on you?"

"Please, let me go. I can't go back to the way I used to be."

"You're choosing not to."

"Eziafa, I've changed."

He had tried to be the kind of man Felix said these modern women needed, and it still wasn't good enough for her. "Then, change back to the person I married."

"I can't!"

"Then you leave me with no choice."

With each ripping sound, as Zina's cries faded into the background, Eziafa's mind cleared. Zina was his. As the ordained head of their home, it was his duty to maintain order and decorum. Zina may be older in years, but she was as foolish as the day he saw her standing in the village square.

The hot pink lace brassiere was new to him. "Oh. This is what you wear for the thief?"

"Let go of me!"

Eziafa's eyes bulged at the sight of the shiny garnet ring hanging on her chest. "What is that?"

Zina covered the ring with her hand. "It's none of your business."

"You are my business. For the last time, what is that thing on your chest?"

She began to sob. "Eziafa, *biko*. You're hurting me."

He tightened his hold on her. "You think I'm not in pain?"

She glanced at the front door. "If you let go of my arm, we can sit down and talk."

"You want to run away."

Zina shook her head. "Please believe me."

"No one believes a lying whore." He pulled Zina to the ground and sat on her. She continued to scream.

"Let this sink into your head. You are my wife. Not Raven's. Mine. Not his."

Zina shook her head. "I belong to me."

"No. You are mine."

"I am mine!"

"You are mine!"

"No. I belong to me."

The maddening scent of the cologne intensified as he ripped off the rest of Zina's clothes. He became determined to put his scent all over her.

Naked, Zina's arms flopped to the ground. Eziafa took it as a sign of surrender. He shifted his weight off her body.

Zina's bloodshot eyes stared at the ceiling. He stroked her cheek. "Zinachidi Okereke, I still love you."

Her lips curled into a snarl. "I pity you."

"Please, don't let us end things this way. It is this strange place which changed you. Let us go back to Oji. I'm sure we can find a last-minute ticket. Once we get home, you'll remember who you are."

"I'm never leaving America."

When he tried to kiss her, Zina clamped her teeth on his lip. Eziafa let out a cry. "What is wrong with you?"

Zina spat at him. "*Anuofia*. Go to hell!"

Eziafa flinched as the warm spittle slid across his face. He didn't wipe it off. Zina, fully in possession of her senses, had broken several sacred vows. But he, Eziafakaego, who had done no wrong, was the wild animal?

Zina's angry words travelled deep into his eardrums and started a loud chant inside his head. *Go to hell. Go to hell. Go to hell.*

For Eziafa, hell was not the feared lake of fire. No. It was suffocation under the bone-crushing weight of despair, the brain-searing knowledge that yet another dream was gone, and there would be no recourse for the great injustice Zina had done to him.

As Eziafa sucked on a bloodied lip, he pinned Zina's thrashing body down with one hand and loosened his belt with the other.

"What are you doing?" Zina asked.

Eziafa felt a sense of calm come over him. While Zina was rolling in bed with her boyfriend, he had visited her kind of hell. And he was told that what he was about to do to Zina was justified.

"Giving you what you deserve."

Chapter Fifty-Four

RAVEN FLUNG OPEN the door to his tri-level closet. He was making space for Zee's things. The goal was to make Zee super comfortable while she figured out her living arrangements. If he behaved himself, she might even change her mind about getting her own place and stay with him. The thought was exhilarating.

One of his big fears, after he ran away from home, was that he would end up alone. When he was a little boy, his grandfather repeatedly told him a story about a biblical figure who broke the law and was cursed to roam the earth for the rest of his days. Raven was in his mid-twenties before he realized that his single state was not because he was intrinsically flawed. It was hard to let himself be vulnerable to anyone. Then Zee happened. She was the best middle finger he could give his grandfather.

Raven began to whistle. The shrillness had a way of drowning out the thumping sounds of his distress. At his age, he shouldn't care about needing approval. Particularly not from those who would say things that reduced him to a snivelling child. Yet, he did. Damn it!

His Oma's face flashed before his eyes. It was because of her that he could not make a clean break. She'd never stopped loving him even when she did not understand the choices he made. He had to tell her about Zee. Oma would keep his secret until he was ready to face the others. Raven took a deep breath. There was no point worrying about it. Zee may not even want to meet them.

He glanced at the bedside alarm clock. It had been almost two hours since Zee called to let him know she was running late. He could push back their dinner reservation for the second time or cancel it. He picked up his cell phone from the bed and dialled Zee's number. The call went to voicemail. He left a message. "Hey, babe. Where are you? I'm getting worried. Call me back. Love you."

Minutes later, his cell phone rang. Nomzamo's name flashed across the screen. Raven smiled. Zee must have told her girlfriend about the proposal and she was calling to make peace. Nomzamo was lucky he wasn't the kind of guy to hold a grudge. "Hey, you."

Nomzamo was hysterical. "Oh, Raven."

"What's wrong? What happened?"

Nomzamo kept sobbing. "I'm so sorry."

"Please, I need you to take some deep breaths so you can tell me what's going on."

"Raven, it's all my fault," Nomzamo said.

He frowned. "What are you talking about?"

"It's Zina."

Raven's heart skipped. "What happened to her?"

"We ... we needed her at the hospital. She didn't pick up her page or cell, so I called her at home. She wasn't there. I ... I spoke to her husband."

Raven gasped. "You did what?"

Nomzamo's voice dropped. "Zina didn't tell me she was going to be with you. On the television, they said the neighbours called the police when they heard her screams. Zina is dead. Raven, my girl's gone."

He shook his head. "You're wrong. Zee went to get her things."

"It's my fault."

Raven pulled on his hair. "Nomzy, tell me this is a sick joke. That Zina got home, changed her mind about us, and asked you to break things off."

"Raven, my heart kept saying that with the number of Nigerians in Texas, it was another Zina Okereke. I've called Zina several times. Raven, she didn't pick up."

"Nomzy, you're wrong."

"No. It's on the news."

Raven dropped the cell phone and ran to the living room. He flipped through the channels until he saw Zee's name scrolling across the bottom of the television screen.

"We have breaking news tonight from our local TV affiliate in Houston, Texas. The citywide manhunt launched earlier today is over. The suspect, forty-five-year-old Eziafa Okereke, led the police officers on a high-speed vehicle chase, which ended after a blockade. The suspect is facing a charge of first-degree murder in the death of his twenty-five-year-old wife, Zina Okereke."

The screen flipped to a police scene. Two police officers fought with a man as they dragged him out of a cruiser. "Zina's death was not my choice. Oji decreed it! Oji decreed it!"

Raven's teeth chattered as he stared at the screen. Who the hell was Oji?

The room swam before his eyes. How could he have been folding clothes while Zee fought for her life?

When the picture from Zee's Facebook profile came up on the television screen, a sob caught in Raven's throat. He shivered as it dawned on him that he would never hold her again. Raven dropped to his knees and screamed until he lost his voice.

Epilogue

GRIEVING VILLAGE YOUTH AVENGE
KINSWOMAN'S DEATH

The Global Press
January 15, 2020, 12:37 WAT
OJI, Nigeria—

Last night, hundreds of Oji youth angry over the death of their kinswoman, Zinachidi Okereke, torched her husband's house. Caught in the inferno, the deceased's mother-in-law suffered severe burns and remains in critical condition at a local hospital.

State police public relations officer, Ndu Mbogu, advised that the riot began when Mrs. Okereke's corpse arrived for burial, and news of the mutilated body spread.

The accused, Eziafakaego Okereke, has entered a plea of not guilty by reason of insanity. He remains under suicide watch at a Houston jail. The state attorney for Harris County has announced her intention to seek the death penalty.

Glossary

Abacha (Igbo): Shredded cassava strips

Achalugo nwanyi (Igbo): A woman of prestige, strength

Anuofia (Igbo): Wild animal

Asa Nwa (Igbo): Beautiful girl

Bia (Igbo): Come

Biko (Igbo): Please

Chei! (Igbo): An exclamation used to express disbelief or
　　distress

Chi m (Igbo): Personal god responsible for an
　　individual's destiny

Chineke (Igbo): Name for God, like Chukwu

Chukwu ga gozie gi (Igbo): God will bless you

Chukwu gozie gi (Igbo): God bless you

Daalu (Igbo): Thank you

Ewo! (Igbo): An exclamatory word said to express
　　sympathy or distress

Ewu (Igbo): Goat

Ezigbo enyim (Igbo): My good friend

Fufu: Popular West African dough made from cassava,
　　yam or plantain; often eaten with stews or soups

Gari: Popular West African food consisting of fried
　　grains made from cassava tubers

Highlife: Popular melodic West African music and
　　dance; originated in Ghana

I ghotara m? (Igbo): You understand me?

Igba nkwu (Igbo): Igbo traditional wedding ceremony

Igbo: A Nigerian ethnic group. The word also stands for the language spoken by the group

Imeela (Igbo): Another word for thank you

Jigida (Igbo): A string of waist beads usually worn by women

Jisie ike (Igbo): A phrase used as encouragement

Ka omesia (Igbo): Goodbye

Kachifo (Igbo): Goodnight

Kedu (Igbo): A short way for saying, how are you?

Kpim (Nigerian term, pidgin): Nothing, a word

Mogudu: Southern African tripe dish served as a stew

Mumu (Nigerian pidgin, slang): An idiot, pushover

Naija (Nigerian slang): Another term for Nigeria or Nigerian

Ndi ocha (Igbo): White person

Ndo (Igbo): Sorry

Negodu (Igbo): See; often used as sarcasm

Nna (Igbo): Father; also used as affectionate term between two men

Nne (Igbo): Mother

Nnoo (Igbo): Welcome

Ntorr (Nigerian pidgin, slang): A mocking exclamation

Nwa m (Igbo): My child

Nwanyi oma (Igbo): A good woman

Nwata akwukwo (Igbo): Student

Obodo Oyibo (Igbo): White man's land

Obu onye k'anyi na acho? (Igbo): Who is it that we're looking for?

Odinma (Igbo): It is well

Oga (Nigerian pidgin, slang): Boss

Ogbono (Igbo): Wild mango seeds ground for a soup base

Ogini (Igbo): What is it?

Omalicha (Igbo): Beautiful. Often a term of endearment, a compliment

Onaghi ezu cha (Igbo): Never perfect, never enough

Onye Bekee, (Igbo): White person

Onye ezi (Igbo): Pig people

Onye ocha (Igbo): White person

Otumokpo (Igbo): Fetish objects used to cause harm; juju

Oyibo (Igbo): White person

Ozugo nu (Igbo): Enough! Calm down

Tufiakwa (Igbo): Exclamation meaning God forbid

Ugba (Igbo): Fermented African oil bean seed

Wahala (Nigerian term, pidgin): Trouble

Waka (Nigerian pidgin, slang): Walk, movement

Wayo (Nigerian pidgin, slang): Cunning behaviour

Wrappa (Nigerian pidgin, slang): A tailored piece of fabric women wrap around themselves. Can be part of an outfit paired with a blouse and headscarf

Yansh (Nigerian pidgin, slang): Buttocks

Zobo: Nigerian drink primarily made from dried hibiscus petals

Acknowledgements

It took eleven long, winding years for this book to become a reality. I'm grateful to the following people who were part of its transformation: Oyindamola Orekoya, Ola Nubi, Unoma Nwankwor, Som Nwegbu, Juliet Kego Ume-Onyido, Toyin Jonah, Mojisola Aderonmu, Susan Dieleman, Uchechukwu Umezurike, Chioma Umezurike, Onyih Odunze, and Deb Babula. I have a nagging feeling that I may have left out some names. If I have, please know that it's due to middle age forgetfulness and not ingratitude.

I'm deeply grateful to Nana Brew-Hammond for saying yes when I needed to hear it the most. And to Okey Ndibe for his generosity.

To Micheal Mirolla, my editor Lindsay Brown, and the team at Guernica Editions, thank you for giving this book the best home and making it shine.

Many thanks to my siblings, family, and friends. I know I can't do life successfully without your love and support.

To my husband Oladele and our children, Oluwafikunmi, Ifeoluwakishi, and Oluwademilade, thank you for your patience. It's not easy sharing me with so many voices.

The glory and honour for this work are to a merciful and faithful God, who gives dreams and sustains them.

About the Author

Yejide Kilanko was born in Ibadan, Nigeria. A writer of fiction and poetry, Kilanko's debut novel, *Daughters Who Walk This Path*, a Canadian national bestseller, was long-listed for the inaugural Etisalat Prize and the 2016 Nigeria Literature Prize. Her work includes a novella, *Chasing Butterflies* (2015), two children's picture books, *There Is An Elephant In My Wardrobe* (2019), and *Juba and The Fireball* (2020). Her short fiction is in the anthology, *New Orleans Review 2017: The African Literary Hustle*. Kilanko lives in Chatham, Ontario, where she also practices as a therapist in children's mental health.

Printed in May 2021
by Gauvin Press,
Gatineau, Québec